HOW TO
FALL IN
LOVE
IN A
TIME OF
UNNAMEABLE
DISASTER

HOW TO FALL IN LOVE IN A TIME OF UNNAMEABLE DISASTER

a novel

MURIEL LEUNG

W. W. NORTON & COMPANY

Independent Publishers Since 1923

For information about permission to reproduce selections from this book, write to
Permissions, W. W. Norton & Company, Inc., 500 Fifth Avenue, New York, NY 10110

For information about special discounts for bulk purchases, please contact
W. W. Norton Special Sales at specialsales@wwnorton.com or 800-233-4830

Manufacturing by Lakeside Book Company
Book design by Chris Welch
Production manager: Lauren Abbate

ISBN 978-1-324-07618-6 (pbk)

W. W. Norton & Company, Inc., 500 Fifth Avenue, New York, N.Y. 10110
www.wwnorton.com

W. W. Norton & Company Ltd., 15 Carlisle Street, London W1D 3BS

10 9 8 7 6 5 4 3 2 1

To the family we continue to choose

HOW TO

FALL IN

LOVE

IN A

TIME OF

UNNAMEABLE

DISASTER

HOW TO FALL IN LOVE IN
A TIME OF UNNAMEABLE
DISASTER

There are many names for surviving disaster. I call it the *after-after*, a pockmarked city leaning into another realm of debris and ghosts, five boroughs smelling of burning flesh. Despite the still-standing buildings on the horizon that beam like a mouth full of chipped teeth, the *after-after* is full of missing. I think of Mal more often than I like—how she stayed, and I left. I sometimes call this period *After Mal*, or *Life After Mal*, or *Fuck Mal*, or *Sorry, I Didn't Mean It Like That, Mal, Please Forgive Me* (all versions a mouthful).

On the radio, I ask others about what name they give their survival. Sometimes their voices are a crackle, but from what I can make out, they are this: *The Rude Bare, Heart Spleen, The Dead on Bowery, Hole-y City, Icarus Mold,* and *That Without a*

Name. It's hard to confirm which of these are exactly as I hear them and which are rough approximations. I do this to offer up something to describe what happened to us. *Dear Listeners*, I always begin. *Can we find a name that is also an apology?*

All apologies are reasonably deferred during this time. Mine cannot come any later.

When I left Mal in Queens to head to Ma's place on the Lower East Side, the quakes had settled, and the debris was just about cleared from most of Manhattan's Financial District. It had seemed, for a moment, that things were on the up-and-up. Then the acid rainstorms started. Every Tuesday, without fail, the rain would come and wash the city in a sulfuric sheen. All of us in Building 4B, Apartment 9A of the Gratuitous Place housing projects call this the *Bad Tuesdays*, though the name itself would eventually become synonymous with any time one of us was in a terrible mood. When I arrived at this apartment just moments before the start of the weekly storms, a broken heart and two large trash bags of clothing in tow, Ma said, "It's Bad Tuesday, isn't it?" and then, studying my crushed face, added, "This will pass too."

I thought of Mal a lot then. How could I not? Everything was haunted, especially with the ghosts of Apartment 9A swirling overhead. ("They just arrived one day and stayed," Ma told me, and it seemed, by her nonchalance, that she had now resigned herself to tending to these additional members of her household.)

As it turns out, the ghosts have their own names for disaster. Grandpa Why—my mother's father, born Li Wai Mo, who was nicknamed Walter, then Wally, and then simply Why after none of the previous permutations stuck—likes to throw open

windows during those cloistered Tuesdays and shout to no
one in particular "Ain't that a *stinker!*" So, I guess that's what
he's calling it now, much to Ma's distress over her acid-soaked
succulents. And then there is Shin, an oversized cockroach,
who calls all of this a simple *catastrophe.* Both were equally
puzzled by the wetness of my face when I showed up at the
door. ("Explain this!" Grandpa Why demanded, finger wagging at me while Ma waved her hand. "You know who she is!"
Though after that proclamation the ghost of my grandfather
had already moved on.) Through the chaos of voices, Shin had
offered back my old bedroom, which the ghosts had come to
inhabit, and there I slept on and off for three days, pummeled
by thoughts of Mal.

When I moved back in with Ma, I did not tell her that Mal
and I were not well. During that first month of the Bad Tuesdays, the apartment Mal and I shared slowly started to fall
apart. Soon after, the landlord stopped answering our calls.
The cell towers shut down across Queens. After repeated wear
from the rain, the power lines split and hung frayed in the
streets. In response, the city set up call centers at markets and
corner stores every twenty blocks. A temporary solution for a
disaster that seems to know no end. The loss of connection
terrified people enough that eventually other families in our
building left for New Jersey, where the latest evacuation site
was stationed. Others in the city had the same idea. With the
tunnels jammed for days, traffic snaking through every street
in Lower Manhattan, the city decided everyone else had to
stay put. With each borough divided into zones and flanked
by checkpoints at various borders, it became increasingly
difficult to leave, let alone move from borough to borough.

Government-certified signatures on travel documents, multiple types of identification, parties of no more than three at a time—the stipulations made it impossible to pass through.

Ma, in her concern, urged me to return home at every turn. I collected the messages at the bodega with Mal, and we would run into JoJo from the floor above us, who had reported the same panic from his mother, Lucinda.

"Shit," JoJo said with an ironic chuckle. "My mom has been leaving me messages all week. You'd think your mom and mine would go in on a message together, split the cost. Save themselves the trouble."

I returned his laugh with an equally strained one, thinking of Ma gathering Lucinda from her apartment two floors down, the pair bundled up in rain ponchos, shoving their way to the front of the call center queue. The comedy of it all was short-lived. In my hands, I held ink-stained pieces of paper, each one etched with some iteration of *Come home now*, their urgency made more pronounced by the rough scrawl of the call center agent's hand relaying the message.

"I don't know what to do. I think Ma wants me to stay with her." I turned to JoJo and then Mal, whose expressions went blank at the notion, and the dangling issue of what to do next became both a question and a plea. "What should we do?"

JoJo looked up at the sky, his face softening against the overcast spool of it. "God, I wish I knew." He looked at me and then Mal. "Troy's got a job working disaster relief in the neighborhood. I don't know if I can leave him behind. What if I can't get back? But my mom . . . I don't know."

We stared at our feet, at the holes in the ground that grew wider each day. I felt Mal's silence most of all, her hands bunched up in her hoodie pocket. A mistake to mention the possibility of my mother's place aloud, I guess, but as I started to make an excuse to part ways, JoJo asked the question for me.

"You guys know what you're gonna do? Head to Mira's mom's?" Sensing our discomfort, he nudged each of us playfully. "Three to a twin bed?"

"Don't know," Mal muttered too quickly.

I nodded just as fast. "Yeah, don't know."

JoJo stretched his arms into an elongated Y before dropping his hands to his head, blowing all the air out of his body. "Well, if you do decide to go home, mind if I pass on some things for you to give to my mom? Just so she knows I'm alive. Give her peace of mind."

Looking at both JoJo and Mal, I offered a polite "Sure," though even the softness of the answer seemed to make Mal bristle.

I felt the tension of that moment course through our days after, a butter knife running along the edges of us, and every once in a while it would nick. Meanwhile, the acid rain worsened around us. Hazard squads gathered in Little Neck, draining pools of foul-smelling pieces of fallen sky from the fields. In FiDi, a giant crater appeared almost overnight, as if the moon had touched down and made an impression right at the corner of Whitehall Station. I saw glimpses of these wounds on the grainy television sets at the call centers where dozens of us would crowd around the screen, pointing to the places we thought would never fall.

At the dollar store, Mal and I would tag-team, crowd-surfing through the thick of people just to grab dish soap, masking tape, aluminum foil—all of which would sell out immediately upon restocking. It was the source of infinite grievances, what we ended up with once we exited the store and who was not fast enough to grab what we needed, many of which Mal issued with great complaint. I never knew what to say. After all, I was tired too.

Soon every little thing became a source of contention. For one, after the city issued an ordinance that every window needed to be reinforced in case of glass erosion from the rain, Mal took it upon herself to direct the placement of duct tape on our windows. She had a distinct aesthetic vision for it, wanting the X to fit each window corner exactly. At first we were responsible for our own windows, each one of us with our designated task to speed up the process, but as the hours passed, Mal saw the need to revise my efforts every so often to realign the X. In turn, I would go over her X, curling the letter deliberately. I designed a flower, a moth, a claw. Then I made the shape of an angry lover's mouth. Furious, she went over each one again, correcting the X until our apartment looked like a series of *Nos*.

"What if we die anyway?" I grumbled. "Would God care how neat your Xs are? Really?"

Mal replied, "At least I'm trying to do something about it. What are you doing? You just keep shoving pots underneath leaks in the ceiling like somehow after you empty all the water from the pots, it'd all be over." She tightened her two fists like angry grapefruits when she spoke.

No, I thought. *I am a person of action. I am a person of intent—a maker.* I retorted instead, "I am a person."

"What?"

"Talk to me like a person who is trying to deal too."

"You aren't, though," she growled. "You keep fucking up the Xs!"

I would say later to myself that it was the product of design that did us in, as if all the reasons that preceded and followed did not have lives of their own.

After the Xs debacle, our fights worsened just as the outer boroughs were declared an "At Risk" zone. After one storm left behind a giant crack in the middle of I-495 on the way from Long Island City to Manhattan, the city decided that in several weeks' time the bridges connecting Queens and Manhattan would close permanently. There was no way to travel through the subway tunnels either, which were all gated off and flooded with sludge from the constant downpour. Mal and I argued constantly about whether to leave or to stay. I insisted we catch the crosstown bus to midtown and walk the rest of the way south to my mother's place for the time being.

"But this is my family's home," Mal would push back, sweeping her hands across the air of the apartment as if it were something more than a leaky room with holes that we were always stuffing with whatever sock or old underwear we could find. Her face fell when she spoke. "It's the only thing I have left of them."

Mal had been an orphan for as long as I had known her. Her apartment was always carefully preserved, as if her parents and grandmother still floated through the space. Even years after their passing, the apartment still smelled like Tiger Balm. The scent lingered on her too, and so it came as no surprise that her life and the fate of the apartment would become one and the same.

I tried, "I understand, but . . ."

What could you say to the person you love, parentless and clinging to the studio apartment where she grew up, sleeping beside her grandmother on the bottom bunk bed while her parents slept on top? Mal spoke often of those early days of her life. When we slept together, our bodies were intertwined with similar closeness, as if we could not afford to leave any space between us.

Our apartment brimmed with the stored life of old wristbands to shows we could not recall, bottles of expired medicines sent from Mal's parents stacked in boxes and crates in the corner, yellowing sheets rescued from the hospital beds where both father and mother slowly passed away. I learned not to question the placement of these assorted objects. I moved a box once, only to find it more fortified the next day—taped shut, labeled, and leaning against the wall, the size of it doubled.

Meanwhile, the Tuesday storms grew feverish. The sky blinked and then the rain cascaded down with such force, the buildings wobbled back and forth. I had never prayed beyond the three bows to my ancestors on the cemetery hill, clutching joss sticks in hand. Yet when the buildings shook, I grappled for any god. Mal would clutch me too while I looked up at her and the towering boxes overhead, wondering when things would finally change. *I'm so sorry, Mal*, I thought during those moments. I understood why she could never leave. And yet my body was already planning its slow departure.

When the storm cleared one day and the Emergency Sanitation and Reconstruction Services cleanup crew (known as ESRS, or simply "the Erasers") had resealed the ground with concrete, I walked several blocks to a call center at a bodega where one of the disaster communication workers was stationed with a white phone and blinking red lights. I was not planning on it, but it occurred to me that something had to be done, and if I didn't act then, I would constantly put it off.

I relayed a message to the worker for my mother: *Can I come*. The response came one day later: *Hurry*.

Leaving was gradual until it was not. The day that I left, the crack in the ceiling of our studio apartment had widened and the acid rain leaked through. We had cleared out several rubber buckets by then, but it seemed futile after a certain point, so we let it spill over, the liquid then seeping into the plastic covering of the floor tiles, causing a trail to bubble over. As the trail expanded, boxes were shoved out of the way, sometimes tilting awkwardly in the middle of the too-small room. Mal and I talked to each other across the apartment through these pillars of forgotten objects, some older than Mal and me combined, and which I was forbidden from opening. Instead, I left Post-it notes on these boxes that read, *I love you, Mal*, and *Maybe today will be better*, and *We're going to be OK*. I thought it all true for a while, until my hope gave out. Then I left another note instead: *We have to talk*.

From behind one of the pillars of boxes, Mal emerged. She shook her head. "Whatever you're going to say, I already know." Her words echoed between the boxes.

I reached for her behind one of the stacks, only to hear her voice move farther away. I called out to her, "What do you know?"

"You're leaving me."

I laid my hand on the side of one of the boxes, hoping she could place her hand there. She didn't.

"That's not it," I began, but the knot in my throat widened. "I want you to come too."

I must have sounded convincing, because Mal finally came out from behind one of the columns to look directly at me. I rushed my plea.

"We can pack some of the things in these boxes. Like this one." I pointed to one of the boxes at the very top, spilling over with aged documents. "This one has your parents' immigration papers and photos. We can put those in a filing cabinet, get one of those pushcarts to roll it all the way to Manhattan. Do you remember that time we walked all the way across the bridge to the city? It was only a couple of hours, and it was doable. We can go to the corner store, pick up some rain gear, be extra careful, and—"

I stopped to study Mal's face, which had gone blank while I was sputtering. No telling if she was angry or sad or both. I begged, "Mal, please. I don't know if I can come back for you."

She said nothing at first and stared out the window boarded up with Xs. You could make out slivers of sky through it all, looming and gray and heavy with impending rain. She told me once that at night, when she could not sleep, she would watch the roaches climbing up the window. Her grandmother would spoon her gently, and together they would count the bugs as they came and went, unsure if a roach was counted once, twice, three times. Sometimes, at night, I would feel Mal awake beside me, whispering the count aloud: *One, two . . . three.*

Mal looked at me in silence for a long while before finally turning away. "Please just go."

I searched her face for more. To leave meant this was over, the two of us—Mal and Mira, Mira and Mal. We had been inseparable, and had said, on more than one occasion, that being apart would be like severing a piece of our own body. In the space between us then, I felt myself saying goodbye to the left side of my own sad sack of flesh.

I looked at Mal as she slowly backed away.

"Mal, I don't want to die." The words came out in sobs. I waited for Mal to say something, anything. She didn't. My knees hit the floor before I could catch myself, and on all fours I crawled to her, placed my face against her thigh. "Please, Mal. We can't keep living here like this. I don't want you to die either."

When I looked up, Mal was shaking her head, and I could see that she was crying too. Through her tears, she cried out, "You said you weren't afraid! You said it. I believed you."

Her palm covered my eyes as if she did not want me to see. I held her by the wrist for as long as she would let me, and together we heaved and wept in unison until the first rumble in the sky jolted us back to where we stood. It was time to go. The rain was coming soon. If I stayed, I knew I would never leave.

"You're right. I said it all wrong. This is the new brave thing. Come with me, Mal," I begged again. Even with her palm still resting across my eyes, I could feel her considering it.

Mal lifted her palm. Above me, her face was wet with tears. She placed her hand against my cheek and said at last, "I love you so much, Mira."

I reached for her. "I love you so much, Mal."

"I'm so sorry."

"I'm sorry too."

Wordlessly, I stood up and gathered my things in trash bags. It all seemed a blur, those next moments. Before I left the apartment, I took one final look back at Mal, who was resting on one of the stacks. Her shoulders were hunched over, and though I could not see her face, I knew she was quietly folding into herself. She was already too far away, and I knew—she was on her way to becoming a ghost.

It was not always this way. At the start of the acid rainstorms, Mal and I would watch the sky change color. Everything wild had a temporary feel to it, and the idea of staying in to watch the tumult outside felt like a bizarre type of camping. We ate caramel popcorn, stale from being at the bottom of the tin, and when we emptied the container, we filled it with paper fortunes that we penned for each other.

You will live a long and outstanding life of many gifts.
Your stomach will be strong, and your heart even stronger.
Your ass will be fat and the envy of all who witness it.

On a dull day, we pulled the fortunes out and read them to each other, feeling our destiny so carefully defined and assured. We took turns falling over with laughter, and then we collapsed against each other, our mouths catching each other first and then our hands. "Tell me about my future," I whispered into her hair. Her fingers reached inside me—an answer.

We started to record our days. From one of Mal's many boxes, she pulled out a handheld tape recorder and two blank cassette tapes. She mumbled something about there being more, she just had to dig around for them.

"Honestly, who besides you would find those around their apartment?" I joked. "I haven't seen that since I was a kid!"

"Oh yeah," Mal said, chuckling, "my parents kept everything."

She blew the dust off the recorder, popped a cassette inside, and pressed record. She held the recorder toward me. I lowered my face to the mic and whispered into it. When she rewound the tape and hit play, a tiny voice sounded out: "This is Mal and Mira from the future. Take off your pants."

Mal stopped the recording and shook her head. "That's not realistic."

"Okay, let me try again."

We greeted the future over and over again, imagining that someone would find us in the debris, fish us out, and hear our voices emanating from the wreckage. Each day, we picked up the recorder and shared about our lives. Sometimes we did it together; other days we took the machine to the bathroom and spoke alone. I talked about the way the windows seemed to be caving in, how Mal and I would cut off the mold from the cheese in the fridge because of the sudden dairy shortage, how we were trying to make it last. I often wondered what Mal talked about when she took the recorder with her in the shower, if she ever mentioned me. We agreed that we would not listen to the tapes, leaving this documentation for the people of the future to hear.

"But what do you talk about?" I could not help asking.

"I don't know. A little bit of everything."

"What if we're really boring?"

Mal considered it, rubbing her chin. "That's possible."

"Did you talk about me?"

Mal feigned confusion at the question.

"Hey!"

Mal's eyes squinted in amusement. "Kidding! Yes. Like I said. A little bit of everything."

I pouted. "Give me a hint."

Mal smiled and lowered her face toward me. "There's a little message for you."

I rolled my eyes. "Great, so none of us will hear it because we'd both be dead by then."

Mal turned the recorder on, the red light blinking in her hand. We laughed for so long that we forgot to press stop until the tape ran out later that night.

Most Tuesdays, I fiddle around with a radio that Yee, the downstairs neighbor in Apartment 7B, fixed up with glue and guitar strings after fishing it out of the East River. In exchange for the radio, I traded Yee a bag of beef jerky, salted fish, and a brief feel of my left breast. His parents disappeared last year when the earth broke open somewhere between Barclay and Rector Streets. Yee watched the fault line vacuum them in and, to his grief, could not find a trace of bone. When he tells me about their vanishing, I do not know what to do. He sobs so deeply into his hoodie that I kiss him just to get him to stop. When he looks up during the height of his bewilderment, I pop the top three buttons of my blouse and press my breast to his hand. He immediately stops crying after that.

I start hosting a weekly show about love, which I suppose I have Yee to thank for. Sometime after holding his head to my chest, I catch him watching me as I unspool myself from his sheets. I ask him if he has ever been in love.

"Before or after the *Big Suck*?" he asks. That is his name for the disaster.

"Both, I guess."

He pauses for a moment before sneaking a glance at my exposed stomach and sheepishly replying, "Not before . . ."

As I wait for him to finish his thoughts, I see his eyes lower to the floor and know it was a mistake to ask.

Because Yee never asks me about love in turn, I talk into a mic about various nothings concerning love. Mostly, I talk about Mal.

Before the rainstorm, when the 7 still ran underground and snaked up to the surface, Mal and I fell in love across the train car. That summer, everybody moved to Brooklyn, and no one wanted to come to Queens. But that was not unusual. It became a season of rooftop parties in Bed-Stuy, of grown-up punks crowding over a makeshift speaker while tíos gathered in the corner, sipping Coronas. Somebody always had the grand idea to barbecue, but two hours into trying to secure a grill, hopping from bodega to bodega looking for charcoal, people's attention would disperse. A faction of the party would head out to the street to collect whatever they could find—meaty pupusas from the pupuseria two blocks away, a large bucket of wings and drumsticks from the Kennedy Fried Chicken that had been there before any of us had arrived in the country, and a plastic bag full of paletas, ice-cream sandwiches, and rainbow popsicles, all sopping wet and melting. It was on one of these occasions of failed plans to grill that I saw Mal walk into the party with three Styrofoam boxes stacked on top of one another. I smelled the grease from where I stood, and that was the last thing I remembered.

The following was relayed to me by Mal: Sauntering over with a half-finished bottle of wine in hand, I put my nose to the boxes in Mal's hands before making my introduction.

Mal was unamused. "Uh, can I help you?"

I pointed and slurred, "What . . . this?"

She opened the top box and heat rushed out—a piling heap

of french fries, most of which I ate by myself that night. When it got late and the party dimmed, the host, always inevitably a friend of a friend of a cousin, pointed to Mal and then me, and relayed an order that was not to be questioned: "Take this drunk bitch home."

At the time, I lived in Flushing, the last stop on the 7 train, a fact I haphazardly communicated to Mal as she guided me through the turnstiles, swiping my MetroCard for me when I couldn't do it myself. Neither of us could remember which trains had stopped working that night, only that it took two transfers cutting through Manhattan to get us home. She too lived off the 7 train, in the apartment we would eventually share, but that information only elicited brief excitement from me before I dashed across the platform. Mal chased me from stairwell to stairwell, a memory she would curse in the months after. ("I quit smoking two days later," she joked.)

When I tired myself out at the Times Square station, we finally hopped on the 7 train. I became subdued and contemplative, remarking first on the alarming language of the DRUG FREE AMERICA posters on one end of the train car and the PSA on preventing teen pregnancy on the other. I spoke about bodies and cellular memory, drawing for Mal on her knee the circulatory motion in which trauma moves. The intimacy of this gesture was lost on me then, though Mal would recall the hair on her legs standing up at the sudden touch, my finger moving along the thin flesh of her knee with bright nonchalance while I talked away. I felt the dizzy aftermath of this moment living in me like a pulsating light: I held Mal's face between my hands. She was astonished by my firm hold. I studied her face, the spots that were most sun-kissed with a light sprinkling of freckles. We stood on two ends of a pole, my elbow gripping the metal while the train shook, bringing her face closer to mine. "Can I just . . . ?" I inquired much after the fact of my doing. "It's just . . . there is so much of your face to remember."

～

I call my radio show *How to Fall in Love in a Time of Unnameable Disaster* because it feels true. With the wires and gadgets from Yee's dumpster-diving, the little ham radio setup I fashioned becomes a more elaborate fixture in my bedroom. I start talking, and then I cannot stop. Although the messages are generally for Mal, the segments themselves garner a following of Listeners.

For a segment on long-distance relationships, I decide to talk about Mal's disappearance as a sort of long-distance affair. Grandpa Why slides through the wires of the program, despite being permanently banned from the show, to offer his two cents: *Don't be cruel to a heart that's true. Why should we ever be apart?* Though his advice is plagiarized from Elvis Presley lyrics, he has a good point. I turn on my ELVIS 3000 karaoke machine and let Grandpa Why serenade me off-key while I drown myself in the last of that month's liquor ration.

Dear Listeners, if your lover is in a militarized zone, consider sending a care package via the few accredited private messenger services. Support local business but also be wary of sending contraband. If you must, wrap it in a wool sweater—that way your lover will have something warm to wear as well.

The mayor's office now defines "long-distance" as anything beyond two checkpoints. In that sense, Mal and I are long-distance, though I never follow through on my own advice. I dialed the call station at her nearby bodega once, twice, and then twenty times, each time receiving an automated government-generated message explaining away the spotty connection in times of emergency. I called friends at various checkpoints, left them messages to pass on to her, but everyone, being too preoccupied with their own disasters, eventually disappeared as well.

In a final effort to reach out, I devise coded messages that I broadcast during each show. We did this for each other before, sneaking stray letters of the alphabet into Post-it notes left inside shoes or scrawled onto the back of hands while sleeping. Eventually the letters come together to form a message.

I hope she knows these letters I am leaving behind for her on the show are for her to collect. If she is listening, they spell out: *MIRA MISSES MAL SORRY MAL WHERE R U MAL R U ALIVE MAL IF U R SEND WORD MIRA MISSES MA—*

I also begin to drink away my devastation.

A caller one day says the following: "My husband has been distant since *it* happened. Of course, since we live by the East River, which is now forty-three percent radium, our daughter was born with tentacle toes and gills. I think she's still cute as a bug, but I suspect that might have something to do with his emotional unavailability. Do you think we'll make it?"

I say, "I live by the East River too. I'm sure my progeny will be part Komodo dragon, but I'd love the child all the same. Your husband could be more understanding. Have you tried talking to him?"

There is a pause and then commotion from her end of the line. "Sorry," the caller says breathlessly. "Husband is listening in the other room and is not happy. I'll have to call you back another time."

Click.

While few call in, there is a regular caller who phones in at the same exact time every Tuesday. The voice on the other end delivers their words slowly and deliberately, and over time it becomes clear that the voice is not human, but one mediated by machine. Whenever the caller phones in, I cannot help but think of their voice as a tattered memory of the ocean.

"HEL-LO," the voice says.

"Hello," I reply. "What's your name and where are you calling from? What are you interested in sharing today?"

"I AM SAD."

"I'm very sorry to hear that. Do you care to share why you are sad today?"

A pause. "NOT TO-DAY. ALL DAYS."

"What makes you sad every day, Listener? I think I'll have to call you Sad, since you didn't give me a name."

"NO HEAD."

"Sad, can you be a little bit more specific? What do you mean by that?"

"NO HEAD."

Click.

Our conversations always start and end this way.

Sometimes I think they are flirting with me. Once, out of nowhere, they say, "DON'T GO FAR OFF, NOT EV-EN FOR A DAY," and that declaration, in their voice like the rip of a wave in far-out waters, sounds so sure of itself.

As I am about to tell them that I am not going anywhere, they say, "PA-BLO NE-RU-DA."

Sometimes they joke. "THIS IS ME BREATH-ING," they relay, and then fall silent for three minutes.

"Are you sure you're human?" I ask after enough time passes. "NO COM-MENT."

Ma, overhearing one of these exchanges, offers, "This is like *Sleepless in Seattle*, but I want to know what Tom Hanks does for a living first before you meet him."

Grandpa Why, on the other hand, is a skeptic. "Finish what you started!" he exclaims, finger wagging in my face. "You know what I mean."

I do not. But with my mother's blessing, I begin to collect facts about Sad. They like Pablo Neruda. They miss being able to swim. They were peeling an apple once during a call and sliced their finger. They have depression and possibly some form of social anxiety disorder. They are an insomniac. They like salty and sweet things. They live somewhere in this building.

Dear Listeners, there is a kindness we need to extend to people we love who are far, far away. Nothing will feel as good as being close enough to touch them. I guarantee it. This holiday, give them the gift of touch. Put yourself in an envelope and puncture three holes. When they open you, reach out and let them know how much they have been missed.

I keep losing Mal again in my dreams. In one, I am sitting in a bathtub with Mal under a layer of white petals. Holding her like a cello, her body wide but light in the water, her black curly hair pillows in my mouth. I kiss the back of her neck with its tiny soft hairs. I stroke her wrinkly knees. I tell her I want us to turn into two raisins and fall down the drain. The more I talk, the more apparent her silence becomes, until finally she turns around, but I do not see her face. I see her hair cascading over her like a widow's veil and then, with gradual horror and grace, the veil washes over her, and she turns into a black eel. She bares her teeth like white bone needles and bites open my inner thighs, pulsing inward with a force that seems to defy the capacity of her new size. Reaching out with my hands, I try to grip her slippery body, only to find it paved with thorns. I hold out my briar-patch hands, and I look down at the pool of my blood pluming beneath me. The eel disappears entirely, but when I wake up I can still feel her swimming inside me for days.

Sad leaves me a message on my machine that echoes: "IN SPAIN . . . THEY ARE . . . GROW-ING . . . AP-PLES . . . WANT TO GO . . . SOMETIME?"

When I start the show that day, I laugh into the mic. "This is for my Listener Sad," I say with a chuckle. "Yes. Let's."

At the end of the program, I play a recording of rain falling in a tunnel and offer the letter *L*.

I will myself to dream of Sad so that I can stop dreaming of eels, and one night it is close to working. In my dream, I am on a tiny sand mound surrounded by a black ocean. Then a flick of silver in the water slowly manifests itself into a merman with hair the same ocean-black as the water that appears to bleed into the tide. He pushes up onto the sand mound with two arms and walks his hands toward me. He introduces himself as *Sad*. Gesturing to my mouth, he seems to be asking, *Salt?* I think, *Yes, please.* He moves his mouth toward my mouth, and I can taste the sand in every shell at the bottom of the ocean floor. He moves his hand to part my thighs, pauses, and looks down. Beneath me, a black eel is crawling out, bloating with a terrible anger that rips through my body. I wake up and put hands to belly and sternum to make sure I am still whole. I am. And somehow, that feels unbearably tragic.

Yee says, "Guilt." He rummages through the dumpster behind Building 6D as I stand guard in a rubber poncho. The sky begins to darken and the workers in rubber suits have started to flip their flashlights on and off anxiously.

"What do I have to be guilty of?" I retort.

From the depths of the dumpster, amid the rustling and clanging, I hear Yee's echo: "I MISS YOU MAL WHERE ARE YOU MAL."

"Shut up. Have you been decoding my messages?"

"Yes," Yee responds matter-of-factly as he rises with two handfuls of electrical wire. "Jackpot!"

"You're taunting me. That's not nice."

"I'm just saying"—Yee lets out a sigh—"you are simultaneously trying to kill and resuscitate a dead thing. It's beyond counterproductive—it's just absurd."

I look up at Yee, who is shoving his latest finds in a makeshift duffel made up of trash bags, his hair decorated with eggshell confetti and rice. He forgot to bring gloves with him once again.

"You're right. I'm the absurd one."

Yee offers an apologetic face and reaches out to pat my shoulder, which I let him do because of the acid-proof rubber I'm wear-ing. "You think you might want to come back to my place for a little bit?" he begins shyly, tucking behind his ear the bit of hair that has fallen over his face. "I fixed up an old Nintendo 64 and picked up this month's rations—Chef Boyardee or whatever the new government brand is. We can eat or, you know, whatever . . ."

Later that night, I let Yee fumble his way on top of me. His mattress has a volatile spring that juts out of the cotton com-pletely when he finally comes. I picture Sad with his computer-ized voice and love of metaphor. I think of him with black hair and a prickly chin. Yee rolls over onto his back. He offers me a cigarette from his father's pack. As I smoke, I brush the egg-shells from Yee's hair while he cries.

On the radio a week later, I wait for Sad to call.

"HEL-LO," the voice says. "RAIN A LOT TO-DAY." Even his small talk feels heavy.

"What did you think of our discussion today, Sad?" That day's broadcast has been about relationship misfortunes and how we move past them. One woman called in about her miscarriage and how her husband wouldn't look at her the same afterward. Another caller wanted to know if it was appropriate to continue her relationship with her boyfriend after he died in the Nova Scotia floods and returned to be with her as a ghost.

"IT IS A-BOUT," he begins, "BE-ING STUCK. WHAT TO DO A-BOUT IT."

"What do you suggest, Sad? For people who are stuck?"

"SWIM."

I laugh, thinking of how uninhabitable our waters have been these past few years, their rising toxicity level, and the fish that washed onto the shore, their bones plucked completely clean of their flesh.

Click.

In the lobby of the building a couple of days later, after picking up a Spam surplus at the nearest checkpoint, I see a series of new xeroxed flyers posted across a bulletin board. They read *LOOK*, and instinctively I whip around in a circle, expecting to find someone or something there. Nothing. I peer into the paper and see that several squiggly lines resembling currents accompany the word. Upon closer inspection, I see that the paper has ink bleeding through it. When I flip it around, I see scratched into the paper with a black Sharpie: *1A.*

I look down the hallway of the lobby, counting down the apartment doors. 1G, then 1F, then 1E, and so on, moving away from the building's front door. 1A is at the far end of the corridor—a red door in a sea of metallic gray, as if it had stood the test of time and won.

I hold on to one of the flyers for days, waiting. *Mira, look, Mira, look.* In the fat letters of the flyer, I see a narrative unfold—a shadow, a pair of rough hands, and an abyss I can fall into for days.

Shin, catching me with the flyer in one hand and masturbating with the other one night, whispers quietly, "Go to him."

Shuddering into my release, I let out a soft "I want to," followed shortly after with a startling revelation: "I can't."

Shin has seen me cry into the night many times before, and so this is no exception. These days, I cry when I come, its relief like an animal leaving me. He crawls toward me, parking himself on my pillow, which is damp with tears. Without saying a word, he lies there quietly, watching me. Finally, with care, he offers the following: "Of the two of us, you can."

I am watching him this time, his small body adrift on the cotton waves of my pillow, so aware of his ghostliness—how I can pass my hand through him, and he will still be there. What a strange thing eternity is. And how short a life.

Dear Listeners, I once met a poet who said that each time some-one broke her heart, she would run through the stretch of Coney Island Beach at night, climb onto a lifeguard's chair, and hurl her-self down onto a pile of broken glass. I was young when I heard this and thought that this dedication to pain meant that you ate glass to become stronger. Then the doctor told me one day that my stomach was full of so much glass that it was cutting into my stomach lining and that is why I have this ulcer. That is why I seek out other forms of nutrition, and, finding nothing else that would taste as good, I rely on Prilosec. I can't offer you any more advice beyond this.

The following Tuesday, I wake up to rapt knocking on the apartment door and open it to find a sobbing Lucinda. Ma rises from bed, hobbling over to her. Lucinda can only cry over and over, "He's dead! He's dead! God took him and he's dead!"

Ma turns on the news, and there is NY1 with a breaking news story about a windstorm that hit Queens in the west, starting from Flushing and then moving into Corona. The windstorm has knocked down more telephone wires, hurled trees onto cars, and smashed into houses. In several neighborhoods, the sparks from torn wires set fire to the dry wood patching up many of the apartment buildings. The fire hopped from build-ing to building until finally it reached an apartment complex at the edge of a park that no one frequented anymore. There the fire died, taking with it twenty-three people who were all surely at some point desperately pawing at the layers of wood plastered over their windows—fire swarming from behind and in front of them, nursing a desperate faith that after diving into the closest flame, they could come out the other side alive.

I watch Lucinda claw at the television as it cycles through photos of charred debris, whispering quietly now, "My baby, my baby, that's my baby."

JoJo. I feel his name like a hard knot in my throat. I stare at the television screen, but after a while the images of burned wreckage and police tape all blur into one storm of color. Who can survive any of this?

And then the thought soon after: *Mal.*

It is possible, I think, and realize the words are coming out my mouth in the form of cold air. To the room of ghosts and wailing women, I say aloud, "Where are you, Mal?"

No answer except the air that crackles. Ma is slumped over Lucinda, who is slumped over the television, the images awash in her tears. Grandpa Why and Shin press themselves against a wall, so far removed from their own immediate grief that the scene suddenly reminds them of their ghostliness, and they howl too. Throwing a sweater over my nightgown, I let this phantom feeling take over. I leave the apartment.

"Where you goin', Lone Ranger?" Grandpa Why calls after me. "Your business is not done!"

I ignore him as I bolt down the stairs, knowing that eventually my feet will reach where they need to go. When I hit door, I pelt through the lobby and the long corridor stretch until I reach the red door marked 1A. Knocking with such urgency burning through me, I am surprised when I hear several locks click from the other side.

The door opens slightly, and I see the clean nails of a man's hand gripping the edges of the frame. Then the door opens fully, and I stare into his square chest. When I look up, I realize the man has no head. At the base of his neck, a surface layer of flesh, so flat that I can place my own head on it and feel assured that everything is going to be okay.

Mal used to say I had no concept of danger. One night I took the train home alone from Canarsie, thinking it'd be fine to put money onto my MetroCard in an empty station. She said she was not surprised when someone clubbed me from behind and took my purse and my MetroCard with inexact fare. In this moment, I imagine she will say, *Now you're just doing it on purpose.*

I open my mouth to speak after a long silence. "Are you Sad?" I ask. "This is Mira from the radio show. Is this a bad time?"

When he doesn't speak for a long time, I think maybe my instincts are right—that a headless person will not be able to hear me. As I apologize, he moves aside to invite me in. I pause for a half second before walking into his apartment.

There is no side table or mirror where a side table or mirror should be, but instead a generator with a line of PVC pipes taped against the wall leading to the living room. There, a large aquarium tank stretches from the floor to just slightly below the ceiling. When I reach the living room, my hands instinctively run along the side of the tank. I feel the weight of its glass, strangely reassured by its thickness. In the tank are looming pieces of pink coral, spiny growths, and leafy plants with glossy petals that start out wide at the bottom and taper off as they reach the top of the water. There are fish too—bright purple ones with transparent skin, spotted brown and yellow sucker fish drifting along the gravel, and peacock eels that ripple when my finger taps against the glass.

I stare for so long at the tanks that I do not realize Sad is standing right behind me. He points his finger at one of the peacock eels and then at my chest.

"You're saying that's me?" I ask, perplexed.

He wags his finger and points again, this time to the left side of my chest, to the space over my heart. He touches his finger to my skin.

"Oh."

He points to my shoes, which in my haste were thrown on without socks and left neglectfully unlaced. I take them off. He gestures, moving his arms up and down his torso. I don't understand. He takes hold of my nightgown's hem and lifts the garment up and over my head, my sweater falling down to the floor along with it. He pauses before pulling my underwear down too.

"How are you going to kiss me?" I ask candidly. I am too ashamed to tell him about all the times I dreamed of him and his mouth pressing against my body.

He places his hand flat against my chest and moves it slowly along the span of my body as if mapping a waltz, and I think about how his hands are also his eyes. When he reaches where I need him to reach me, I feel him trace a somber wetness that rings like a siren upward and through me.

In the corner of the room, I see Grandpa Why camouflaged against the ceiling cracks, shaking his head disapprovingly and then covering his eyes. I see Shin looking on, his antennae twitching every which way.

Sad hoists me up, at first lifting me to his hip, and then over his neck, until I am standing on his shoulders, holding on to the top of the fish tank for balance. He points emphatically to the top of the tank and then to its floor. I throw my body over the edge of the tank, diving headfirst into the cold water, salty and sour with aquatic life. I see the many fish disperse as I splash into them and then quietly and surely return to center, gently nudging against my flesh. They understand how my body has become a box over the years—that I will do anything to be smashed open.

Later, when Sad joins me in the tank, I tell him about Mal and how the first time we slept together I grew to love her strangeness. Plagued by night terrors, the only thing that could calm her at night was to fashion a bed in the bathtub. She would sleep there, and then in the morning drink water straight from the metal spout. She said it reminded her of being in the womb, which even she knew was ridiculous. And yet, she said, the body knew things that memory had no footholds in. We were always building surrogate wombs while living—to sleep and to dream in. On one occasion, she lowered herself to the tub, her eyes watering with sleep. She had pleaded softly, "Can I stay here for a little bit longer?" I nodded, and before I knew it, I was nestled there with her. She did not ask me to, but I knew—that night, she wanted me to stay there with her too.

HOW TO GROW A GARDEN

Dear Listeners,

Let me tell you a story without end. I'm dedicating this segment of our show to the letter *I*, though this story has little to do with me. In fact, it is about a mother and daughter who lived in a tiny studio apartment somewhere along Mott Street where Chinatown borders Little Italy, a place so small that the closet would eventually become the daughter's room when she grew older. They lived a quiet life with the usual routine—the girl gets dropped off at school on Henry Street before eight a.m.; after, the woman takes herself to work at the garment shop off the York Street station; dinner every night by six, which the girl, once she is old enough, prepares for her mother before she comes home from her work of sewing and unstitching the hems of assorted denim; library on

Saturdays for free morning programs; free food line at the community center on Wednesdays; and grocery shopping for cheap cuts of meat, preserved sausages, canned fish, slightly bruised vegetables at Hong Kong Supermarket on Thursdays after school lets out. The rice cooker would open to a steamer carrying a tiny dish of spareribs, often more rib than meat, the heat filling the apartment. The girl and the woman would clink their bowls together like little princes.

"One day," the girl begins to promise her mother over dinner, "I will buy you a big house with a garden where you can grow bitter melon and squash, large and juicy red tomatoes."

Mothers love when little ones relay these impossible dreams, but the woman feels something gnaw at her chest. *Is love not enough?* she was probably wondering.

One day, the building caught fire in the middle of the night. Most of the residents were able to get out alive, but not the woman and her daughter. With the entire building engulfed in black, peeling apart, the firefighters found them in their respective beds (the room, the closet), each appearing to be sound asleep.

But their story is not over. When I tell you that disaster is a ghost machine, I mean it literally. A decade before the acid rain, they rebuilt this building, which became a version of something far removed from its original form—a salon downstairs, white and pristine from ceiling to floor, and a lobby with more than one security guard who kept watch over several cameras. Nothing happened during that decade of rebuilding until the acid rain came—that's when mother and daughter returned for good.

You might be wondering what every ghost's first order of business is upon return. Grandpa Why would say he felt a freedom much like a belch, and that's what he did. He belched. Shin, on the other hand, didn't speak for days after Ma tried to end him a second time with the back of one of her slippers. So, you see, no one ghost thinks alike.

The woman and the girl, the two of them took over the new building, wreaking a special kind of havoc. On nights when meat was served for dinner, the two would turn the stove or oven up to a roaring broil until the stench of black smoke would fill the room, and from the thick veil of it all you would just hear their twin cackles. This they would do every night, in unison, until eventually everyone turned vegetarian, which would soon have been the case anyway, given the slim pickings of our food rations.

During the early days of the acid rain, you might remember, in some zones we were given packets of seeds—lettuce, green beans, cucumbers, tomatoes. Not enough potting soil to go around, but some of us had enough knowledge of composting to make things work. Some of us might have sold these seeds for something else, and others grew tiny pots of what would eventually sprout and vine through our apartments.

This new building was no different. Though the residents pooled their seeds together and made a rooftop garden, shielded by an acid-proof tarp during the Tuesday rain. No protective layer would ever last more than a couple of storms, but what they did manage to grow—though never as tasty and flavorful as the vegetables they remember—was undoubtedly impressive. The lettuce was most abundant, and the green beans dangled, heavy and long. The tomatoes, extra beefy, were a swirl of green and red, already bending their stalks toward the ground.

It was here, in sight of all of this, that the woman and the girl could be spotted sitting, one hand over the other, folded on each other's laps, looking into this garden on the rooftop pooling with questionably edible things. Funny how it happens, isn't it? How some people can make a home by haunting one.

Yee took me to this rooftop once on a mission I cannot disclose, and all I could do was cry. That week's rations: canned peaches, canned corn, everything in a can. I must have been so hungry that day. That must have been it.

THE MA (妈) LIKE MĀ, NOT LIKE HORSE (马) RADIO SHOW

Guest Spot #1: There Are No Rules to This Haunting

妈 is pronounced Mā. The tongue is flat as plasterboard in your mouth. If you try to complicate it, moving the sounds back to front, you would be saying Mǎ, which is how you get *horse*, and that is not what I am.

Like yesterday, when Mira says, "Mǎ, can you do me a favor?" I know she is trying me. She thinks she's a regular Stephen Chow, that one, following up with a real ask like I didn't see it coming. She says, "I want you to come on my radio show and talk about something," to which I say, "Okay, you want me to talk about *something*." In case you're missing it, I'm rolling my eyes.

Then, as usual, she puts her head on my shoulder, and smiles like a dumb fish into my ear. "Mǎ, I mean something that matters to you, and you only." Which is how I got to be where I am today talking to all of you about God knows what.

Mira, you spend a lot of time on this radio show, talking all kinds of things about love and heartbreak. I don't know how you do it. What is there to say? You're looking at me like I'm a spool about to unwind. I can tell you this: Love happens and sometimes it goes away. No need to dwell on it.

Mira says to start with an introduction. "Something easy," she says. She's handing me a note now with a list of topic ideas. I see now she's thinking this is a bad idea, but it's too late.

It is Tuesday and there is a hole over New York City from which water keeps pouring out. Just our luck, I guess, though you can't say that other parts of this country are doing any better. The hurricanes in Florida dragged the whole state through chemical sludge, earthquakes opened chasms in California so deep that they had to retabulate zip codes. I hear about it on the radio and sometimes it is too much. We should be so lucky that at least we are on a schedule of some kind—a siren ringing out every Tuesday morning, city workers in hazard suits passing out protective gear, yelling at us to stay home. Some people do, some people don't, though if you don't . . . well, you know. In any case, it is very ABC.

The water is the hardest part—to hide from, to seek out. Each family with our own plastic drum that we roll down the street on a not-Tuesday on a metal hand truck. No one likes this, by the way. I see Mira now shaking her head.

The other day, for instance, I waited in line with Mira for half an hour—and that was what they called a quiet day—only to be offered the bottom-of-the-barrel stuff. You know, the water with all the dirt and grit floating on top? Like I told Mira, this was unacceptable. The kid working the water rations shift that day—she had no idea what she was doing. I said I wasn't going anywhere until they brought out clean water, and we stared each other down for a good ten minutes. In the end, she mixed the purifying tablets into the water, and I can't understand for the life of me why she didn't just do that in the first place. Wasting everyone's time.

And me. I have lived here most of my life, this apartment overlooking the East River where the Pathmark used to be a long time ago. I couldn't have been more than one year old when I boarded the plane from Hong Kong to New York with Grandpa Why, could barely recall anything of that memory that your grandfather did not relay to me himself. He said we slept on every cousin's uncle and auntie's floor for several years until we found ourselves in this apartment. It is strange to recall it now, but I do remember that first night here when we laid out the one sheet that we shared between us on the floor and that was our bed.

Grandpa Why and I had, by some miracle or habit of having slept on floors for the better part of the year, just fallen asleep when I was woken up by a roaring outside the window. I looked out the window and saw that the water of the East River was slapping (really slapping!) against the concrete barrier. But the roaring did not come from the water. To this day, I'm not sure if what I saw was my imagination or something else, but there, walking on the water, was a row of young girls, each one wearing the same identical braid down her back. They were lit up by the moon and highway lights, these young girls skipping as if they were on a playground and not floating atop the moving water. When they opened their mouths and closed them, out came a roar, which sounded nothing like human noise. I could see them so clearly, but when I told Grandpa Why the next morning, he looked at me and scoffed, "You children are always making up stories! This country is already scrambling your brains."

Had I believed in ghosts before then? I grew up on ghost stories told by Grandpa Why and all the uncles and aunties we ever stayed with—tales of abandoned women, children who left the world too soon, each of them with their hair grown long and sweeping to the floor. They were not so much ghost stories, but stories of people who kept losing themselves after death. They were not moaners or screechers, though on occasion they've been known to steal a child from their bed. I understood their loneliness, why they would drag their fingers along a living body with such longing. I always felt there was good reason for their haunting.

Since I've lived in this apartment, I've not heard anything about the haunting of the East River, though I knew of the early days when the water was the mob's dumping ground. Now they're fishing up all sorts of animals with gangrene and piss-yellow eyes sunk deep in the water, and I say animals because I don't know for sure what else comes and goes in there, human or otherwise.

When Mira was very young—and I doubt she'd remember this—a girl went missing in her school. She could not have been older than ten, the Fujianese girl—there was a whole wave of them that came to New York then; you could hear the sharpness of their dialect from down the street. She had immigrated with her parents not more than one year before and barely spoke any English. Some said they saw a man—tall,

white, and bearded—who walked next her, and to anyone looking it seemed like they were just a pair of odd friends. That was
what the papers, Chinese and American alike, said when they
interviewed witnesses. The young girl stayed silent the whole
time, apparently. Can you believe it? A city full of people, and
no one could recognize a face full of terror? They found her a
week later, lifted her out of the East River, bloated and with
only her shirt on.

When the rain started, I thought we would see her again,
that she would, like the hundreds of ghosts newly arrived in the
city, come back to haunt us. So far, the ghosts have only come
to haunt the insides of homes. No one had any clue who would
come to visit and who would stay for the long run.

From what I know so far, the dead girl hasn't paid any of us
a visit, so I imagine there is no rule or pattern as to why some
decide to return and some just prefer to stay away.

(Is this good enough now, Mira? Am I supposed to say more?)

Some advice regarding the lost girl: If you do see her, set
out an altar, fill it with red candy, light some incense, and bow
three times each in four directions. Perhaps she will come to
you when you really mean it, and so, you mean it.

What matters to me, and to me only? In no specific order:
Mira, the left side of Buddha, a life where I get to stay right
here, unchanged, even when all around me the world is a
sneeze away from collapsing.

Guest Spot #2: The Doctor

I have never liked hospitals. Not even the waiting rooms at
free clinics. Can't stand the sight of syringes, sharp metal

objects on a plate. I have not gone to a dentist in years. (I prefer to keep my cavities.) When I get my blood drawn, Lucinda comes with me, holds my hand. The skin where the needle pierces through blooms into a large purple bruise that stays for weeks.

I suppose it makes sense that it has come down to this, though I still don't care for the mandated doctor visits. All of us, packed like sardines into the clinic, what did the city expect except disease to spread? Thankfully, for this building at least, there has not been anything serious so far—mostly colds, some upper respiratory ailments, a strange case of ringworm among the kindergarten lot, and of course the seasonal flu, which took so many of us down. I suppose the idea is that making regular checkups a requirement of the law would enable the city to treat any disease before it spreads. With so many of us, though, and so little time before preparation for the next rain, the lines for appointments can wrap around multiple blocks.

You may have heard about Dr. Wu already, the old man with hair so shiny and slicked back it was like a big black helmet. He had somehow found a way to keep dyeing his hair during quarantine, never a single gray spotted on his head, as jet-black as the day Mira first saw him as a child. Do you remember him, Mira? His receptionist, older than he was, would give you her old erasers for you to play with. She's long gone now, but Dr. Wu managed to stick around.

Dr. Wu's old office was in a basement off Bayard, where he saw many of us, and by some miracle none of his appointments ever lasted more than five minutes. It was an ideal situation for me, as I told him: "If I had a choice, I wouldn't even be sitting here." To which he then replied saucily, "Good. I don't even want most people to be here long enough to sit down." I admit that I like that kind of bedside manner.

Lucinda and I would go to him during these checkups, and he would see both of us together. With JoJo gone, Lucinda is beginning to tell me more and more about her health, and I tell her as much as I can about mine. Who else is going to look after us, after all? I learn from Dr. Wu that Lucinda has a hyperactive thyroid and that my blood pressure could be lower. Neither of us should be eating as much fat and oil as we do, so he sends us home with supplement packages, courtesy of the city government, and the business card of an herbalist right next door.

To think I was starting to get used to the idea of going to a doctor. But of course nothing good can stay for long. The city shut his business down after finding out that he had not been following all the rules for routine visits and was prescribing medicines not on the authorized checklist. We found this out when we arrived at Dr. Wu's office for our checkup, only to see a sign on the door with some version of this explanation. Mayor's signature and all. Such a shame.

When we leave Dr. Wu's office for the last time, the herbalist waves us into his shop, which he shares with the shoe cobbler. Says that Dr. Wu has since moved to New Jersey, where he shares a house with two of his mistresses. How that works, I can't begin to know. Then the herbalist hands me a pouch of something brown and full of roots, stinky so you know it works.

"For your daughter," the herbalist tells me, "from Dr. Wu."

When I ask Mira what the medicine is for, she shrugs, so I ask her again. With the same tired sigh that she always gives me, she covers her eyes with one palm and then places her other hand on her chest. She says, "For my head and my heart."

I tap at my watch—its hour hand has been stuck at three for a while now—and then look back at her face. "You've mourned for a while now. Is it not time to let some things go?"

Mira's face scrunches up into something miserable. I mean it in the sense that no heart should put itself through so much torture. What is the point, after all? When people go, they go. She doesn't think of it that way.

Mira looks away when she remarks, "You'll never see it, will you?" Her face so very sad.

Very confusing, how she gets like this sometimes. I never know what to say. What am I not seeing, after all? The rain that won't stop? The seemingly endless unspooling of our days? I want people to see I'm tired too.

Mira begins to walk away as I call after her, "What did you tell Dr. Wu?" She pretends not to hear me, so I joke, "Maybe I need some medicine too!"

Guest Spot #3: The Dream

It was in a dream that I saw the rain before it came.

In the dream, I was a tortoise, and I was both hard and soft. I knew my way around the land, which was New York City through a tortoise-eye view. The buildings were large, imposing, and sharp as a knife cutting into the sky. I walked through the city from Rector Street all along the East River up to Pike, where I lived or remembered living as a human. It was a strange thing, walking through the city in this other body, which moved so slowly even in a dream. The ground was dry, but it spoke to me; it said it would not be long.

I've heard that animals always recognize the first signs of

disaster before humans do. The ants file out in thick frenzied black lines before the rain. The way dogs bark or horses kick when they sense a disturbance. I felt it all in my body, walking as I did, block after block, that something was sure to arrive.

When I reached the steps of Building 4B, I thought about how it would be like to live the rest of my life as a tortoise, surprising myself with how quickly I came to accept this new life. What parts of my humanness did I miss? I guess they were all forgettable.

Then a cannonball fell from the sky, and it was not until I rocked my shell back to standing that I saw that it was not metal but water that came crashing down. It splashed and sizzled, burning thirty-five holes in the ground. I blinked (could tortoises blink? I did), and in the moment that passed before the first impact and the shutting of lids, another came down just ten feet away.

I thought, *I'm going to die.*

I thought, *What does it mean to die as a tortoise?*

But the rain never came down on me. It fell instead all around, knocking over the metal railing, flattening the ramp to a cobbled dent. The trees fell too, smacked down to the ground in swift finishes. It left craters bigger than SUVs on the street, and suddenly the Lower East Side was a terrifying moon.

When I woke up, my joints were aching. I made myself some tea, thinking of how I would have to take the bus to Chambers since the C train wasn't running at Jay Street that month, which was usually where I would transfer from the F on my way to work. *Like a joke*, I said to myself: Well, if the world would just end today, I'd save myself a trip. And then the rain came, and it didn't stop. It burned holes in every pocket of the city. Even now I can smell the bodies after the rain.

Guest Spot #4: The Return of Grandpa Why

How do I explain the strange sensation of meeting my father again, who you all know as Grandpa Why or the flatulent king, after he has been dead for twenty-one years?

We never talk about what it means to miss someone, my father and me.

My mother died before I knew her, and so, how do I miss her? I asked your Grandpa Why once if he thought of her often, but he said nothing, would not even look me in the eye.

To miss him, then? I don't know what well of feeling to draw from.

Mira says, "One thing." I want to say, *I remember the length of his eyebrows, the hairs so long I thought they were there to cast shadows for his eyes.* So funny to think about, those eyebrows, but for those first few years after your Grandpa Why died, I would be walking down the street, and any time I saw an old man with very long eyebrows, I would feel it in my chest. I don't know what to call that feeling.

When Grandpa Why died, I thought, this was it. I did not cry, could not with Mira at my hip. (Mira, you were so little, but even then you knew it was time to cry.) I bounced my Mira in my arms while the monk chanted, the chanting eventually putting her to sleep. My father was a stern man when he was alive, so humorless that it was no surprise attendance at the funeral was sparse. The people who did come had very few things to say. There was your Grandpa Why's old boss who came up to us after, giving Mira such a hard pat on the head that it woke her up and reminded her that more crying had to be done. I was trying to wrestle her back to sleep when the old boss muttered something about your Grandpa Why being a "hard worker" before scurrying away.

It is hard to imagine him as anything but the very serious man I knew him as, though there were always signs, I suppose, of some other life we did not know about. For instance, when the funeral home laid his body into the coffin, I touched his breast pocket to find, tucked inside a handkerchief, a blue kazoo.

I could not remember him laughing much. He had no tolerance for jokes, not even when the other factory workers took the buttons from the bins and placed them over their eyes, hopping around like vampires. "The spoiled cabbage society rises again," he'd say when he got home. Then I'd play the same game with my own collection of buttons, and he'd smack the back of my head, the tiny rounds falling from my eyes.

I asked them to wipe the cancer from his face with heavy foundation and a bit of coloring. It was what he would have wanted, the little dignity cosmetics could offer.

I watched as they lowered him into the ground.

The small procession and I waited at our apartment door for his spirit to pass through.

Every year, we burned for him, paper money, paper mansions, paper cars.

We were quiet for a long time.

Then your Grandpa Why returned, and he was not himself.

When he came back to Apartment 9A, he seemed to know his own ghost body better than he had ever known his human parts when he was alive, stretching his whole self from one end of the room to the other, fascinated by how much he could flex, bend, loop, and spin.

I just sat on the couch, my jaw hanging loose.

I called out to him. "Baba?" I reached out for him. It was as if he could not see or hear me. He kept on spinning through the room, yelping as he did. As he pelted through the space, I could make out his face through the blue blur of him—his crooked nose, his long brows, the hair spilling over his ears. I had to check, you know? Just to be sure. All his parts were there.

He didn't answer. I was stunned. I thought, *Maybe he doesn't remember me anymore?* My chest hurt at the thought. In the air, he was like a fish, all that fast movement. I wanted him so badly to slow down.

I called out to him again. "Baba?" and then, "Do you not see me?"

Grandpa Why paused long enough to study my face. He lunged forward jokingly, as if he were about to strike me in a head butt, but I did not flinch. He seemed disappointed, the way one would if their punch line missed the mark. All he murmured was "Oh, I know you." And that was that.

When my father came back, the first thing I thought of was what he said to me before he died: "It is just you now." We do not say *I love you* here. It is not something we say at all.

Which is not to say that he did not care in his own way. There was a time when he cared so deeply, in fact, he made himself sick. When I was little, I would watch him comb his hair back with oil and wait for the hair to stiffen before touching it. He was always a different man after he was done with his hair—glasses on, pressed collar, and shoes polished so cleanly you would think they could never scuff. All this just to go to the factory, which seemed to be a maker of as much dust and accidents as bobbins and wheels. His pressed shirt would be wilted, soaked in steam and sweat by the time he came home. Still, even when he was coughing up tar and blood, he made sure to set his hair straight before he went to work. At night, he repolished his shoes, ironed his shirt again for the next day. Toward the end of his life, he was spitting up red clots into the same polishing cloth, folding it in half so that I would not see. He never spoke of disease himself, did not go to any doctor, except, after much pleading on my part, he did see an acupuncturist on Baxter Street who said that he could purify the toxins in his blood, but as the culprit lay deep in him, there was little else he could do.

You would not think the circumstances of his death were anything this tragic by the looks of him now—foulmouthed and mirroring the sounds of the air sirens during the most ridiculous hours of night. God forbid any of us should get any sleep if he cannot. These days, he seems most alive in his boredom.

The other day, Grandpa Why and I were traveling through the stairwell of the building, as it was my turn to do the monthly repairs. He had decided to come with me to the Liang family's apartment, whose toilet was backed up after their youngest tried to flush a pack of screws. Grandpa Why was no help, of course, plunging himself down the drainpipe, kicking up water as he went. The youngest Liang, who saw that her bad move was celebrated by all this mess and noise, clapped and fell over laughing. I do not think the Liangs were happy with me after that. When Grandpa Why and I left, the repair half done, I was fuming. I told him to walk five steps behind me, which he took literally, counting out each step along the way. I'm not proud of it, talking to my own father like this, and I imagine Mira might have picked up a thing or two from me.

Then the counting stopped, and I turned around to find him crouched over a step. He cried out, "Well, boy howee!" He motioned to the darkened step.

I pointed my flashlight toward where he was bent over, seeing nothing at first until I moved closer. Beneath my father's ghost was an etching about half an inch tall: my full name in Chinese carved into the side of the concrete.

"You, you, you," Grandpa Why said as he started pointing my way, and then I remembered. During a blackout one night many years ago, my father and I were walking up the dark stairwell to our apartment. I had been complaining about writing the Chinese characters for "mountain" and "sky" and "human" over and over in thin green composition books my father kept in stacks lining each cabinet. He put me down and took out a pocketknife, squatting over a step with a conspiratorial look in his eyes I could make out even in the dark. We struck a bargain that night. If I could write my name there and do it perfectly, Grandpa Why said, I'd never have to do lessons with him ever again.

I studied the dark, the way that the shapes of our bodies folded within it. The knife moved tentatively in my hand and then more surely as I corrected myself with the other hand, feeling for each stroke. I had heard that the friction between two hard surfaces could create a spark. I thought that with the heaviness of each stroke, I could make a fire.

When I was done, my father clapped his hand on my shoulder and folded back his knife. He carried me on his back for the rest of the way up the stairs. In the morning, we went to go look at the etching. We found that although it lacked the kind of grace that he had when he wrote, it was, more or less, readable and correct.

When he asked me what I wanted to do then, I said I wanted to play from now on, and that was what I did.

I wouldn't recommend doing what I did, which was slack off for years, so much of my language lost that it took some time to get it all back. "Mountain," "sky," "human." "Human," "mountain," "sky." I tell Mira now that she has to write them over and over. She says, "Why, Ma? This is so boring." But you know now, Mira. It is hard to get back what you lose once you lose it. Do you get it now? Have I said enough?

Guest Spot #5: The Other Dream

It would happen again.

Most nights, there was a great big hole in the sky. I dreamed it. A swirling mass that moved like a whirlpool. Like the world had turned upside down and water took the place of the sky. In the dream, I was looking up, and the sky had a face, so bright with the color of fury. All of us stood in front of the apartment building—Mira, your Grandpa Why, the neighbors—forming a long line that snaked around the corner and for many blocks onward.

I thought to myself, how typical the way things go these days—another line, another wait for some undetermined time. And I was so bored at first that the alarm took some time to settle in.

The air was heavy with something electric and with sirens that flickered their forever red. Then the buses would come, the way they used to arrive in five- or ten-minute intervals during rush hour on a weekday. My god, were they beat up, these buses. They meant to take us away.

In the dream, I kept asking, "Where? Where?"

Every bus driver a faceless man wearing a shadow veil—they would always say nothing.

Then the people would cram onto the buses, abandoning all hope for order. The ghosts stayed behind, tethered to the building and whatever life lingered between its walls. The sky darkened, the whirlpool churning itself into black tar. And then the water would begin to fall slowly, hot and burning against our shoulders, our temples.

There was no time for questions. We had to go. I grabbed Mira's hand, but in the chaos of the crowd, I could not look back, and so it could have been anyone's hand. Each time I dreamed this, I would try to memorize the shape and feel of her hand.

Here, Mira. Give me your hand. I'll show you. The mounds of your fingers identical to mine, though with less roughness. We should know this now, just in case.

Though I never made it inside the bus, I was determined to stay afloat in the crowd, grabbing hold of Mira so tightly. This was all I could do, after all. Wherever these buses would take us, I was sure we would find out in due time.

Guest Spot #6: What I Know About Love

"What do you know about love?" Mira, you asked me this once.

On the day you returned to Apartment 9A, you were unwell, and you remained unwell for weeks after. I could not understand it, and even now I have questions.

That day you arrived at my door, your eyes were like two red clouds.

I looked you up and down, the same torn jeans you wore when you left home. I said to you, "What's the matter with you?"

You just shook your head and rushed past me, and it was as if you knew that your room was still there, that it had remained untouched since you had left it.

I stood by the door, watching your body slump onto the bed. Your back rounded and became concave again in a pattern of heaving sobs. I asked you again, softly this time, "What happened?"

You rolled over and pointed to your chest. You said, "It hurts, Ma."

Okay. I placed my hand on your back and rubbed it in circles, just like I had always done when you were little and upset.

I asked you if you had a fight with your friend. I knew it was about Mal, the Korean girl with big hair, who looked like a boy sometimes, wearing jeans with bigger holes than the ones you would wear. Because you became so quiet, I told you what I knew, which was that it was always a bad idea to live with friends. It's no good, you see? You have one fight and then suddenly you have no home and no friend.

What now, Mira? Are you upset again? You're looking at me now with the same look you had then.

It is always the same argument, which I still cannot understand. Can you explain it to me now without dumbing it down, Mira? Back then, you declared that I knew nothing about love, that I cared about nothing. Who talks to their parent like that? Take Grandpa Why. In his living days, he often talked about the cruelty of daughters when I acted out—came home late, played too rough with boys. Even then, I knew when he cuffed my ear or slapped the back of my head that he meant well, that he cared, which was more than what most parents did. To say that I know nothing about love! Well.

When you were five years old, you were so, so small, the unfortunate target of many bullying girls twice your size. You came home one day, your backpack emptied of your stickers and gel pens, the tiny things you loved to collect and which I knew you spent hours keeping in careful order. You denied anything had happened, but I knew. Mothers always know. And so I went to your school the next day, spoke to the teacher, an older white woman who seemed clueless about the unkindness of Chinese girls bullying one another in two languages. You were in your seat, avoiding eye contact, but I knew by the way you kept looking across the room at one of the taller girls that I had found the ringleader of the bunch.

I approached the girl, who must have seemed giant to you then, but her two missing front teeth and spray of hair shooting up from a red scrunchie made her seem not so big to me.

I said to her, "Hello, do you know who I am?" The girl seemed confused, so I repeated myself again in Cantonese. "你知唔知我係邊個呀?"

This time the girl's eyes grew wide with alarm. If she had ever known the wrath of aunties, then surely she knew the vengeance of mothers learning that their child had suffered some injury. We were in public, and, gathering by her expression, she had assessed this. She knew I wouldn't dare knock her across the face. (Some slight relief there.) But then it occurred to her too that Chinatown was not so small that I could not find her. (Panic flared again.)

She glanced over at Mira almost pleadingly.

"佢係我嘅囡." I pointed to Mira. That one, she is mine. In English, I said to her, "Do not forget."

I'm older now, but I find that I remember everything sometimes so clearly. I see Mira with Sad, a very good man, and I think this does not come from nowhere. We need each other very badly during these times. These days, the world is a giant hole in the sky that is leaking. What can we do about it but try our best? I tell Mira, "You must be good to Sad and let him take care of you. It is not good to be alone." Sometimes when I tell her this, she cries.

What do I know about love? What a silly question. Mira, you silly, silly girl.

Guest Spot #7: The Sadness of Fruits

Bananas are the only fruit to have survived. This is the market's most singular truth. You don't believe me? Ask Paolo at the Henry Street fruit stand and Min too at East Broadway, if you really care to make sure. To call it a fruit stand anymore is pure nostalgia, as if we have more than one thing to choose from. The banana is lab-grown, said to taste like strawberries in some cases and like regular bananas other times. I read about this once in the Chinese papers. It was a failure in flavor splicing, the scientists wanting to make two memories—the creamy and sinewy banana with the seedy tartness of a strawberry—for the price of one. It was too costly to expend so much energy on replicating either strawberry or banana alone, so why not fuse both? The results are these little shrubs carrying bananas no bigger than the size of your thumb, the peels sometimes peppered with black seeds. The labs tossed the seeds for these fruits anywhere they could, practically dumping them on the doorsteps of local farms. This was in the trial phases, of course, and now I'm sure they're charging them plenty to keep going. They were desperate for any takers. And so the farmers in Jersey came to grow these banana-strawberry plants, funny as they were, and the wholesale markets, seeing that there were no other options but these hybrid fruits, ended up just taking them.

We eat them all the time now, especially on the days when food rations are a little lower than usual. Bananas mixed with rice, some hoisin sauce on the side to sweeten. They are one of the most hated things to eat around here. Eating too much of them, people have discovered, is a digestive nightmare. Some of us may have eaten a little too much of them, though you know what? I don't mind it so much.

Guest Spot #8: Lucinda

To my good friend Lucinda on the eighth floor, I dedicate this program to you today.

It seemed impossible for some time to make a new friend at my age, what with being quarantined here once a week and working all day during the others. I tell you it was much easier when I was younger, and for many reasons, the acid rain included, it is just far more difficult now. I won't say how many years ago, but I will say I remember playing jacks made with sewed-up rice packs that looked like tiny pillows that fell on your fingers. That was a fast way to make friends. Now it matters less what toy you have and more what you can barter.

Lucinda, though, she never asks much of me. Maybe once she asked me to find a button that could match her blouse, and because I had many saved from the days Grandpa Why hoarded buttons from the factory, we found one that was so exact it terrified us a bit. Lucinda has a way of saying with her eyes how scared she is and what makes her very, very happy, the two sometimes being one and the same. There are things people say about Lucinda, about how she's a witch, but I think these are just things people say about old women who live alone.

They call me an old widow. I hate that word "widow," and for anyone who has seen a black widow spider, you would think twice about giving an old woman that sort of name. It is true that I felt like I was capable of something deadly when Mira's dad died. I won't talk about that. It's not seemly to talk about the dead in such detail, especially not publicly. Though I talk to Lucinda about this all the time. And she agrees: What good are the men, living or dead? What have they done for us alive that we can't do ourselves?

How unfair, that even as the past year has changed so much for all of us, the men don't show up, and when they do, they make a mess of it all.

"Has your son come back to visit?" I ask Lucinda of her JoJo.

She shakes her head and tells me, "Still working on it," which I think is very commendable, urging any man to return.

JoJo was a sweet one, though, a very artistic boy who looked like any slice of wind could bowl him over. So we are eager for him to visit us as a ghost soon. I know Lucinda would prefer it sooner. I imagine it's just a matter of time.

Sometimes Lucinda and I play a game with the workers who come by in hazmat suits. When they sound the alarms, do floor checks, and barricade the doors, we sometimes peek out our windows to watch them. We like to think some of them have got something going on underneath all that good rubber. One day, when Lucinda and I were walking into the building, one of the workers held the door open for us, and we gave each other this look like, *Ooh, check out this good-looking piece of—* and then, of course, Lucinda let out a loud whistle. The hazmat suit, still holding the door open, took off their hat, and in front of us stood one handsome woman. She gave us a wink, and though we were embarrassed, we both winked back.

Guest Spot #9: The Business of Being Sad

Let me tell you what makes a good man. That Sad, he's a good one. I've said this before, and I don't say this often of many men. You would think all this time the problem with men is that they don't have much going on in their heads. Not to worry with Sad, though—he lost his head a good while ago. *It's okay to joke*, Sad says. *Just don't take it too far.* So, I'll leave it at that.

Sad takes Mira on walks through the building. They don't go outside, I think because Sad prefers it that way. And I don't know how he does it without a mouth, but somehow he tells her about flowers, their Latin names, and the light they grow best in. He learned about them from a botany book, one of the few left behind in the basement with braille, and because there aren't many around, I suppose, it makes it easier to study the one over and over, to memorize the way the book feels. Mira comes back to the apartment, the names of things I cannot see or place spilling out of her, and it makes me relieved to see her so excited about something for the first time in a long while.

What a skill that is, remembering—something Mira was never good at. I know my girl is smart, but, my daughter, you have always had the hardest time in history class, always mixing up dates and events, confusing one president for another. Once, when you were in high school, you failed a history test on the presidential executive orders that took place over the course of two world wars, and you needed my signature. I demanded, "What's your excuse for this?" You stomped your foot and said, "Ma, it's not my fault these pasty-white men look and sound the same to me." Which is a fair point.

Sad says remembering can be easy, like a muscle you train to stop forgetting. Or at least this is what Mira says he says. I can barely understand him. Maybe it's good that you're recording this, Mira, so you too can remember this a year from now.

Mira tells me, "Sad says it's not about what you remember but how you remember it." I think that is a very wise thing to say.

Guest Spot #10: The Last Dream

Funny how it happens. I would dream every once in a while before the storms began, but now the dreams feel especially vibrant. So it goes: Last night, I dreamed that the East River became row after row of submerged scales, gleaming in the moonlight, so shimmering and metallic that I thought I had stepped into an oil slick. There, on the water, were the girls again. They glided along the water, sometimes skipping in unison as they went. They were coming toward me.

I ran to Mira's room, but it was empty. I touched her bed to find it soaked through; lifted the covers to discover tiny silver fish, flapping and barely alive.

There went the roaring again, and this time I chased it through the streets to the edge of the river where the noise was loudest. The girls were still walking, their braids still pristine. Not a single hair moved throughout these decades of haunting. I could see their faces now, sunken and darkened around the eyes, hollows where once the cheeks might have been full. And in their orderly procession was Mira, the only one without a braid, her hair splayed out against the wind. She held the hand of another girl, slightly younger than the others though she shared their gray complexion. I thought I had seen her before, trying to remember where and when, before it occurred to me that, yes, this was the one who was drowned here. The Fujianese girl who could not or was not allowed to speak.

I suppose you think I should be terrified, but what I felt then was the opposite of horror. In this dream, I held out my arms to them. I wanted to welcome them all home.

Guest Spot #11: A Story Worth Telling

Here is a story Mira says is worth telling, and despite her hearing it many times, she has asked for me to tell it again to all of you: Mira was conceived on a purple day without help from anyone. She had a father, yes, but the conception—that was something she did on her own. Like an idea, she thought it and then she became it—a seed in my belly. The world was purple because I fell asleep in a field of purple irises, dreaming her into life. We met in that moment, my girl and I, and then she was.

The birth itself was less magical, and don't believe anyone who tells the story of giving birth like it is a religious experience. I cursed God and so many other gods I didn't even believe in, gods whose names I didn't even think I knew, and I cursed Mira's father, of course, who was in the hospital room with me, probably with a thumb up his ass.

Before the contractions started, I thought I was seeing purple. They were bright as sirens. During all the months of the pregnancy, Mira craved purple things, and I would cook ubes in water, salt them, and eat them by the pound. I went to Red Ribbon in Woodside, stocking up on ube cakes and ube sweet bread. I tried to trick her once and ate a blue potato, but I only threw it up.

Mira's father said that this made sense—that I would have a child as bullheaded as me. I told him to get out of the hospital room and pushed Mira out by the end of the hour.

The other day, I asked Mira if she remembered any of it, and did she feel like purple in the womb when she was inside me all those months.

She said, "No, but what's a purple iris look like? Does it look like an eye?"

No, I explained to her, and then I drew the flower on a napkin.

"Oh," she said. "I don't remember ever seeing anything like that."

HOW TO GIVE A EULOGY

Dear Listeners,

There is, to my knowledge, no one way to perform a eulogy for a ghost. Assuming they already had one on the occasion of their first death, most were not present for it. That was Grandpa Why's chief complaint—his arrival into this world as ghost occurred many years too late to hear what people had to say about him. While I pointed out that Chinese Buddhist funerals did not usually include eulogies on their agenda, he was still insistent that I do the research and instruct others on how to say the proper words about his unlife.

"Which life or unlife is this eulogy grieving, though?" I ask him. "Do you plan on passing again?"

I don't mean to imply that he is going anywhere, but he takes offense to it anyway. "Say what?" he exclaims. "Ungrateful. You wish your grandpa away? Let me tell you where we end up next—"

I tell him sorry, sorry, forget I said anything.

Grandpa Why lets it go, but barely. Though I take it upon myself to go to the library on Broadway anyway to see about the topic. I invite Sad to come, but he never wants to leave the building. *Too many sensations, too many feelings,* he tells me. I understand that. So the library becomes a solo mission.

Unluckily for the library on Broadway, which had just gone through a round of renovations before the acid rain struck, the building is starting to fall apart once more. With the library reverting to its analog cataloging system, there is a certain quaintness to sifting through the index cards, I admit. They smell like a *before time*.

There, I find the *Big Book of Greatest Eulogies*, which I have to lift with both hands to bring to checkout, the book sealed into a protective plastic bag. ("Everything, in case of the rain," the librarian says, and then, "Twenty-dollar fine for damages.") According to the book, which features a wide collection of mournful writing from grievers, amateur and famed writers alike, the key to an effective eulogy is to identify one pivotal theme or defining aspect of someone's life that you wish to highlight, and to frame the rest of one's speech around that feature. Sure, a funny story here or there will do, but anecdotes are only as good as their relevance to the main point. Never forget the main point.

"But I was a baby when you died the first time," I express to Grandpa Why, who does not mask his disappointment. "Doesn't it make more sense to eulogize you as if you would pass again today?"

Grandpa Why sniffles and runs off to tell Ma about my foul attitude, to which she says, "Okay, fine. Your grandpa wants a eulogy. I will give it." She pauses to scratch her chin. "Tell me what to say."

I tell her that the book suggests finding a central feature of Grandpa Why that her words can orbit around. "You know, like the thing you missed the most when he died the first time," I elaborate.

Ma looks at Grandpa Why, who squats in the corner in anticipation. I can feel her thinking, the way her face flashes through at least two types of feelings. Finally, she says, "To be honest, I never really knew my father. I mean, I knew he provided for me. But he was always full of secrets."

Grandpa Why boos her from his corner and tells her that if she's got nothing nice to say about him, to not say anything at all.

"I'm not done!" Ma exhales so loudly, the front tuft of her hair flies up when she blows air out of her mouth. She continues. "I didn't know what to miss when he died. And now, with your Grandpa Why back, I am learning about him a second time. So many things I missed the first time. I guess I am grateful for that. I still may not understand him, but if he goes again, then I have much more to miss now."

Grandpa Why, from his corner, shows a quiver of something in his expression, which I take to mean he is a little bit touched. Still, he cries out, "Oy! Where am I going? I'm staying right dang here."

Ma and I both nod. Okay, okay. We get it.

I am always examining Ma's face during these moments when she shares something surprising, just a little bit tender but not too much—mostly when she is pushed to the point of expression, but still. We do not give eulogies. We keep our secrets close. That's a marker of our family, I guess. And maybe I am turning out the same way.

I don't know if it's pointless to offer up any letters anymore. Like F for today or really F this day and F the need for eulogies in the first place. After finishing the Big Book of Greatest Eulogies, all I've come away with is how terrible I am at saying goodbye.

You, if you're listening. Whether ghost or disappeared into the beyond. I don't care where. I don't know how to eulogize you. I lost the main point a long time ago.

TO MOLT AND
TO LOVE YOU

When Shin thinks about his first molt, he recalls the shape of his loneliness. He remembers being surprised to find the molt looking so much like him—the left antenna pointed askew, its puffy upper lip, the whole container of him engorged with a longing he would spend the rest of his life trying to explain away. How bare he felt that instant, not like the roach he is but something other. He had reached out to touch it, the translucent shell, wanting to touch something within himself through it. Had it not been for Ren beside him, he would have stared forever at his loosened self.

Shin never thought he would long for the days of molting until shedding his shell was no longer a possibility. Shin is dead— and a dead roach, at that—so his loneliness is quite often doubled. As ghost, Shin is still his original size, half of a human palm, which once made for scurrying away undetected at the flicker of kitchen lights incredibly difficult. Not that it would be an issue now—as a sheer blue haunt that can pass through anything. With some conviction, the other person-sized ghosts can harden themselves, turn opaque through sheer will such that they could slam a door or hold up ever so briefly a glass cup without spilling any of its contents. The other ghosts are more interested in the capacities of their new forms, however, and prefer to squeeze themselves through pipes, sink through the floorboards and through various apartments (much to the alarm of their unsuspecting residents), and pass through a live body with all its murky guts and splendor. That last one never fails to embarrass Shin, that he can spy of someone's innards, that curious rush of blood and muscle like fast-moving twine. Learning quickly that it was impolite to linger too long in a person's body, he has since curbed that practice of bodily haunting. Working against him too was the ever-present knowledge that even in his ghostly form, he appears still to these looming human bodies as just another roach.

But harden? He cannot. He passes through doors so easily. Since the start of the acid rainstorms, it takes nearly all his energy to keep from slipping through the floors. At the height of his overwhelm, the falling feeling seizes him, and he grips the floor, his legs sliding and passing through.

It is possible, it occurs to him, that this stage of ghostliness is only a momentary state before the next one, and another molting is in order. He had only seen it happen once before, with a person-sized ghost a couple of floors down from where he resides with Ma, Mira, and Grandpa Why. A young man who was once part of a family of ten crowded in the same apartment, the ghost kept mainly to himself such that he and Shin never spoke, and so when he no longer appeared in passing, Shin paid the family's apartment a visit. It was as if he weren't there at all, the way the family bustled with their usual routine, clamoring over each other, the large black-and-white photograph of the young ghost still hanging above the dining table. Yet when he looked closely, Shin saw the light touch of a blue glow against the wall where a long crack ran along the surface. Over the course of the next days, the blue faded away completely. Shin does not know the human version of a molt, but he suspects that some iteration of it has occurred. And if something can happen once, then it surely is bound to happen again.

"Do you believe in an after to the *after-after*?" Mira asked him once, and the question rattled him because Ren had asked the same of him before. But whereas Ren had quickly added, "Wherever you go, I'll go, and you do the same," Mira had wept. They had only just met.

Shin didn't know what to say at the time. She looked at him imploringly, as if he had special knowledge about ghosts that he could impart. She seemed to want an answer to something else, though, which he did not know how to provide, and so he said only, "I believe so."

It comforted her then, and, moving forward, they grew close, sometimes nestling together in the same bed, where she spoke, and he listened. He was always listening. It was fascinating how much the humans could remember and care about, especially among the living. In his aliveness, he never looked so closely at a human face, and no one before this but Ren had ever looked at him without wanting to kill him.

With so much conviction about an *after-after* among humans, there has to be one for ghost roaches too, surely. This he wrestled with on his own while Mira's eyes glazed over with sleep. He wished he could know for himself too, because, *Quite honestly, Mira*, he thought, *I'm not sure I can do forever here.*

So Shin practices. He squeezes himself taut as he can as if to make a molt out of the nothing that is his body. *Do it, you stupid jerk*, he says to himself in the mirror. But as he tilts his head toward the reflective glass, he tumbles through it with ease. He does this every day, each attempt to harden proving as futile as the original. At first he would shrug the disappointment away. Over time, the disappointment turns to devastation, and one day Grandpa Why finds Shin frantically passing back and forth through the mirror, making sounds he assumes can only be weeping. "Friend!" Grandpa Why cries as he lifts the mirror from the wall. "You are not okay!" And Shin knows he is not as he shudders into Grandpa Why, who, being a ghost himself, cannot, even to the best of his ability, hold him.

※

There are no words to describe Shin's affliction.

Over time, the city turned itself into a concrete lot. It brimmed with holes. The acidity of the rain grew more pungent, its assailing power now tough enough to erode the three-decade-old surfaces of Building 4B. Now the city has regulated the use of thick black resistant rubber covers, which engulf the building in a totalizing darkness every Tuesday morning before the downpours. In an instant, light ceases to exist.

On the first day this regulation is put in place, the building manager comes by Apartment 9A to hand Ma and Mira a box of flashlights. Upon first flicker, the lights lit up the room with tiny fluorescent moons. It has become a game for Ma and Mira, this exercise of dancing light and shadow. They trace their names into the walls in the dark and it is not long before Grandpa Why joins in, taking the light to his chest like a bullet wound while singing to the moon goddess, Chang'e, "I'm sorry, so sorry for your sacrifice, my lady! Bless me! Bless me with your touch!" Ma and Mira barrage him with a chorus of boos.

Looking at Ma and Mira squeeze the light between their fingers, making it as small as a pinprick against the wall until it is no more, Shin thinks about the smallness of his in-between life, how it can sometimes feel like he is waiting for the shadow to descend upon him, wiping him out. During a break, he turns frantically toward Grandpa Why and asks him, "Do you ever think about what happens next?"

Grandpa Why places one finger on the side of his nose, teasing in a singsong voice, "I know something you don't know."

"Please, I have to know."

"If I tell you, you won't believe me. Nobody listens to me."

Shin pauses. "So, you have seen something. What is it? Tell me."

Grandpa Why observes the deep concern in Shin's shaking antennae and decides against saying more. "Friend, you worry too much."

That may be true, but before Shin has a chance to insist further, Grandpa Why is already holding up several vases with his arms and head, preparing for his next act. While Ma and Mira giggle at Granda Why's careless balancing act, shining the light at distant corners to throw him off intentionally, Shin feels their laughter move far away from where he stands, and he realizes he is sinking into the floorboards once again.

On the week before Qingming, the feeling continues to sit like the puckered darkness inside him. Although the ninth floor brims with the noise of shuffling bodies, his insides feel sedimented. The humans and ghosts move around him, carrying trays of plastic-wrapped food, bowls covered in newsprint, joss sticks, and gold-flecked paper. Sometimes there are visitors, and other times a whole family from down the hall comes in to see Ma, the apartment filling with half-drunk cups of tea.

If this is the season of ghosts, then why do I feel as if I don't belong here? Shin wonders as he watches the flicker of activities before him.

It continues to be impossible to talk with Grandpa Why, who has been bouncing off the ceiling with excitement for Qingming.

"Please," Shin whispers to the old ghost under his breath when asked to join in. "A hint about what's to come after this."

It seems that it takes great strain for Grandpa Why to focus, though he scrunches up his face in a brief instance of concentration. With some solemnness, he finally declares, "It's better here than there. I can tell you that."

Shin has given up on asking Grandpa Why for clarification by the time the suddenly spritely poltergeist shoots off to his next act, though where *here* and *there* reside at the moment feels one and the same.

To Mira, he confides, "I don't know what is happening."

Mira pauses while sweeping the floor to peer deeply into Shin's eyes. She relays, "You look the same as when I first met you. Maybe something is happening inside." She gestures toward her chest, at where Shin assumes is the nebulous organ that is the human heart. He hears Mira talking about the human heart often during her radio show, and it is mystifying to him how much emphasis people place on something no bigger than their fist, that it should symbolize something more than what funnels blood throughout their body.

Shin is not convinced. "What did I look like when we first met?"

Mira takes a moment to consider the memory. As for Shin, he remembers it vividly, the barging weight of her coming through the entryway after abusing the door knocker. Her face was wet, and the rain was about to start that day. How she was allowed to storm into the building so recklessly when security armed every corner and stairwell, he had no idea. She had flopped onto the bed, spoken briefly with Ma, and then, looking up as if realizing the apartment around her for the first time, stared at Grandpa Why and Shin, who were both sitting and watching on the top of a bookcase.

"We have ghosts now," Ma had said, waving her hands toward the two, and, then to Mira again, "You were gone too long."

"Oh," Mira uttered, her mouth forming a tight O. "How long do they plan on staying?"

While Grandpa Why ranted on and on about Mira's unfilial self, Shin remained quiet on the shelf. Only later, when the others left the room to let Mira finish her crying, did he come down and sheepishly say, "Uh, we've been using this room, but you can have it back."

Mira looked up and around, her eyes finally landing on Shin. Shin moved closer then so she could see him better. He found that this was the easiest way to mitigate human shock, to move closely and with some determination so that they were forced to look before reacting.

Mira opened and closed her mouth several times before asking, "I know why Grandpa Why is here . . . but who are you?"

"I'm Shin," Shin replied, and added honestly, "and I don't know."

"Where's your family?"

Shin tried to recall this. No one had asked him this before. Trying as hard as he could, he had no visual for mother, father, or any number of siblings. A perfect blank. He answered honestly, "Don't know."

"Partner? Lover? Polycule? Roach consortium?"

Ren. That much he did remember. But if Ren was there too, they would have found each other by now. There was nothing comforting about this fact. More softly, he said again, "Don't remember, don't know."

Mira nodded as if to say, *Fair enough.* She twirled her finger in the air, asking Shin to do a turn for her, which he did and thought uncomfortably funny.

"Huh," Mira considered, tilting her head as she examined Shin's ghostly blue body, which seemed to hum electric as he spun one way and then another. "Where did you even come from?"

Shin had no answer for her then and was no closer to answering this question now. Back in the swirl of Qingming preparations, Mira catches the faraway look in his beady eyes.

"Are you remembering again?" Mira asks with concern.

Shin shakes his body in a defeated *No.* Truthfully, he sees flickers of Ren from time to time, though he always assumes he is simply losing his mind. Ren running behind the houseplant, withered down to its last brown leaf. Ren rattling around in the silverware drawer. When he rushes over to check, no one is there, so he must be imagining it. Each appearance seems to shake something loose within him, and he can almost feel his old lover touching him, leg to leg. It feels cruel, whatever is happening to Shin, but there also seems to be no end in sight.

Ma calls for Mira in the kitchen. Mira turns to Shin. "Will you be okay?"

Shin does his best to imitate a human shrug.

The day Shin met Ren, a food raid was under way, and every roach was fending for itself. In the dark, they each descended upon an open trash can, the lid nudged off by a nuisance dog who was more afraid of them than they were of him. The garbage overflowed with fruit peels and sour meat, their juices soaking through several layers of newsprint. Shin had always moved slowly, tentatively, and had burrowed himself so deep into the trash can that he had a tough time climbing out. On top of an apple core, he chewed and groped his way back to standing. In the middle of grasping for leverage, he felt another leg clamp onto his, and in the blue darkness he could make out Ren's broad face, so eager and full of mischief.

"I see you like sweets too," Ren said, plucking off a sizable chunk of the fruit and handing it to Shin.

Back then, Shin did not know that what Ren was doing was called flirting. He thought it a jab at his own inadequacy as a scavenger. *Okay*, Shin thought, *well, fuck you too.* But Ren's face was bright and optimistic even in the gauze of night, and he had taken Shin by the front leg, dragging him up toward the night air, a piece of apple hanging from his mouth.

They ran so hard they nearly smacked into a thin crack in the wall they mistook for a wider crevice that some of the other roaches had burrowed through. When they found the hole at long last, they nestled themselves within the bricks, and there Ren flirted again. "You know, they say that apples are an aphrodisiac," and all Shin could say in return was a sheepish "Oh, I didn't know that." It was not until Ren kissed his antenna against his that it became a bit clearer.

"Have you ever . . . ?" Ren asked.

Shin shook his head.

"Would you like to . . . ?"

Shin nodded his head so vigorously, he thought it would snap. His front legs on Ren's face, he saw through a sliver of light that he was so beautiful. His eyes like black marbles, the burnished honey of his shell. Shin felt he could look at him forever, and a tiny hurt grew inside him.

Ren touched him lightly on his head and Shin flinched.

He trailed his leg along Shin's back, which made him wince and whisper a litany of *sorrys*.

"Are you always this nervous?"

Shin thought about it for a while, feeling quite strongly that he had been this way for as long as he could recall. *Yes*, Shin said with his eyes, *I have always been this afraid.*

Ren smiled, his leg stroking Shin's face. "I have a little trick I use when I'm nervous. Do you want to try it with me?"

Shin nodded, his legs falling by Ren's side.

What Ren said next, Shin would never forget. Stroking Shin's face, Ren spoke of the safest place for a roach to go, the second-closest thing to an egg sac. The place where they both once grew, lively and abundant. Picture the sac as a hole in the wall, he said. Picture it big enough for us to get through but too small for human hands. The hole fits two. *You and me and no one else*, he emphasized. The hole is damp and cushioned by the dark. It is a place where you can sleep for days and no one will ever know, and no one will ever find you. It is a place where no one else can go, just the ones you let in. *This* . . . he declared again, and by then he had stopped stroking Shin's face, *this is the safest place.*

Lulled by the drawl of Ren's voice, Shin did not notice at first that Ren had begun undoing his skin, plucking apart his shell with soft bites peppered between words. When Shin realized what was happening, he leapt to catch up, fastening his legs to Ren with sudden urgency. Then they were taking each other apart frantically, moaning into each other's mouths, their backs rubbing against the harsh bricks behind them. Looking upon Ren's face, its honeyed brightness like brown liquor hitting the light, Shin felt that he was taking him into his body.

When they woke up together the next day, they saw that their molts were lying beside one another like twin lovers frozen in time. Where they were bronze once, they had become a pale nude. They looked different to each other, bare beyond bare, and they were fascinated by the other's body, its new ridges and shapes, softer and clearer than their former selves. Eventually Ren caught himself staring and roused himself to leave.

"I had a wonderful time," he said as he skirted backward toward the opening.

Before Shin could respond, Ren had already darted out of the hole, leaving him alone in their safest place with their two molts, the pair already having untangled from each other's hold by some slice of wind that had snuck in at some point when neither one was looking.

As Qingming nears and the piles of food in Apartment 9A start to look like staggered towers in the corner of the living room, the kitchen having been exhausted of its counter space, Ren seems to appear more often to Shin than before. One day, while Mira is lighting joss sticks for Grandpa Why, Shin sees the smoke wafting from the yellow sticks convulse in the air, eventually becoming the shape of a handsome roach, the wings of his back readying to ascend. Just as he spies Ren in the white puff, his old lover disappears. He thinks of the shape of Ren all the time, but to see him there, dispersing just inches from Mira's face—it jolts him. When it happens again later the same night, a hole in the wall humming and glowing, Shin dips his head in to investigate. When he peers into the hole, he sees the scuttering butt of an insect turning the corner. He thinks about running after him, of yelling, *Ren! Ren!* until the figure hears him and turns around. It has become hard to know what is true and what is a vision of his most fantastic imagination. In this world, it is possible that all of this can mean the inauguration of Ren's eventual arrival. A ghost is made, after all, as the product of one's dying. And Ren is most certainly dead.

The night that Shin does not chase the figure in the hole, the humans and ghosts of Apartment 9A gather around the coffee table, which is littered with saltine cracker crumbs and salted black beans. Mira calls it "Chinese caviar" and she eats until her belly hurts. This Shin knows because she offers lush descriptions of its taste from its hearty beginning to lodged end. It does not matter what any of the ghosts are doing at the moment—they always pause long enough to hear her contemplate her words while chewing, going, "Hmm," and then offering up an assessment of its flavors, something that the ghosts know only through memory. There is a strange comfort in hearing someone describe what you can never again experience.

When Mira describes the soft pungency of preserved black beans, everyone's eyes, living and dead, glow bright with nostalgia. The conversation turns to favorite foods, what has been lost or misremembered or simply would not grow again after the acid rain.

"Papaya," Ma shares immediately, nodding as she recalls scooping the dark green seeds out with a large spoon. "To have a slice of it right now would be very, very nice."

Grandpa Why spits into the air and shouts, "No one here yet has been able to make proper stir-friend snow pea leaves with garlic! A travesty, if you ask me!"

Ma and Mira look at each other, each hesitating to share that even the heartier vegetables like cabbage, lettuce, and potatoes are struggling to grow since the acid rain. Certainly there will be no snow pea leaves to set by Grandpa Why's altar. Neither of them has tasted garlic for a very long time.

Shin has nothing to contribute to the conversation. When he tries to recall the taste of apples, he can only sense their bitterness. The taste of Ren, however, is a different matter. Looking at Mira, he sees an idea circling like a storm above her head. He prays she will not ask him to join in the discussion.

Mira excitedly works her way to standing. "An idea!" she

gasps. "We'll try to make imitation dishes of everyone's favorite food for Qingming. How about that?"

The room resounds in deep agreement, while Shin remains silent. In watching Mira over the past few months, Shin sees how she has increasingly filled her days with activities. Between her mournful first arrival and now, she has not stopped moving. It is the most curious thing, especially since he can feel himself slowing down.

Suddenly everyone seems to grow aware of Shin's silence.

"We can make your favorite food too," Mira offers with a smile. "Did you have a favorite from . . . well, you know?"

Shin looks at Ma's face, then Mira's, and then Grandpa Why's, each of them looking at him expectantly. Since his arrival at Apartment 9A, he has shared so little of his previous life, remembering almost none of it. There are his memories of Ren, but what good will that do anyone now? They are waiting for an answer, and, try as he might, he cannot recall the taste of anything so great that it is worth celebrating during a day of remembering what has passed.

Their eyes are still watching him.

"I think . . . a sweet rice cake."

The answer seems to satisfy. In truth, he cannot recollect even the taste of that, only the sensations of the spongy cake that Mira once described in full, and even so, he knows that there are differences between the human and roach mouth that even Mira cannot begin to bridge.

The group begins to disperse, until only Mira and Shin remain.

Mira holds her hand out to Shin as if he can take it with his own. "Wanna take a walk with me?" she invites.

Shin nods. Together, they make their way down several

flights of stairs and toward the back exit of the building, Mira pausing every couple of steps for Shin to catch up. They are an odd pair—the one, tall, fleshy, and always with her shoulders hunched forward in a permanent sulk, while the other barely fits in her hand. In a past life, he would have been squashed flat on a forgettable surface.

How different this ghostly life is for Shin from his living days, and though he cannot confirm the difference through memory alone, he feels it reverberating through him. He recalls the first day he arrived in Apartment 9A, his body and mind coming together, feeling himself designed particle by particle, as if trying to fill the mold of what he used to be with sand, one grain at a time in a panicked rush. It was so dizzying, this scramble of time and his remaking, that he felt himself come in and out of consciousness.

When he finally came to, he felt the coldness of Ma's floor, her loud shriek, and then the bright pink slipper above her head, waiting to be smacked down on him. He was prepared to die a second time then. When Ma's slipper slammed into his body, though, he was surprised to feel not the crushing sound of his own mass, but the impact moving through him like a current. Then he opened his mouth and spoke a meek "Wait!" at the sight of Ma's slipper raised again for a second blow. It was in that moment that Ma fainted.

Mira enjoys the story a little too much at Ma's expense. She has Shin tell the story over and over, poking her finger through him in jest. By the time the ghosts had all settled into the building, one by one at first and then seemingly en masse, the presence of these haunting figures was no longer a surprise to anyone, least of all to returnees like Mira herself.

Walking with Mira now out the door of the building is like living another life, one in which he can look out across the East River and feel nothing of his attachment to it. The river roars at the two of them. Above them, workers are hoisting the rubber cover over the building, tending to the ropes and folds of it for a more efficient drop.

Mira is deep in thought as she props herself up onto the railing and takes a seat on the highest metal bar. She looks up to the top of the building. "How much longer do you think we can do this?" she asks aloud.

Shin thinks of Mira, with her promise of papaya, snow pea leaves, and the fatty recollections of a time before. He cannot recall ever involving himself with humans in his life before, so talk of endurance in people-time is outside of what he can immediately assess.

Sensing Shin's silence, Mira speaks again. "Sad and I are together now, you know?" She looks down at her feet, dangling over the lower bar. "I mean, it sounds so juvenile. Him and me, a couple. Boyfriend and girlfriend. Like we're twelve or something."

Shin has heard Mira and Sad's courtship evolve over Mira's radio show, how she stumbled into his apartment one morning and returned soaked head to toe in salty water, nearly giving Ma a heart attack, thinking she had been drenched in acid rain. Mira's eyes have moved sleepily ever since as if permanently dreaming. Still, Shin hears the heavy fluttering of Mira's eyes when she sleeps, and he can tell something else haunts her dreams.

Shin considers his next statement carefully. "Oh?"

"It's . . . new."

"Oh."

They sit in silence for a while. Grandpa Why has often said to Shin that talking to him feels painful. The former ghost zips and spins in the air and the latter can barely form a sentence unpunctuated by an "um" or an "uh." The quiet unnerves Shin. He looks up at Mira, who seems to just let the silence hang. It is as if he is not even there.

Mira turns to him suddenly. "Did you ever love someone?"

Shin thinks of Ren, who by now has become his entire world.

At his lack of response, Mira posits another question: "What would you do if he was with you right here, right now?"

Shin tries to imagine Ren coursing about the building, covering every wall and surface. He would leave no inch of the building unexplored. Together, they would make their way to the back exit, staring up at the graying sky, and then with some ceremony back their way into the building once again. Ren too would have limits as to where he could go, but he would make a second life of uncovering how far he could take it. And Shin would gladly come along.

Mira does not wait for Shin's answer when she shares, "We are a lot alike, you and me." Upon seeing Shin's antennae twitch in confusion, she goes on, "Someone lives inside of us and won't get out."

Shin thinks of his insides as a house's interior where he and Ren can live nestled together in peace. He imagines the warmth of that space, the softness of the light, almost as if . . . But no, he cannot go there. Not yet.

"Sad is wonderful," Mira interjects again. Shin looks up at her, and she looks almost sad. "I feel so lucky."

"It's going to be okay." The sound of Shin's voice shocks him. He does not know if it will be okay.

Mira nods once, twice, and several times more as if to assure herself. "I'm trying to do a nice thing. For everyone."

Shin is confused at first and then remembers the food for the party. It does not matter to him whether there will be rice cakes or fake papaya or torn-up paper painted to look like leafy greens. He thinks of telling Mira then that something inside him is changing and rice cakes cannot cure it.

"I just—" Mira's voice comes shaky, cracking a little at the last word. "I want everyone to be happy."

Shin inches close to Mira, his own way of saying, *There, there,* or at least he thinks this is what you are supposed to say in these moments. He does not know for sure.

Mira turns to look at Shin on the ground beside her as if she has just noticed him there. She asks, "Are you happy?"

The question makes Shin stumble a little. Honestly, he is not, but she is asking for confirmation of something else. Her question is a stinging reminder of what plagues him and sinks him into an unpleasant place. He would much rather think of a home with Ren, but now all he can think about is how it can never be.

Shin finally speaks. "Thank you for making the sweet rice cake," he says.

The answer, for what it's worth, suffices for now.

It did not take long for Shin to figure out that Ren was a frequent guest at the love motel stationed at the back cupboard of the kitchen. With full neon armor, the love motel managed to be both gregarious and hidden in plain sight. Shin had heard of such places in passing, knew the lure of its sugar-lined walls. He heard of roaches who had given up on midnight food raids, left their packs, and drifted toward the beckoning call of the love motel's hot pink glow. Once they were there, they never really left, only visiting the outside world every once in a while. Their legs were always sticky with an unknown gel and their words slurred. They moved slowly, weakly, and tasted food differently, remarking on how the apples and beef chunks that they once lapped up with pleasure no longer had the same exhilarating flavors. A temporary home for wayward roaches, for those who could not divorce their longing from their hunger—the love motel fed them plenty of both.

A roach nearly twice his size, Ren would stagger out of the place, drenched in its sweetness. Shin would follow him at first to make sure that he made it from open floor to shadow safely. Whether Ren pretended not to notice or was truly oblivious to Shin's scurrying steps behind him, it was unclear, only that this ritual would go on for days at a time. One day, though, Ren turned around, blurry-eyed, and asked, "Do you have a light?"

They found an empty matchbox and tucked themselves in it, the dark smelling of sulfur. Ren did not recognize Shin at first, only managing to mumble that he needed a break, pressing his head against Shin and falling asleep shortly after. Shin let him sleep on top of him, careful not to move too quickly. He could smell the love motel on him, a candied scent with a ripe pungency. It gradually filled the space of the matchbox, and it was the smell that eventually put Shin to sleep as well, dreaming of the two of them, their limbs knotted and tangled together.

But Ren would never stay long, and when Shin awoke again, his love would leave only a sticky trail behind him. Shin continued to watch Ren from afar, his brazen body swaying to the rhythm of the open air, exploring its own time. From the love motel echoed a choral tune that sounded like wings rubbing together in rapid succession. The pink of its signage glowed and waned in careful rhythm. When Ren entered its doors once again, the music pulsed louder. Shin could almost see why someone would give themselves to this place, why they would stay a little longer than they intended.

On the day of Qingming, Shin finds Apartment 9A completely transformed. In a radical revision of a typically austere holiday, the apartment was flooded with people, ghosts, and music playing from a disc honoring the best of songs from the last decade. The streamers, originally limp and tangled in the center of the living room, have now grown in volume and feature intricate designs. There are balloons, tiny half-filled ones pumped by a weak lung, but someone has arranged them on the wall like clashing and noisy bouquets. A cascade of newsprint confetti swirls overhead when Shin walks into the room. Packed wall to wall, the apartment feels unrecognizable, with rows of fold-up tables lined with sweet rice cakes, flatbread, fried corn with sugar, potato salad tossed with ten-year-old Miracle Whip, and bathtub vodka in old water bottles labeled with a dried-out Sharpie and a haphazardly drawn skull and crossbones. As people come and go, they grab joss sticks, bowing in whichever direction their drunken bodies sway before planting them in one of the many mounds of clay. Some forget that they are holding joss sticks and take to shimmying to their knees on the floor when the music tells them to get low, the ashes from the burning sticks coating the floor. As people dance, Grandpa

Why slips through their legs, occasionally spooking the dancers so much that they fall backward onto the floor, though they keep dancing anyway until they are pulled back up.

For a second Shin thinks that he might enjoy himself. Sidling up to the sweet rice cakes, he finds himself moving to the music, tentatively at first, but then with a little more gusto. On occasion, someone will walk by, warn him about the vodka while pouring generous portions into their cup, and dance their way to the center of the living room. He imagines Ren would use this as an opportunity to sneak a few crumbs, feeling a bit smug for having pulled one over on a crowd like this. *Go on, dance*, he envisions Ren teasing, bumping his body against his own. Shin can already feel his whole body blushing, shyly shaking his way to a coy *No, I don't think so* . . .

Then, with a forceful tug of his antenna, Ren would go, *Why not?*

Shin feels a thousand pinpricks rain throughout his body. Through the music, he hears the skittering feet of someone close to his size, and when he looks into the crowd, he swears he can see a tiny body gleam between stomping feet.

Ren, Shin thinks loudly to himself. And then he says it to the room: "Ren!"

The party continues, Shin's voice lost in the din. Suddenly he feels very tired.

Mira emerges from the kitchen wearing a heavy necklace made of aluminum foil. She stumbles when she approaches Shin, a mug filled with clear liquid sloshing in her hand.

Mira opens her mouth wide, full of teeth, and shouts, "Come on, now! It's conga time!"

It is exactly as Shin feared. Mira's announcement is a beacon to a fast-forming unruly train of people and ghosts. In his effort to flee the scene, Shin accidentally finds himself thrust into the middle of the action. Though the conga line starts to make room for him in between people, the growing number of bodies in the apartment means that everyone eventually is shoulder to shoulder, feet to feet. Shin feels the bodies closing in on him.

When the first person steps on him by accident, he does not mind, their shoe passing through him without consequence. Shin tries to move out of the way to keep in rhythm with the conga line. When he is trampled once again, the sensation of the foot against his back almost takes the wind out of him, much to his surprise. He dodges one foot and then another. When a third comes down on him, he can hear a slight crunch in his backside, and instinctively he winces.

Finding Mira bouncing in the crowd, Shin plants himself on her shoe, hardening with all his might, and pleads, "Please—"

"It's okay! Dance with me!" Mira shakes her boot, and Shin, trying to follow the motion of her feet, feels close to being sick.

"Please!"

"Just go with it!"

Shin does as he's told, his head spinning. The crowd blurs into one terrifying color, their sounds like a collective gnashing of metal against metal. When he squints, he can see Ren shaking his head as if to say, *You're not supposed to be here.* When the song slows, Shin catches himself agreeing. His movements taper into a low sway and he is reminded just then of his final days with Ren at the love motel.

When he first came to the love motel, it was to find Ren and tell him that he longed for him, could not stop thinking of him each night. Inside the pink box, every roach was twirling, drunk on some music in their heads. Ren was splayed out on the floor, his wings tapping out a quiet rhythm. In any other place, Shin would have thought this charming, how Ren's eyes glazed over with mysterious delight, but this was the love motel; the rules governing joy came laced with something else.

"Did you follow me here, handsome?"

Ren spoke first, startling Shin, who could only mutter in return, ". . . Worried about you."

Ren offered him a dollop of white sugar, its bitterness punching through Shin's senses. Shin shook his head, declining with some shame.

"What's the matter?" Ren's face contorted quickly into one of concern, suddenly lucid.

Shin shook his head again.

"Oh baby," Ren cooed. He reached over to touch Shin's face. "Things are moving a bit too fast for you."

At the party, Shin feels that same sensation again, of being so near Ren, the dizzying scent of him. The music seems to crawl up walls, the whole apartment shuddering. The people jump up and down to a song that pelts its instructions across the crowded room. Every cup that has not been turned over now gives way to spill. Every frame has been toppled, and the people too are draped over each other like dominoes. Shin backs himself into a corner, his insides pulsing with noise. It is so loud, the rest of the room goes mute, and suddenly it is as if everyone is just thrashing aimlessly into the night. When he looks around, he can see all the cracks on the walls, the thin ones and those with their own sense of cartography. They brim with heat, every single one of them, and they beckon to him, *Come on, now. It is time.*

No, not yet, Shin calls out to the air. What about Ren? Is he still waiting to arrive? Has he already passed over? These are the things Shin does not know, but the spaces in the walls have their own sense of time. Shin darts in between dancing bodies, coursing through their damp flesh. In their liveliness, he sees their fear, how intently they move to avoid the rush of death.

He stumbles through, plants himself on a table, and crawls his way to a plate of something spongy. Though he cannot taste it, he knows the smell of sweet rice cake immediately, its gooey texture like a cushion for his weary ghost body. He hardens himself, surprised by the ease in which his back can bristle against another surface. He crawls deeper into the crevice, an opening in the cake leading toward its center. *So soft*, he sighs to himself. The day has made him so tired. He stops and closes his eyes, feeling the familiar wave of sleep kiss his body.

Shin kept returning to the love motel. Once he made it in the first time, the hosts learned to expect him. They handed him piles of sugar at the door, but he always refused. There, in the love motel, Shin and Ren would lie together, their bodies clinging and pulling apart like Scotch tape. Even as it grew hotter, they still fastened themselves to each other, and it was the only time life felt truly good.

At first Shin stayed only a couple of hours, timing his visits meticulously, and left with enough time to purge his stomach of the place. He swore each time he'd stop, would drag Ren out of the love motel, to some place far away—a field of apples, maybe, where they could eat their fill and then some. Shin was wild with plans, but each time he came to the love motel, he would sink into its sticky floors, grow drowsy and languid, and collapse on top of Ren.

Then he touched his mouth to Ren's mouth one day when it was dusted with sugar, and he did not hate it.

Each day, Shin came back to the love motel to find Ren and touch his mouth to his, the same sugar passing through them both until Shin was just as dizzy as his love. It happened gradually and then all at once.

He sprinkled sugar on Ren's back and lapped it up greedily.

They would fuck and take turns drizzling sweetness on each other.

At the front door, Shin would collect the sugar offerings, stuff himself so full that he had only energy enough to lie on his back by the time he reached Ren.

"It is like daffodils," Shin said. "My mouth feels like flowers."

Ren loved the description so much, he worked it into their lexicon. "My daffodil boy," Ren called him, "my brightest bulb in the garden."

Shin loved Ren so much, it made his stomach turn. He was sick so often, not even the air outside the love motel could alleviate his nausea. In fact, it made it worse, so much so that he decided there was no reason to ever leave the place. When Shin told Ren as much, he seemed relieved, and they held each other as the air inside the love motel grew heavy as a curtain.

During their final days, time blurred together into a mesh of legs and slow bodies colliding into one another, unsure of where they began and where the room ended. They ate so much that their heads hurt, and they would say to each other, "I love you so much, it hurts." They fell asleep in their own retch and woke up to begin the same ritual again. It was unclear who died first and however many minutes apart.

Dying the first time was the hardest part. On his second death, Shin is relieved to confirm this much. This time is not unlike sleep, or whatever he can remember of it, his body sinking deeper and deeper into the passing layers of time. Occasionally Ren would cross his mind, those final moments with him, but they do not press upon him anymore with the same gnawing weight. Perhaps this is what they call *surrender.* He feels himself riding a low wave, pulling him forward toward a horizon of unknowns. Wherever he is going, he senses there is no rush.

By midnight, only half of the party has made it through without passing out on the floor or hallway. Shin can hear the lessening clamor, the apartment finally quiet enough to hear a human cough and sneeze. How he will miss all of this.

From the corner of the room, he hears Mira's sandals clacking against the floor. "Have you seen Shin?" she asks someone, and that someone must have shaken their head, because the sound of her heels becomes more urgent. "Please," he hears her say faintly this time, "can you find him?"

I'm here, Mira, Shin calls out, realizing that it is his thoughts that cry out loudly. As for his voice, nothing will come out.

Tired, he thinks. *I'm just so very tired.*

Outside, the rain has subsided, the thick rubber tarp lifting from the windows, exposing a tiny sliver of sun between the departing clouds. From wherever Shin is, he can feel that soft touch of light upon the shell covering him. For those who are sobering up, the glow from the window incites the smallest exhale.

It is not clear how Mira comes to find him. He hopes that it has something to do with the invisible thread that tethers him to her, and her to him. He will never forget Mira, just as he will never forget Ren. All the memories rushing back, colliding into the painful present. He cannot see anything in the dark, but he recalls Mira's face, the full flood of her tears. Suddenly the darkness splits open like a rice cake peeled from the center, and the last vestige of the ghost of him peers out from the sweet and gummy mold he has found himself in. The final molt. To drown in something that he can neither taste nor smell now—he can almost laugh at the tragedy of it all.

Above him, Shin can make out a gasp and then a long silence punctuated by a shuddering cry. Someone yells out, "What in the actual fuck?" and others continue to stare. They take turns poking at Shin's molt, having seen nothing like it before. The molt glows like an oceanic body. Perhaps in all their study and admiration of the beaming shell of a once-Shin, it occurs to them that after one ghostly phase, there can be another. What becomes of a life when one dies a second time? The question hangs in the air, each person in the room surely puzzling over the consequence of this in their own life and death.

Grandpa Why's voice resonates up close as he speaks with emphatic staccato, "DO NOT FOR-GET." Then, just as quickly, his voice becomes a distant echo. Shin can barely register it in his state.

"It's too much." Shin cannot make out the voice at first, but the cry that follows is too achingly familiar. *Oh, Mira*, he thinks, and prays this could come out in words. *Don't cry.* The voice gives out one last sputter. "When is this going to stop?"

A crowd of murmurs gathers around Mira, and Shin wishes he could rise from his molt to embrace her cheek. He feels himself come up in the air, unsure at first where he is headed, and then realizes it is Mira lifting the rice cake up to her face—the heat of her breath the most alive thing he has ever felt. He cannot tell for certain, but it is possible Mira has kissed the whole of the rice cake where the molt is flickering its bright blue hue. He feels a rush of warmth course through him—fear or grief, it no longer matters what—which he comes to identify as the sensation of eating to the point beyond fullness, the body wanting to pry itself open.

Sleep, his body says. *I'm so tired*, he thinks once more. Letting himself sink deeper into time, he feels his body funnel through its layers, achingly slow, as if moving through honey. This is it. It is happening. The current ushers him through, and then noise vacates itself. The honey sighs. Is he dreaming? There, before him, is a never-ending field. A stretch of grass and the world washed in gray. It is teeming with humans, but at his level, he can see his fellow roaches tucked away in the grass. A feeling of having been here before, but he is not so sure, and he surprises himself with how much he yearns to be there. Here, where he has belonged all this time.

HOW TO CONJURE
A GHOST

Dear Listeners,

Find me someone who hasn't lost someone. I've lost several now. Emphasis on the letter *I* this time. I keep losing them. And now I know that you can lose a ghost too. This life is a sucky portal that can take back its ghosts at will. To think, just a few summers ago conservative pundits were comparing the influx of ghosts to an immigration issue, wanting the state to pour money into ghost-busting solutions. That didn't last for too long. As it turns out, people get attached to their ghosts.

By now I must have read every book on mediumship, books on Wiccan spell-casting, *How to Speak to the Dead for Dummies*. I go to the underground botanica near Essex and Delancey, where I stock up on white candles, special knives with ivory handles that bind to me if they catch my blood. I am told that my blood is what brings a ghost into this world. I speak to brujas, shamans, witches, everyone who has dealt in some form with the dead, and everyone agrees it's not a good idea unless I'm prepared to potentially encounter more grief. *Who are we without our desperation, though?* I tell them. Death makes seekers of us all.

Have you heard about the ghost-conjuring gone wrong that took place on Cherry Street? An old man with a hex on him, calling for his ex-wife from another realm to come lift it from him. Apparently he had developed some type of boil that spread, possibly through contact with the acid rain. It wasn't clear what he used exactly for his ritual, but at some point he took a cleaver to himself. It appeared he was trying to split himself in half. Something to do with the hex, I suppose. Not sure if this would qualify as a success.

Then there was the trio of girls on Pike who saw a chance to revive a dead classmate. They held a séance at their school in the middle of the night under a full moon. To their surprise, their classmate did come back, though in pale blue form and screeching wildly for a full week before she quit speaking at all. "Where did you go and what happened to you?" people asked the ghost girl. She would look sick in the face and say nothing at all. Now all the girls are in therapy, ghost included.

So, I know there are consequences. And still, if the afterlife is so close enough to touch, I want to touch it. Don't you? Wouldn't you try everything in your power if you knew someone you loved was just within reach? Perhaps they are trying to reach you too.

WE'RE GOING HOME

The thing about JoJo was that he was a really good boy. Not just a good boy in the way that all mothers seem to inherently believe their sons to be immaculately good; when Lucinda thinks back on JoJo's life, she honestly cannot recall a time in which she was ever disappointed in him—he never talked back, never cussed in the same room as her, never smoked or drank to excess, and always, when his friends came by, would say their *Hello, titas* and *Thank you, titas* without fail. At eight years old, he was translating permission slips from school for her, going, "Nanay, put your name here." Observing how tentatively she held the paper in her hand and that a small part of her pride was injured there, he would lean his head on her shoulder as he had always done since he was a toddler, feeling her soften and

touch his small face, as if to say, *I'm still your boy, right, Nanay?*
By the time he was fourteen, he was already bagging groceries
at Pathmark, setting aside the greater portion of his monthly
pay to help with rent, which ultimately was a godsend when
Lucinda's husband, Joseph, finally left them for good. Then,
when the acid rain arrived, he managed to send her a single
message: *I'm coming home, Nanay.* They would be the last words
she ever received from him.

When JoJo moved out, the apartment became eerily quiet,
and quieter still when the storms came, the rooms of the apartment echoing a vacuous drone. She cannot move around her
home without hearing the sound of her slippers loudly slapping the linoleum tiles. Each time the rain comes, the roar of
it fills almost every unpatched hole of the apartment, and its
terror reminds her, more than anything else, that she is very
much alone.

Ma comes often to break her out of her grief stupor, and
with the unspoken rule that her friend can march into her living room at any point, plop down on the couch, and turn on
the TV to the latest rerun—and it is only reruns these days of
Dallas, General Hospital, All My Children, or that one about the
puppet and the witch and the bizarrely watery-eyed girl who
went to hell and survived—the days have become a little bit
more bearable.

Lucinda likes Ma because she does not gossip. She is more
interested in trying to reason out the plot choices in these televised stories than anything else. Lucinda can get up and light
the day's candle for JoJo, and it is not something she has to
explain. She can say offhand, "Oh, JoJo always liked his coffee with more cream and sugar than there was coffee," or "JoJo

used to say that Susan Lucci is 'like the ultimate queen,'" which neither Ma nor Lucinda can deny is true. It is a relief to not talk about JoJo or talk about JoJo or even forget for a moment the desolate state of the world around her, which seems to walk hand in hand with her in mourning.

Recently, Ma has been a constant fixture in her living room, likely due to the arrival of her daughter, Mira, some odd months ago. If JoJo possesses so much of Lucinda's mind and heart, Mira has a similar effect on Ma, though more on the ornery end. The other day, Ma walked into Lucinda's apartment with a large pot of jujube tea, huffing as she scooped the water into a pair of chipped mugs. Handing one to Lucinda, she complained, "I don't know what's wrong with that girl. She never gets out of bed. Barely does anything all day."

Lucinda nodded and offered, "Well, there's her radio show."

Ma rolled her eyes. "How's that feeding us now?"

"It's a hard time right now. No one's hiring except the Erasers for these streets."

That hardship Ma is well aware of. Even with unemployment as high as it has been this past year, the cleanup crew has had trouble incentivizing people to come on board, to no surprise to those who have worked the shifts. According to the former crew members employed there for a short while—and these stints never last more than a month, it seems—they would rather have chosen no work at all. Besides, Ma said before that she would rather her household cut its rations in half than have Mira picking up mangled bodies off the streets.

Still, Lucinda can tell there is more to what Ma is trying to say. She has known Mira since the girl was five years old, when Lucinda moved into the apartment two floors down, pregnant with JoJo. Even then, Mira was a strange, moony-eyed girl who ran up to her, pointed at her large belly, and cried out loud, "Ma! Ma! A watermelon!" Ma had rushed over to apologize and knock Mira on the head, but Lucinda never needed that, grateful for the friendship that came after. Ma would send Mira to her apartment every week with tea leaves, dried fruit, herbal soups that smelled of mushrooms and bone. Mira would always linger, ask many questions about babies, even after JoJo was born, wanting to hold him, calling him hers, and then asking if she could borrow him for a while. "Maybe someday when you are older," Lucinda would say, and Mira's eyes would glow bright with excitement. Even now, with the girl returned—hardened, thin-bodied, and moving lifelessly through her days—it is hard to let go of this image of Mira as a young girl.

"She is a good girl, you know, but say what you want to say."

Ma has barely touched her tea. "I wonder if it is me. Something I have done wrong."

"Oh, love, why would you say a thing like that?"

Ma pinches her forehead, a move that Lucinda recognizes as her friend's attempt to stop the tears. It always works. "Why does she make life so difficult for herself, as hard as it is right now?"

Lucinda purses her lips. This is not an answer to her question, but she permits it. "She is grieving, isn't she?"

With a flutter of her hands, Ma dismisses this. "Who's she shedding tears over? Shin? How much of a friend can a roach be?"

Lucinda purses her lips, biting down her disagreement. "Perhaps. Though there's also . . . you know."

Ma's eyes flash hurriedly. Of course, how can one forget the fire in Queens, and JoJo too? With the constant news of tragedy these days, neither of them can seem to keep track of every loss and its corresponding event. This one, though, Lucinda can never forget, especially when JoJo's body remains to be found. The girl, Mira's friend, likely shares the same rubble.

"I'm sorry, Lucinda. I didn't mean to be so careless . . ."

"It's all right, love. I barely dream of him anymore." This is not true, and Lucinda is not sure why she forces herself to lie. "What is Mira's friend's name? The one who died in the same fire?"

"I think . . . Mal. Her name is Mal. I met her once or twice. A girl who dressed like a boy. Very pretty, if not for the sweatpants she always seemed to be wearing."

Lucinda holds the girl's name in her mouth and says it aloud, "Mal," as if fashioning her out of her own breath.

Something about the way Lucinda says Mal's name seems to soften Ma a bit. All she can offer in response is a small "Yes."

"I'll light a candle for her tonight."

Nights are always hardest, especially when the apartment buzzes with the sound of ghosts as the humans sleep. Lucinda always wonders where her ghosts are, why JoJo has not made his way back to her. Ma has her father, albeit in a warped poltergeist form, and even the Espositos downstairs had their whole clan come back, every great-grandparent and the great-greats, permanently seated at their too-small dinner table. Sometimes family-less ghosts show up too, and no one knows what to make of them. Even these homeless ghosts have not chosen her to haunt, and she does not know how to feel about that.

That night, Lucinda rolls aside her rug to begin her ritual.

When the rain first began, she felt her skin prickle with something awaking in her, and whatever arose was ancient and far preceded her. She knew it did not come from nowhere, having witnessed her mother and grandmother with "the gift" when she was younger. None of that telekinetic magic that you see on television, no wiggle of the nose for hijinks to ensue—the women in her family brewed remedies for heartache, scooped other women's tears into vials and then buried them with their cheating husbands' pubic hair. Of course, the passing of this gift stopped when her father prohibited her mother from teaching her. As her father would have it, she went to Mass, received Communion, and then, when all was said and done, returned home to find that the ghosts always came knocking. She felt them everywhere. Everything Lucinda has done since has been scavenged and ad-libbed from memory.

The ritual always begins the same way. First, the floor is cleared and swept. The votive candles laid out in a circle surrounding her. She nods at Santo Niño, who watches in full ornamental garb above the television. She crosses herself. A thumbprint of day-old incense ash on her forehead. In an abalone bowl, a picture of JoJo sits, slightly wrinkled from the coins and sage weighing the image down. In the photo, JoJo had her orange silk scarf wrapped around his neck, and when she had asked him about it, he had quickly stammered to say that he was playing pilot with his friends. The orange was so bright against the blooming darkness of his skin, he was luminescent. She snapped a photo of him with a disposable camera, and it remains her favorite picture of him.

The night is deceptively quiet this time, but Lucinda can

feel the quake of ghosts waiting behind a thick veil. She sits cross-legged on the floor, lighting the candles around her. Anointing herself with oils, she holds the bowl of JoJo close. In her other hand, she fingers her rosary, counting each bead with her thumb. This goes on for hours until her legs start to tingle from sitting so still for so long. She can hear the ghosts in the floors above and below her, but occasionally the whistle of something farther away emerges from the din. She tries to call to it, pull its hands from the reaches of the shadow. Once in a while she comes close, a touch so light, it could have been her imagination.

"JoJo," she murmurs to the room. "Come back to me."

With her eyes closed, she envisions her boy at the dinner table, eating more than his fill of macaroni and Spam, which he likes to mix with portions from a large pot of chicken adobo. He wipes his mouth and makes an audible "Mmm" sound so that she knows for sure that he is grateful to her. Every night unearths a new memory, and this one creates a soft knot in her gut.

Like each night before, she opens her eyes and the room around her remains empty. No ghosts, just the rattling of wind against the windows. She does not wait around like she used to, getting up to put the room back in order. The clock says two a.m., but time fails to resonate with her these days. Massaging the needles from her legs as she rises, she slowly makes her way to bed.

Lucinda has barely laid her head down on her pillow when she hears the sound of someone sighing beside her. She opens her eyes and waits for the darkness to take shape. Nothing. But when she closes her eyes again, the sigh deepens. Her eyes fly open, and she looks around the room. There, by the barred window of her room, is a woman close to her in age, maybe slightly older, with permed black hair and deep hollows under her eyes. When the curtains blow, she sees the fabric pass through the woman, who slowly turns to her, back hunched and somber.

The woman starts to speak, but Lucinda cannot hear. Without thinking, she moves toward the woman. Face-to-face, she sees that the woman is much older than she thought, the wrinkles preserved on her pale face, somewhere between pewter and ash.

The woman looks back at her, eyes filling with water. "Con gái," she says, trying to grasp Lucinda's hand and failing.

"What's your name?"

"Con gái!"

"I don't understand."

The woman dissolves into sobs, and out of habit reaches for her face to conceal her tears.

"Come lie down, sister," Lucinda murmurs. She gestures for the woman to lie down on the bed beside her, but she does not budge, only cries. All Lucinda can do is console her, but even so, with her arms passing through the specter of the woman, there is only so much she can do.

Finally, Lucinda relents. "I'm so tired . . . Let me help you in the morning."

"Con gái, con gái," the woman urges when Lucinda lies down to rest.

Throughout the night, the woman cries out the same word. The stamina of ghosts! Lucinda can hardly believe it, but then again, she never had to endure this before. Even when dawn arrives and she expects the woman to tire herself out, she does not. When the sun rises, it is as if the woman's voice has only escalated in urgency. Pacing now, the woman insists and insists. Eventually, left with little recourse, Lucinda emerges red-eyed from bed to see the woman kneeling on the edge of her mattress.

"Con gái."

Lucinda tries to drink her coffee, but her hesitation seems to irritate the woman even more. Forgoing her coffee for the first time in years, she gets dressed. The woman gesticulates with her arms as if to say, *Hurry, hurry.* She follows Lucinda out the door and into the hallway.

Lucinda tries to think. In the building, she knows of three Vietnamese families, none of whom she recalls having lost a mother or grandmother during the acid rainstorms, but then again, this loss could have preceded all of it.

She stops at the Nguyens' on the second floor first. As soon as the youngest son opens the door, the ghost barrels in, sniffing the air smelling of incense and dried flowers.

"Con gái!" the woman calls into every room.

The youngest Nguyen, visibly annoyed, demands, "What is this?"

Lucinda throws her hands in the air. "Who knows! She's looking for someone, I suppose."

The young boy rubs his chin, calls his mother to the door. "Mẹ! You know something about this?"

The young boy's mother comes to the door. Lan, a rougher version of her boy, acknowledges Lucinda with a nod. Half her face is covered in purple scales that at a distance could pass for a large birthmark, the consequence of being caught in the acid rain during its early days. When she catches Lucinda staring, she glares, the scales on her face shimmering under the fluorescent light of the hallway. "Not one of ours," she says, a little too coldly.

"Any idea who she is looking for?"

Lan glares at the ghost still wandering through her apartment. "Chào!" she calls out to the woman. "Con gái của bạn không có ở đây!" She disappears after the ghost, shooing her back outside. Out of sight line, Lucinda can hear Lan whispering harshly to her son.

The young boy makes his way to the doorframe again and sheepishly says, "Mẹ says to tell your ghost that her daughter is not here."

"Yes. Thank you."

The door closes on Lucinda sharply. The ghost reappears beside her with renewed energy for the mission.

There is no luck with the Phams either. Widowed old man Hien and his two adult sons squint at the woman but cannot place her. When Lucinda ducks her head into their apartment, she sees the faint light of Hien's long-departed wife, Linh, still trying to set the table.

The last stop is the Trans. Sensing that they are at the end of the line, the woman wails again. To the best of her ability, Lucinda tells her to have some faith whether the woman can understand or not.

A young girl answers the door, her round face made rounder by her hair pulled back into a high ponytail, which sits on her head like a tiny spitting fountain of water. "Hello, how can I help you?" she performs brightly.

Lucinda smiles. "Good girl, so polite."

Before Lucinda can ask her question a third time, she hears a voice from within the apartment call out, "Jessica!"

The young girl waves and points to herself. "I'm Jessica."

From behind Jessica emerges a slender woman with long hair pulled into a beehive bun held together with countless pins. She has the look of someone who once dressed in business-casual clothes. She now wears a T-shirt with holes tucked into an office skirt, a dozen hair ties wrapped around one wrist.

"I'm so sorry," the slender woman says to Lucinda before glaring at the young girl. "I'm Thuy, this little girl's mother. She knows she's not supposed to answer the door alone, but she's learning this whole etiquette thing at school. It's super weird. But it's dangerous, right, baby? Answer the door alone, and someone's gonna hack your face off."

Jessica nods and turns back to Lucinda and the ghost, making a sweeping gesture with her arms. "Would you all like to come in for some tea?"

Thuy smacks an exhausted palm over her face.

Lucinda smiles at Jessica and lowers herself a little to meet the girl eye to eye. "Maybe another time, my love. But maybe you can help me." She points to the ghost beside her, whose hands are covering her face as if embarrassed, suddenly very quiet and still. "Do you recognize this woman beside me?"

Jessica looks up at the ghost and without hesitation nods vigorously.

"Now, who is this woman to you?"

"That's Bà Ngoại!"

"And what does that mean, my love?"

"Grandma!" Then looking to Thuy beside her for confirmation, she asks, "Right, Mom?"

Thuy's eyes open wide as she stares at the ghost beside Lucinda. The ghost's embarrassment seems to peak as she tries to hide behind Lucinda now.

Thuy takes several steps out the door until she is close enough to embrace the ghost. "Mẹ? Is that you? I can barely recognize—"

The ghost nods and starts to cry again. Thuy begins to cry too, and suddenly the reunited mother and daughter stand, unsure of what to do next. Eventually the ghost follows Thuy and Jessica into the apartment and, flustered, Thuy can only manage a small wave of gratitude to Lucinda before the door closes behind her. Despite the shut door, Lucinda can hear Jessica's voice calling out, "Bà ngoại! Welcome! Welcome! Would you like some tea? Are you hungry?"

Word gets around that Lucinda has been conjuring ghosts. For her, it is only the one time, and she does not even know if she can do it again, but the rumor snowballs before she can get a handle on it. She finds out that Thuy has started bringing her ghost mother, Anh, to every floor, introducing her to all the neighbors and ghosts. In Thuy's account of what transpired, Lucinda had called the spirit out in the middle of the night, pulling Anh out from the plane of suffering in which she had lived, a restless spirit adrift in the boundless eternity that is the afterlife.

When this story comes back to Lucinda, she feels immediately embarrassed, unsure if her rituals had anything to do with Anh's arrival. And even if it did, what if the mother ghost returned greatly disturbed? Anh has yet to utter any new words and frequently hides behind her daughter. *If* Lucinda was responsible, *if* that was truly the case, then what would be in store for JoJo if she could reach him?

Lucinda barely has time to consider all the possibilities. Before she knows it, the Esquerras are at her door, searching for a long-lost cousin. Then Gloria Lopez wants to know if she can find her dead father and shutter him in hell where he belongs—a request that Lucinda awkwardly turns down. Thuy returns with Linh, a photo album of dead relatives in tow, asking if Lucinda can retrieve the rest of the maternal line. Following soon after them are the Fedorovs, an elderly couple, each seeking their own parents at this late stage of their lives, wanting to know what awaits them.

Lucinda never knows what to say, so she says she will try. The stacks of photographs of family members that are not her own collect on her coffee table next to prayer cards. She stares at them as she drinks her coffee in the morning, pondering the lives of all those faces before her. Some vibrate with an intense urgency; some unfold like a song.

She tries every night, putting the conjuring of JoJo on hold so that she can speak to others across the veil.

"Sorry, JoJo," she whispers to the photograph of her son wrapped in orange.

The nights are quiet each time. Although the images and sentimental items left behind by her neighbors quake with energy, when she closes her eyes she can only envision blackness, a curtain enveloping everything. By the time she opens her eyes, hours have passed, and the sky has the milky color of dawn. She goes to bed blanketed by the silence of her home.

Ma comes by the apartment with Mira and Sad. Ma walks in

empty-handed, while the two others maneuver dollies stacked with rations for her. Thanks to the messiness of relief efforts, Lucinda can still claim JoJo as a dependent, and thus acquire twice the amount of rations, so she redistributes the extra rations among the building residents. Ma and Mira typically go to the rations site to pick up her items, on account of her bad knees. To her knowledge, Sad does not leave the building, but he helps when he can.

When Ma sees the bags under Lucinda's eyes, she is quick to comment. "Ay! What is this? Are you not sleeping?"

"No, sister. Afraid not."

Ma shakes her head and turns to Mira and Sad to confirm her disapproval. Mira only shrugs, and Sad, headless and expressionless, simply stands there. "Not sleeping is no good! Are you still trying to talk to these people's dead relatives?"

"Trying. Not very successful, unfortunately."

Ma's nostrils flare. "This is wrong. How can they exploit you like that?" Again she looks to Mira and Sad for agreement. This time Mira turns to Lucinda and makes a funny face as if she is about to ask a question, until the moment passes. Sad remains still.

"No, no. It's fine. I'm happy to do it."

That is not true either, though Lucinda is not sure why it comes out like that.

"Let me talk to the people," Ma insists. "Tell them to find someone else to bother."

Lucinda swipes her hand in the air. "Oh please. Don't do that."

"If they want a ghost, tell them I'll loan them Grandpa Why. That'll teach them a thing or two about willing a ghost to appear."

Lucinda and Ma chuckle, Ma's laughter slightly louder than her friend's. Meanwhile, Lucinda has noticed that Mira's eyes are trained on her intently.

Ma parks her dolly at the threshold of the apartment. "You want me to tell them off, you just let me know." She gestures to Mira and Sad. "You two, help your auntie carry the boxes into her kitchen. I have to go rest my back."

Once Ma leaves, Sad begins lifting the first box from the dolly. Mira places one hand on his arm, tapping him twice. He seems to understand, and places the box back on the dolly, giving Lucinda a small wave before leaving.

With Mira finally alone with Lucinda, they perform the same dance they do every month—the older woman offering to help with those boxes, Mira refusing, going, "No, please, sit." Then, finally, Lucinda relinquishes the boxes to Mira's authority, and she sits in the kitchen, watching the rations fill the refrigerator and cabinets.

Mira stands on a stool in the kitchen, placing the cans, label facing out, in the appropriate cabinets, a job which she can do in her sleep. Lucinda watches, this curious girl whose calves grow skinnier by the day, a kite of a body about to fly away at the slightest breeze. Since JoJo's passing, she cannot help but look with greater tenderness at her young neighbor, so close to JoJo's age and yet so distant from everyone else.

Lucinda finally asks, "How are you, my dear?"

Mira pauses, a can of whole tomatoes in hand, before turning to Lucinda with a too-bright smile. "I'm good! Great. Yeah."

"Must be very difficult with your friend gone."

"What?" The comment seems to take her by surprise. Sensing the softness of Lucinda's voice, though, she lets her gaze fall and her shoulders follow. "Yes. It's hard. Shin and I were very close."

"Any sign of him since he vanished?"

Mira cocks her head at Lucinda with a look that says, *Come on, now.* "I don't think he vanished. Ghosts don't just . . . disappear."

Lucinda offers a slight nod of understanding. "Then we can only hope he is happy where he is now."

Mira continues to stock the shelves, less quietly now, the metal of the cans colliding into one another. After the last of the canned pineapple is shelved, she shuts the cabinet door and turns to the older woman.

"Lucinda."

"Yes, my love?"

"How do you do it?"

Lucinda cautiously considers Mira's face, bright with urgency. "Do what, my dear?"

As she suspects, Mira responds, "The ghosts. How do you bring them here?"

Lucinda studies the young girl before her, not so much a girl anymore, but someone who aged through the early grief of her life. She recalls seeing her once in the lobby of the building, her body pressed against another's. She had thought the contours of the person looked like a boy, and she had made a note to inform Ma of this immediately. But when the body turned, the person possessed a soft, feminine face, long hair tucked inside the collar of her hooded sweatshirt. Their faces only an inch apart, their lips moving in low whispers. When they spotted Lucinda, they pulled apart quickly, waved goodbye. Lucinda had never really given that moment much thought. It was so innocent, after all, the closeness of two girls. Yet in this moment she returns to it, the wide-eyed emergency of Mira's eyes, so familiar, as if approaching something secret.

Mira's gaze grows more intense, her eyes like two mirrors.

"I'm not sure," Lucinda answers honestly. "It just happened."

Mira shoves her hands into her pockets, unsure of herself just then. "Do you really think you can do it again?"

Lucinda catches herself reaching out to touch the girl's wrist, so thin and small it could almost crack if her grasp was any clumsier. Gingerly, she tugs at Mira's wrist until she pulls out her balled-up fist.

"Ask what you want to really ask, my love."

Mira lets her hand open like a flower, and in her palm's center is a small cassette tape. Lucinda stares too long, and Mira quickly shoves the tape back into her pocket. "It's all I have left of her," she says.

"Of who?"

Mira bites her lip and shakes her head. "I can't tell you. Can you just help me?"

"Is it Shin? You want me to reach him?"

The young girl's mouth turns into a deep frown. "No. I mean, I miss Shin. But I know he is where he needs to be. The person I'm thinking of . . . they want to be here. They have to."

Although Mira stands a foot taller than Lucinda, she seems so small in that moment. Her voice comes out like a plea, and suddenly she is a child again.

Lucinda has said yes to several neighbors at this point, though none as close to her as Mira by way of Ma. Although never formally discussed, the understanding between her and Ma had always been that if one saw something concerning the

other's child, it was imperative that something be said. What-
ever Mira's secret is, she intends to keep it to herself and from
Ma. So, as the law of friendship goes, she will need to approach
Ma first before making any promises.

"Let me think about it, love, okay?" she finally offers.

Flustered, Mira shoves her hands into her pockets again,
fumbling with the cassette. "It's okay. Forget about it," she
quickly mutters before making her way to the door.

"My love—"

Without another word, Mira slams the cassette tape on
Lucinda's kitchen counter and leaves. Mira's fast exit leaves
Lucinda flustered, staring at the tiny plastic box on her counter. She has not seen a cassette of that size for years and
tries to remember for a minute if she still has a tape recorder
stored somewhere in the back of JoJo's closet. The closet,
being the biggest one in the apartment, was storage for not
only JoJo's things but the family's retired objects that were
infrequently used, possibly broken, but somehow too sentimental to let go. The thought of digging through that closet
seizes her heart. She had been avoiding the room altogether
since JoJo's passing.

Lucinda shakes the thought from her head as she considers
what she will tell Ma about Mira's request.

That night, Lucinda performs her ritual with only white candles, dressed in ash. Mira's cassette tape lingers in her mind,
even as it continues to sit untouched on the kitchen counter.
This time, she envisions the walls of her mind collapsing into
rubble. Beyond the cracks of those walls are stars whose light

pierces through the darkness. She thinks: *Clear heart, clear heart.* She wills it so.

This time there is no one specific that she is trying to reach. She will cast as wide a net as the spiritual plane will allow her. *Come one, come all.* Her hands open, two palms willing to receive. As her mother and grandmother taught her, the spirits can read your heart. She hopes that they know her heart is purified by grief, her want so clear, even if she is filled with fear.

The wind rustles through the open window, and the air around the room produces a soft sigh. Her eyes still closed, Lucinda envisions the room filling with the voices of people dead and gone, imagining that among the din, JoJo will be one of them. She shuts her eyes tighter and prays. Yet when she opens them, the room looks exactly as it always has, empty.

She is accustomed to the disappointment of her rituals by now, but tonight the absence feels particularly loud. Just as she is about to put away her candles, the door to JoJo's old room slowly opens. An act of wind has nudged it ajar, maybe, but to be certain, Lucinda makes her way into the room, tiptoeing as she used to do when checking on sleeping JoJo at night. Peeking in, she sees only the shadows of the dark room, illuminated by the light from outside. The air inside is stale, untouched. She makes her way inside and sits on the bed.

Before JoJo moved out, Lucinda reminded her son that if he ever came home for a weekend, the room would be just as he left it. As frequently as he could, he would sleep over on Sundays, and there would always be enough of him there that she could put in the hamper to launder, cups to be taken back to the sink. Now only traces of him remain—a fake gold watch on top of a pair of boxer briefs on the floor, unopened mail peeking out from under the bed.

She follows the traces to the closet now, bombarded by the smell of mothballs when she opens its doors. Stacks of boxes lean against each other in disarray, some spilling over with appliances, others with old winter coats. JoJo's three button-down shirts and tie hang on metal wires. She pulls a box from the back and starts rummaging through its contents, finding the tape recorder she was positive she still had, but unsure if the cassette Mira gave her would fit. Just as she is about to return the box to the closet, she sees a photo strip hanging out of one of JoJo's shirt pockets. Fishing it out, she sees a black-and-white triptych of JoJo and another boy, darker than JoJo and with a smooth fade, a funny contrast to the black mop that is JoJo's hair. In the first two images, the boys are making silly faces, a pair of tongues stretched out, showing off their length. In the final picture, the other boy has both arms wrapped around JoJo, his fingers running through his chest hair as if he is grazing water, and he plants a kiss on JoJo's cheek, only an inch away from his mouth.

Without thinking, Lucinda pockets the photo strip and tape recorder, returning the rest of the items to the closet. She has seen every photograph of her boy, and this new one presenting itself to her is like having him home again. She brings the photo strip, tape recorder, and cassette to bed with her, and realizing that the cassette does in fact fit the old device, she hits play. The photo strip still clutched in her hand, she sinks into bed, watching the wheels of the cassette turn in the player. Before the voice on tape begins to speak, she is already sobbing into the photograph.

The room is dark when Lucinda wakes up, not able to recall at first when and how she fell asleep. It is a noise in the apartment that wakes her, a rattling somewhere outside her bedroom though she cannot place it. The rattle happens again, and this time she figures it to be the apartment doorknob being jostled. She freezes. The thud of footsteps approach, and there is not much time for her to react. She pulls the blanket over her head and prays that the ghost is a benevolent one.

The light switches on, and Lucinda feels a heavy tug on her blanket. Someone is yanking it out of her grasp. She squints once, twice, trying to make out the figure in front of her, a face so familiar and gradually becoming clear.

"Joseph!" she gasps. Even with his overgrown hair and scraggly beard, she still recognizes his face behind all of it. More fatigued, and certainly older than she remembers, this man she has not seen for years has returned to her.

Joseph's eyes are bloodshot when he squints, and from the smell of his breath, she can tell that old habits die hard. He collapses onto the bed beside her. "Shh," he implores. "Did not mean to scare you. Let me sleep awhile, please."

He barely finishes his sentence when he starts to snore. Lucinda stares, scanning the body of the old man beside her, the gray hair on his belly, which spills just a little bit over his belt. Just to be sure, she pokes him in the chest; he responds with a loud cough. The finger touches something hard, fleshy, so yes, Joseph is alive, not a ghost. She is not sure whether to be relieved or disappointed in that fact.

With Joseph sprawled on the bed, she decides to move to the

couch. There is no going back to sleep now, not with this black hole of her past sleeping in her bedroom. She ought to knock him with the clock radio, honestly, for the way he left things, that stupid drunk. But instead, she sinks herself deeper into the couch, pulling a worn blanket up to her neck.

It has been years since she has seen Joseph, but so little seems to have changed. Some gray in his beard, sure, but the way he bulldozes into her life—that is devastatingly familiar. How has she managed to conjure him now, of all times, when the silence of the apartment alone is enough to drive her crazy? How can she forget the time he nearly missed her head when he threw a half-drunk bottle at the wall? That day he showed up at JoJo's school for pickup and grabbed Lucinda's wrist so roughly that every parent and teacher looked at her funny for the rest of the year? As a father, Joseph proved far worse. When JoJo came home with one pierced ear, a tiny sterling silver stud, Joseph had called out to him in passing, "So, what? You're like a ladyboy now or something?" And when JoJo made the dash to his room, Joseph swooped in quickly, yanking JoJo by his freshly pierced ear toward the bathroom sink. Poor JoJo's cries came deep from the back of the throat, pleading, "No, no, Tatay, please, it hurts! I'll take it out, I'll take it out! Let me do it myself!" Joseph stuffed JoJo's head under the sink faucet, where he ran the water over the back of his son's ears, trickling down his eyes and mouth, his cries becoming garbled. The earring came out, plucked by Joseph's hand, and he help it up like a pirate collecting his treasure after a bloody pillage. She wishes she could say that she and JoJo left Joseph eventually, but it was in fact the man who left them behind. Lucinda and JoJo woke up one day to find that their apartment had been ransacked, papers strewn everywhere, the television gone, and every bit of cash she did not hide from her husband emptied from its tin.

Knowing all this to be true, her body boiling with a rage that she has carefully kept dormant until then, one simple fact remains: She is tired. Since the quarantine began and JoJo could no longer visit her, she has lived in the silence of the apartment, feeling its quiet festering beneath her skin. She was restless at first, and then that became a fatigue that would not lift. Even knowing the terror that is Joseph in the other room, she cannot help but find relief, in some small way, in his company. It is either him or the descent into a totalizing silence. Who knows where that will take her?

That night, she falls asleep to the sound of Joseph's snores in the next room. No other ghosts come to visit.

In the morning, Lucinda blinks herself awake. The air in the room carries a soft white cloud. In the kitchen she hears the crackle of something hitting oil, and she sits up suddenly, aware that everything is not a dream. Joseph stands beside the stove, a greasy spatula in hand.

"Good morning, mi reina!" he shouts brightly. The spatula dips down and flips a chunk of ground meat in the pan.

"Don't 'mi reina' me." She looks down at the pan, all the wasted oil for the precious meat, which is quickly burning. "What are you doing here?"

Joseph runs his free hand through the back of his hair sheepishly, and it is almost boyish how his fingers thread through it. "It's a long story . . ."

"Tell me."

As is turns out, the Erasers really do live up to their infamy. Joseph had signed up for the cleanup crew in the early days of the rainstorms, having exhausted his network of friends willing to let him sleep on their couch. They had converted several YMCAs into housing for the crews, which worked out for a newly homeless Joseph.

At first the job was not so bad. Having worked some brief stints as a grave digger back in Manila, he told himself that the proximity to dead bodies was nothing to him. They were usually facedown anyway by the time the crew got to them. He even made a game of it, counting their two arms, a set of gills, and once a child with a small fishtail nub on the small of their back. Some bodies looked like they were yanked out from the river, sulfuric and rattling with swallowed dead fish. Either way, it did not matter. They all went to the same place in the end. He had the routine down: wrap their heads in a plastic bag, grab a fellow worker, and lift the body on three. This way, he never had to look into their eyes.

The death toll kept rising, and so the job got busier, longer hours with stricter rules for breaks. Run-down and tired after working two back-to-back shifts, Joseph skipped the first step of body removal one day, and the eyes of a young boy stared back at him. He did not say anything when he bagged the body, but later he could think only how the boy was no bigger than JoJo when he left. The eyes haunted his dreams, their milky whiteness a thin film that stretched across the sky of his nightmares. "I can never seem to outrun it," he tells Lucinda, his face in his palms.

One day he woke up and found that he could not move from

his cot. His ESRS supervisors sought him out, sat him down, and said something akin to "We don't have time for your tantrum. Plenty people without work. We can replace you if we have to." At those words, his body felt like Jell-O, and he dissolved where he was, laying on the floor until someone came to resuscitate him. The ESRS higher-ups issued him $1,000, which he immediately spent on liquor. And this is what has brought him here, back to Lucinda's apartment, begging her to open her good woman heart to him again, or at least to let him stay there for a while.

"It's been years, Joseph," Lucinda finally says with a sigh. "You have no idea how much has happened since you left. How could you ever . . ." She does not finish her sentence. Watching the meat on the stove burn, she grabs the spatula from Joseph's hand, plates the meat, and turns off the burner. She tosses the spatula onto the counter, letting it clatter loudly. "And here you are, eating up all the meat already! The first day!"

He takes her balled-up fist and holds it against his chest until her hand blooms like a flower, spreading over his heart. He holds it there, even as she struggles to pull away. "Mi reina, feel this," he insists, pushing her hand farther into his chest. "I owe you everything. I abandoned you. I abandoned JoJo. I am a cockroach. I am the bottom of your shoe. But you must believe me when I tell you that I have suffered too."

Lucinda sighs again, much deeper this time. She has stopped trying to pull her hand away. Joseph, seizing the moment, takes her hand and places it flat on his head, raising and lowering it as he says, "Bad husband. Punish me like the dog I am. Go on. I deserve it."

Lucinda balls her fist, preparing to slam it down hard on his head. She imagines him sprawled on the floor, cowering from her, for a change. Instead, she feels her hand fall heavy on his head, her fingers massaging his hair like grass. How long has it been since she has touched a blade of grass? It seems Joseph shares the same thought as he takes her hand and places it against his cheek, his scraggly beard in wild disarray.

He seems to turn puppyish in the moment. "I did not mean to be wasteful. I just wanted to do something nice for you for a change."

Lucinda's eyes shoot back to the plate of meat, lamenting the charred meat that was supposed to last her the week, now barely edible. She pauses for a long time before finally relenting. "Fine. But next time, I do all the cooking."

To Lucinda's surprise, the days with Joseph quickly begin to feel routine. Sensing that atonement will take a while, Joseph follows Lucinda's instructions to sleep in their old bedroom while she takes JoJo's. She cannot bear to relinquish JoJo's room to him, and at her mercy, he lets her tell him where and when to sleep—the floor, even, if she wills it.

They wake up at the same time, brew coffee, eat their breakfast of saltines and whatever canned fish is available that day. All day, he patches up the cracked windows of the apartment with polymer glue, tightens every screw that has gone loose, fixes the television static. She makes dinner, now for two. He compliments her often, waxing nostalgic about the early days of their marriage—an arrangement by their parents, but so what? He tells her he has always known his luck, to lock down the prettiest girl in their hometown before she became someone else's.

One day, Joseph borrows a pair of clippers from the neighbors and shaves his hair and beard, leaving behind a neat tuft on his head that he can slick back with pomade. When he finishes and presents his fresh look to Lucinda, her mouth hangs open just a bit, and, catching herself, she tells him coolly, "Eh, it looks better now."

Meanwhile, the neighbors' reaction to Joseph's return is even more unexpected. He has made himself useful, offering to take over repair shifts in the building. With little else to do, he spends his time fixing the wiring inside apartments, relighting the pilots of old heaters, and even emptying mousetraps. When a task is done, the neighbors ask him to stay awhile, offering him tea and cookies, and it is not uncommon for him to return to Lucinda with an armful of dried fruit, pickles, canned beans, and more. Those who knew him seem to forget that he once pulled his wife by the hair into the hallway, and that another time he drunkenly pissed himself in the elevator. They want his stories of working on the cleanup crew, how he was instructed to bag bodies quickly before the news crews arrived.

"But is it really as bad as they say?" they want to know.

Joseph's face turns dramatic and sullen. "Oh, it's far worse."

At first Lucinda had a hard time tolerating the willful amnesia of her neighbors, so quick to accept Joseph back into the fold. Joseph seemed to notice too; upon seeing her arms crossed in the hallway, he would wrap up conversation with the neighbors and shuffle back to her side.

She had heard his stories from the sidelines enough times to pique her own curiosity, however, and gradually found herself beginning to linger behind him, even as he described the mutilated bodies he had disposed of. Once, he told a macabre joke about lifting a heavy dead body that looked as if it were in the middle of performing one last sexual act before passing, rigor mortis having set in. He and his team had to stuff the body into the bag with the poor corpse nowhere near completion.

"Oh, Joseph, you're always exaggerating," she found herself exclaiming, letting loose a tiny laugh. She clapped it back with one hand over her mouth, the other playfully batting his arm. He seemed surprised at the lightness of this gesture, and for the first time since his arrival, she smiled at him.

The only person not impressed with Joseph's arrival is Ma, but that has always been a given. When Ma first laid eyes on Joseph after his return, she immediately pulled Lucinda aside and hissed, "I can't believe you haven't slipped some rat poison in that man's booze by now." When Ma noted Lucinda's hesitancy to respond, she prodded. "What did he do? Did he blackmail you into letting him back in? Say that he would put you in jail for not reporting JoJo's death to the city?"

Lucinda looked away. "No, not exactly."

"Then why is he still here?"

Lucinda did not know how to answer, could only offer, "It's too hard to be alone."

It was clear that Ma was growing increasingly annoyed. "So? I'm alone."

"Yes, but it's different. I'm not like you."

That would not suffice. "Is it money? Do you need money?"

Lucinda shook her head and then her hands. "No, no. It isn't about money."

"I told you that if you ever need anything, you call me."

Lucinda nodded, opening and closing her mouth as she worked out what she wanted to say. "Yes, but . . . it is not enough."

Ma's sigh came heavily through her nostrils. "This will not end well. You know this."

They were quiet for a while. The two rarely fought, and when they did, it was usually about what happened in *General Hospital* many seasons ago, nothing that replaying the old episodes could not resolve. But this, Lucinda felt it in her gut, the ache and humiliation of it all.

"I'm so lonely all the time," Lucinda finally said. She felt her legs tingle, her bones so, so tired. "Can you please understand?"

"If you are lonely, you come to me. I told you . . ." Ma bit her lip and seemed to swallow the next words.

"I don't understand why you are mad."

"I'm not mad!"

The two sighed at the same time. Silence fell over them, but this time it was Ma who spoke up. "I don't think I want to come over to your place if that man is still there."

"Fine. Don't come over, then."

Each was surprised by the response of the other, but it was too late to take any of it back. Lucinda, unsure whether Ma had expected more protest on her part. Ma, a storm brewing in her chest. They took turns opening and closing their mouths, but neither could pull out an apology. Not knowing what to do, they turned from each other and walked slowly away, neither of them looking back.

As it turns out, Ma is a woman of her word. She no longer comes over unannounced, no soft pitter-patter of her slippers coming up the hallway. In her place, Mira arrives every week with little offerings—a twelve-pack of raisins, sour plums, a dusty bag of peach rings.

"How's your mom?" Lucinda inquired once.

Mira shrugged, unaware of what has transpired. "Fine."

Joseph, blissfully ignorant of his role in Ma and Lucinda's falling out, immediately opens the packages and devours their contents.

During one of her visits, Mira stops to say a few words to Lucinda before leaving, "I'm sorry about how I responded to you the other day . . ."

With the whirlwind of Joseph's arrival, Lucinda has already forgotten the instance Mira is referring to. "My dear, I have to say that I don't remember what you've done that would offend me."

"The tape . . . when I wanted you to . . . you know."

Lucinda suddenly remembers Mira slamming the small cassette tape on her counter. "Ah yes. I remember now."

"Can I tell you something?"

"Of course, my love. What is it?"

"I'm trying to get ahold of someone I love. That's who I want you to bring back."

"Oh."

Lucinda's mouth forms a tight circle, unsure of what to say next. She thinks of the last time she strolled through the lobby, seeing Mira emerging from Sad's apartment, her hand caressing his chest. Since they have been together, they have been inseparable. Even Ma has said at certain points, "At last! The girl is a little happier these days!" That has certainly been true for a while, but recently Lucinda has noticed the heaviness come back to Mira's steps.

Lucinda sits down. "I should talk to your mom first before I—"

Mira swipes her hand through the air. "Don't bother. She'll tell you not to do it."

"How are you so sure?"

Mira snorts. "I know my mom. She's never approved of this person."

Lucinda pauses. "Who is this person?"

Mira bites her lip. In the silence that passes, Lucinda once again has a vision of Mira in the lobby, pressed up against the girl who looked like a boy.

"Her name is Mal."

Mira lays out each word of her sentence. Lucinda nods like she understands. Mal. She lets the name roll around in her head. Of course. Something within her had known this all along.

Mira continues. "She died in the fire. The same one that took JoJo."

Lucinda keeps nodding, even as her hands start to shake.

"Mal was the one who helped JoJo find the apartment down the block so he could move in with—"

Lucinda looks up at Mira. who has stopped herself abruptly. She feels the sensation of water welling up inside her, rocking against her chest. "Tell me," she finally says. "You knew JoJo very well. Was he happy?"

Mira seems to regret bringing up JoJo at all, but when she recovers is finally able to reply, "I think so."

"Good."

Mira's face softens. She sits across from Lucinda and takes her hand. "I want to let you know that he was very loved until the very end." She pauses. "Do you understand what I mean by that?"

The water inside Lucinda crests, spilling over. She catches herself, sighs until her eyes swell. "Of course. I love him. He must know that."

Mira tightens her grip on Lucinda's hand. "There's someone who loved him as much as you."

Lucinda tries to blink back some of her tears, but it's no use. "I don't understand."

"Think about it, tita. You already know."

Lucinda thinks back to the photo strip she discovered in JoJo's shirt pocket, the look on JoJo's face when the other boy kissed his cheek, eyes squinting shut as if joy rattled inside him. She saw the bright orange scarf of his childhood wrapped around him, gentle as the hand that rested against his chest, all light and everything good, just as JoJo was, just as JoJo will always remain.

Mira watches Lucinda's face and allows her grip to soften. "Does it change anything for you?"

Lucinda is quiet, lost in the color of a bright flame.

"Tita?"

"I hear you."

"Do you understand now?"

Lucinda nods, and the water seems to spill from her chest now in deep, long sighs. Mira gives her a minute to complete her sobs, and throughout that silence Lucinda's mind rushes to the memories of everything JoJo was and continues to be—a very good boy.

Lucinda sniffs and wipes her free hand over her nose. She gestures to Mira, "And your Mal?"

"Yes. What about her?"

"Did she know that she was loved?"

Between the two women, an entire ocean swells. Mira sighs into her hands. "I'm not sure," she confesses. "We didn't end on a good note. That's why I want your help to tell her."

Lucinda gently removes Mira's hands from her mouth, placing them gently on the table. "Okay," she finally relents. "I will help you."

Mira's eyes fly wide open with surprise. "You will? But what about my mom? You said . . ."

Lucinda considers what Ma would say to this. If they were still talking, it might be a different matter. But now, here, with Mira in front of her, she feels something stir in her.

"I'll do it," she tells Mira once again. Mira pulls her hands back to her face, sighing relief into them. Lucinda adds a warning. "But I don't know if it'll work. I've been trying to call to the spirits. To JoJo. Every night. Nothing."

Mira lets Lucinda know that she understands and will appreciate anything she can attempt. She does not have many of Mal's things beyond the cassette tape, though she does not say more about it than that. She gives Lucinda a tight hug before leaving, saying, "Thank you! Thank you!"

Lucinda walks Mira out of the apartment to the sound of the young girl's platitudes. Joseph has returned home, sitting in the living room with a dozen questions written across his face. He points to the door where Mira had exited and asks, "What did I just overhear?"

Caught off guard, Lucinda is unprepared to answer. She stammers. "What? Don't be nosy. It's nothing. The girl just wants some love advice. Leave it alone."

When Lucinda begins to make her way to the kitchen, Joseph grabs her by the wrist. The force of his grip startles them both. He lets go quickly, clears his throat. "Ghosts? You're trying to bring back ghosts now? Is that what you've been doing every night?"

Lucinda does not answer at first, the two of them locked in

their current positions. Finally, the words come out soft and quiet. "Wouldn't you want to if you could?" When Joseph's face turns to surprise, she goes on. "To see JoJo again?"

Joseph's expression falls flat, lifeless. "No."

Stunned, Lucinda can only muster, "What?"

"I said no."

"Why not?" She thinks she should strike him, should pummel his face with her fists. Fear ignites within her as she reels from the sharpness of his knuckles, so deeply embedded in her bones—she tucks these thoughts away as quickly as they appear.

Joseph rubs his face, exasperated. "I don't think he wants to see me."

Lucinda spits out her words. "That's your fault."

She does not regret the harshness of her response, and Joseph does not fight her on it either. He nods in agreement. "I hope he is better wherever he is. Why disturb him?"

Lucinda shakes her head. "You cannot possibly believe that. He died in a horrific fire. He did not choose that for himself."

"All the better to let him be."

"You selfish, selfish man."

They turn away from each other, letting the tense quiet of the room pass through them. It is Joseph who finally speaks. "Does it work, though? Are you able to do it?"

"Do what? Bring back ghosts?"

"Yes."

Lucinda looks down at her hands, thinking of the one ghost she was able to bring back, if only by sheer accident. "It happened one time. But yes, just the once."

Suddenly Joseph's face lights up. "And you think you can do it again? Like you told Mira?"

"I don't know. I'm going to try."

Joseph rubs his chin. "What are you charging Mira for this?"

"Pardon?"

"Money. Is she giving you money?" Observing Lucinda's nonresponse, he raises his voice to a shout. "Is anyone giving you money for this?"

"It's fine!"

Joseph waves his hand in the air. "We're in hard times! Lucinda, you can't be this naïve. I've seen what's out there. We need to protect ourselves. You can't let these people leech off the kindness of your heart, woman. As soon as you're down on your luck, they leave you starving on the streets and pick apart your pockets."

Lucinda shakes her head vigorously. "Oh Joseph, what a life you must live if you give only to take."

"Trust me, Lucinda. You will want a safety net when things get worse . . . and they will get worse."

"Stop."

Lucinda holds out her hand, erecting a wall between the two of them. Joseph opens his mouth to speak, but she pinches her hand shut and he knows to obey that gesture. Joseph throws up his hands and walks away, leaving Lucinda the victor.

Lucinda starts her ritual anew that night in JoJo's room, feeling as if she has conquered something. Sitting on the floor by his bed, she recalls the vision of her boy's orange scarf, only this time it is wrapped around him and the other boy like the string of fate. She breathes in the air of his room, the scent of him that remains there beside the musk of untouched space. Something like Pantene and Old Spice, and somewhere in there the warm smell of a humid summer day.

The candles surround her, a bowl now overflowing with JoJo's things pulled from the drawers—old receipts, Trident gum. She lays the photo strip of JoJo and his love on top of it all. Finally, she casts her eyes up to the ceiling and says aloud, "Come back to me, JoJo. Nanay is here."

As she expects, the nothingness of the void is returned to her.

She sighs. "Okay, JoJo. You need some more time. Nanay understands."

In the next room, Joseph snores so loudly the walls seem to shake. Each time Lucinda closes her eyes to focus on her ritual, her concentration is broken by the rustle of her husband shifting and groaning in bed.

Eventually she gives up and lies on JoJo's bed, ready to call it a night. Before she closes her eyes, she sees Mira's cassette tape inside the tape recorder resting on the nightstand. She sees that the tape has been played all the way through. Suddenly she recalls the night she had let the cassette play, though she barely remembers any of it.

Without thinking, she rewinds the tape and plays it again from the beginning. From the recorder comes a throat-clearing, a shaky "Um," and then a small voice speaks: *Hello from the other room.*

Lucinda quickly presses pause and listens for sounds in the next room. Joseph's snores have subsided. The voice unnerves her with its quiet, the faint hum of the recording like prickling static across the room.

She exhales slowly, lets the voice resume: *I don't understand what is happening right now. All I know is there is you and me, and I am here recording this in the bathroom while you sleep.*

The voice trembles a little and some time elapses before it continues.

I'm scared. I'm scared all the time. I'm scared while we're awake, trying to fix these windows, waiting for the inevitable. I don't know what will happen from here, and that scares me too.

Lucinda realizes that the voice belongs to Mal. The tape is a message left behind for Mira. Poor girl, she thinks. How she must have replayed this message many times over.

You know what doesn't scare me, though? The fact that you're here with me. That I can look over at you in the middle of the night, see your face, and think, Okay, we're going to get through this together. *I don't know what I'd do without you here. I love you, okay? So much. Whatever happens, if we get separated or whatever, let's promise we'll always find each other. Okay?*

There is a sniffle toward the end, and then a long period of soft static before the tape ends. Lucinda sighs, holding the tape recorder to her heart, which aches for her best friend's daughter. How can anyone move on from a message like that?

After Lucinda extinguishes the candles and heads to bed, she feels herself drift into a peaceful dream. The thought of JoJo lolls in her mind and then fades into pitch-black. From the darkness, a field eventually emerges, a bright green horizon. As she walks across it, she sees the field fade into the same gray as the sky and everything around it. Above her, the birds fly in perfect formation, never a stray body breaking position.

In the distance, she sees specks of people congregating in the center of the field. She walks quickly to them, and as she approaches, she sees that they wear all black or all white. She moves past them, and no one bats an eye.

Eventually Lucinda spots a friendly face in the crowd, a

young woman with her hair pulled into a low ponytail. She has a broad and strong face, but her lips are full and soft, familiar.

"Excuse me," Lucinda interrupts the woman's stupor. "Do you know where we are?"

The woman blinks, noticing Lucinda for the first time. She opens her mouth, but no words come out.

"My name is Lucinda. Do you know who you are?"

The woman's eyes grow wide. She speaks at last. "I remember you."

Lucinda blinks with surprise. "You do?"

"I remember you."

Lucinda combs her memory, and the image of Mira and the woman who looks like a boy in the lobby lights up inside her like a flare. When she finally remembers Mal, she gasps and immediately leans in to tell her, "I have a message for you from Mira."

"Mira?" Mal's voice comes out small, perplexed by the sound of Mira's name.

"She wants to tell you she is sorry. She loves you."

"Mira?"

The sound of a loud horn blasts through the air, and everyone ducks down in unison. Mal presses two hands over her ears, wincing. When Lucinda tries to repeat herself, the dream suddenly comes to an end. She wakes up in the dark of JoJo's room. Mal is nowhere to be found.

The next day, Joseph surprises Lucinda by apologizing for trying to force her hand. She accepts, more out of fatigue than anything. After waking from her dream, she could not go back to sleep, and so she played the cassette tape over and over again, hoping to go back to the field, to find Mal there, to complete the message. When the sun finally emerges, the field still not returned to her, she gives up, and makes herself some coffee, more red-eyed than the day before.

She mulls over what to tell Mira. Where do you begin, when a dream is not a dream but a premonition? Had her body astral-projected somewhere beyond this plane? Or was it simply the drive of her imagination, to want the ghost so badly that she conjured it in her head?

In the lobby, Lucinda runs into Ma and considers telling her about the dream that may not be entirely a dream. They lock eyes just as Ma is about to exit, and for a moment they both stop and look at each other. Mouths opening and closing until, finally, from Lucinda's throat comes a sound.

"You're well?" The sound comes out a croak.

Ma nods, clears her throat. "You?"

"Could be better."

"Uh-huh."

The two of them turn their glances elsewhere. Lucinda thinks about how to share what she thinks she knows, remembering Mira's insistence that Ma will not understand. But what if she does? And what if Ma can advise better? Would this not allow her daughter some peace?

Before Lucinda opens her mouth to speak, Ma says, "Well, I should go soon. Errands outside. Need to get back before curfew."

They offer each other a halfhearted wave goodbye, and then Lucinda is alone again, still the only one who knows about and harbors the details of the eerie dream.

She thinks maybe she will have the opportunity to talk with Mira at the next rations drop-off, but it is Sad who shows up in her place. Despite his being headless, Lucinda reads every expression of defeat on his faceless body. He rolls the boxes into the living room, and they teeter a little before he catches them with the weight of his body.

She touches his arm, and almost instantly he collapses against her, his body sobbing. She guides him to the couch, where he folds himself into his arms, rocking back and forth. Between them, no speech passes. She sees that his keyboard, through which he can communicate, is not with him, so she takes out a pen and notepad, placing it into his hands.

"Tell me," she ushers quietly, worried he cannot hear.

Sad fumbles with the pad, finding its edges, and then writes the message: SHE DOESN'T LOVE ME.

Lucinda lets out a deep sigh, knowing that Sad can feel its soft vibration in the air. "That isn't true, my love. But yes, it is complicated."

Sad does not react at first. Then he resumes his writing: MAL?

Lucinda considers the nervousness of Sad's body, wondering if she should tell him what she found. She admits, "I think I found her."

He writes back immediately: WHERE IS SHE?

Lucinda is not sure, and that is precisely why she cannot commit to telling him what she saw. She relays only what she knows: "I don't know. But she is close."

Sad quickly scrawls: WHY?

Lucinda feels waves of guilt flood her. To know so intimately the pain of someone so far gone and perhaps irretrievable—what if there was a way to bring them back? Who would refuse that?

Very quietly, she tells him, "So we can all have some peace."

Sad pushes the pen against the pad so firmly that the ink almost pierces through the paper: *PLEASE DON'T DO THIS.*

Lucinda looks down at Sad's hands, quaking against his own words. "What are you afraid of, my love?"

Sad absently touches the base of his neck where his head used to be, letting that hand fall back down to his lap. His whole body sighs, and he finally writes: *WILL I LOSE HER?*

"My dear . . ." Lucinda begins softly. She places his hand firmly on her throat. "She is already lost."

Lucinda can tell that it is not the response that Sad wants to hear. She rubs his back slowly as he slumps over, the notepad falling to the floor. "I'm sorry" is all she can say, over and over. "I'm so, so sorry."

In the nights that follow, Lucinda performs the same ritual, as she has done for days now. This time she plays Mira's recording before bed, hoping that she can visit Mal again in her dreams or whatever afterlife she is transported to. Each night, her sleep is peaceful and dreamless. She wakes, frustrated by the waywardness of her magic. It seems nothing she sets out to do goes as she desires it to. It is enough to wonder: Is it a sign to stop wanting?

Meanwhile, as another Tuesday approaches, the building calls for a residents' meeting in the basement. It is a gathering that the residents begrudgingly attend. A representative is sent from every apartment, and the basement is packed like fish in a tin. Several folding chairs pepper the floor for the older residents, corners sectioned off for mobility scooters and folks who just need a wall to lean on.

Lucinda joins the meeting along with Joseph, who seems oddly eager to attend, having never expressed interest in any of these activities before. She sniffs his collar every morning when he passes, always expecting the burning smell of alcohol to seep through his pores, but as far as she can tell, he has stayed sober. As they pass through the basement door, he touches the small of her back, and it makes her almost giddy again.

Over a microphone, the building manager announces that the meeting will begin shortly and urges everyone to file in so that the doors can close behind them. Joseph urges Lucinda to take a seat, but she passes, letting another older woman sit instead. He takes her hand and squeezes it.

Lucinda spies Ma walking in, and, without thinking much of it, drops her grip on Joseph's hand. Their eyes meet and instantly avert. Ma places herself close to the doors, a safe distance behind Lucinda and Joseph.

As the residents clamor in, Lucinda sees another familiar face in the form of a young, bouncing girl. Jessica, in an oversized shirt that hangs to her knees, observes the room with wide eyes, and, spotting Lucinda, rushes toward her.

"Auntie! Auntie!" she ambushes the older woman.

Lucinda allows a polite embrace, asks her if she has been a good girl.

Jessica looks up at her with wet eyes, which takes Lucinda by surprise. The young girl places her hands on Lucinda's hips as if to shake her. "I'm a good girl! I promise. Please don't take bà ngoại away from us." Lucinda's mouth hangs, stunned.

"Jessica! Let her go."

Jessica's mom rushes through the doors to her daughter, who has yet to let go of Lucinda. Thuy wears her hair slicked back, neater today for the purposes of the big gathering, but within seconds of wrestling Jessica from Lucinda, her hair has fallen out of place.

Lucinda smiles at Thuy and nearly makes a joke of it all, but the younger woman seems to be avoiding her eyes. She tries again to say hello, to which Thuy responds, "Sorry to bother you. We will get you your money soon. It's just . . . I'm still trying to get ahold of unemployment . . ."

Before Lucinda can respond, Thuy has already marched Jessica to the other side of the room. Shocked and confused, she can only turn to Joseph, who seems nonplussed by the whole affair.

"What's this all about?" she demands. "What did you do?"

Joseph shrugs, scrunches his face into an expression of bewilderment. "Nothing!"

"Joseph! Don't lie to me."

"Okay, fine!" He rolls his eyes, but stops when he catches her glare. "I know that family has some savings somewhere. I see where they're getting their extra rations. I just thought . . . you know . . . if they have the means, they can at least compensate you for your time. You work so hard—"

"That is not for you to decide."

Joseph rubs the back of his head, flustered. "I'm trying to help you."

"Help me?" Lucinda's voice comes out higher pitched than she expected. "Help me? Help me?" Around the room, people start to turn and look, but her voice only gets louder. "What have you done to help me? Tell me."

As Lucinda peers into Joseph's eyes, she sees a flash of fear and remorse, but it is brief. Soon the familiar fire in his eyes emerges, and he points his finger at her. "I have done nothing but provide for you and your damn ladyboy of a child. Help you? That's all I've done!"

"You keep JoJo out of your mouth! He is not yours anymore." The volume of Lucinda's voice surprises even her.

Joseph looks mad enough to spit into the ground. "I knew it! You're a whore like they said. I knew that child could never be mine."

Suddenly the memory of something old returns to Lucinda—her weakened body in a soaked nightgown, wrestling a tiny life between her legs. She thought that she had forgotten this moment, but now the memory is as clear as the sky after rainfall. There was a doctor, sure, but what she recalls is her own hands pulling the baby out. JoJo, slick with blood and placenta, his skin translucent under the light. *Mahal kita* echoes from her mouth over and over. *Mahal kita, mahal kita.* Every sound in the room disappeared, and she heard only her own screams crying out to the child whose life unfolded before her, every joy and possibility and laughter suddenly realized.

There is a perverse pleasure that Joseph seems to take in Lucinda's tears, which pour out now, remembering JoJo this way. The tears eventually turn into laughter, a soft chuckle as she thinks about the first nights she spent with JoJo in the world, alone and without Joseph. He was drunk somewhere, probably draped over a snooker table, and yet she recalls those first days of JoJo's life as some of the most peaceful times she has known.

Shaking her head, she finally relays, "I pity you, Joseph. You are a sad man."

This pushes Joseph over the edge. He reaches for her, and because she is too late to dodge, her shirt is pulled up to his knuckles, and he shakes her violently. When he raises a hand to slap her, she looks away out of instinct, but then a voice calls out to her from somewhere, and she turns her face to look back at him. They meet eye to eye, and for a moment, he seems locked in his movement—afraid.

A hand reaches out and pulls Joseph back. It happens so quickly that Lucinda can barely track the sequence of movements. All she knows is that she hears Ma's voice call out, "Enough!" and then Joseph is on the floor, Ma's knee against his neck. Joseph groans under the weight of her, and at this point several others have come in to intervene so that Ma can stand up.

Lucinda is stunned into silence for several seconds until she can gather herself. The others who are now holding Joseph up and back seem to be waiting for her instructions. With a level voice, she tells her husband, "You have to leave."

"What?" Joseph's eyes grow wide as he casts his gaze to the basement doors. "But . . . but it's raining outside! I'll die out there."

"After," Lucinda emphasizes. "You will leave after the rain is done."

Joseph slumps, defeated, into the arms of those who have been holding him back. Lucinda can tell that he has more to say, perhaps a final dig, but the many witnesses surrounding them deter him. They shove him through the doors, where he will wait in the lobby until the rain clears.

Lucinda looks back at Ma, who has started to move away. She follows until they reach the very back of the room, a rare quiet corner where the sounds of the meeting are muffled slightly.

Ma turns to Lucinda, knowing she has followed her. With some bitterness, she says, "I told you."

Lucinda nods. Ma's words are perfunctory more than they intend to wound, and with this exchange the two friends fall back into each other's grace. Lucinda touches Ma's hand, which touches her back, and they hold each other like that for a while.

"I have something to tell you," Lucinda eventually whispers. "It's about Mira . . ."

Later that night, Lucinda returns to her apartment, her arms full of paper notices, new guidelines for building safety during the Tuesday rainstorms. Out of habit now, she collapses onto JoJo's bed, the remains of the previous night's spell still scattered on the floor. As she looks around her, the apartment radiates with emptiness, but something has shifted. Perhaps it is the rain subsiding, its wind outside picking up speed one last time and making its way through the crevices of the old building. The curtains flicker against the windowpane, catching the last bit of light left in the day. She thinks she may be dreaming when she hears a chuckle much like her own, a voice deep and familiar in its throatiness. She closes her eyes, and the electric veil of orange passes over her sight, enveloping her.

"JoJo," Lucinda mouths into the room's soft interior.

When she opens her eyes, the walls are painted over in orange, every object coated in light. She knows instantly it is a gift. Within her, she feels her spirit fill up with the vibrating waters of her faith. She wants to call to JoJo with her loudest voice, but she knows he needs time. He is elsewhere, not yet here, but he is coming. Lucinda stretches out her hands in the air. She will be ready for him. She is here and waiting to welcome him home.

HOW TO LOSE
YOUR FAITH

Dear Listeners,

I believed once that time could in fact heal everything, but then I saw what time could do to a person, the way it corrodes us, makes us bitter and cruel. I believed once too that love has no shelf life, that it could live on, but when the other is no longer in front of you, human or ghost, what else can love tether itself to? I believed like everyone else that the rains would end soon, but the water comes down harder each week, and Tuesdays no longer feel like an indoor party but a crowded box that we share, sifting through everyone's shit and grime. I believed too that once the ghosts are here, they are here, but apparently, they can leave too. Ha! Joke's on us. Nothing is for certain, not even death.

I wish the power of my will alone could make me believe. I once thought I would live in a tiny apartment filled with boxes on a shitty broken bed with all my love pouring into one person. But she decided she would rather die than come with me. Maybe my belief started its death journey there. I searched for faith that things could work out for so long that I pushed her far away, and when we said goodbye, I abandoned all my faith with her.

Lucinda says that if we can pray over a dead body, then we can pray over a ghost too. I don't know how to do that if the ghost is not standing before me. See Grandpa Why squirreling away at any given moment. Every ghost is on some mission we can never know. Who do I pray for anyway? "All this talk of ghosts is understandable," she says sagely, "but don't forget about the living too. Pray for them as well."

I forget that hope strays. That faith alone is a wild currency that does not take us very far. I mean I don't know how far it has gotten me. I am so, so lost without you. You must know that, or you must be lost too. I miss you so fucking much, Mal. The days feel like they're peeling away at my skin. The letter is N this time—put this shit together. Are you getting any of this? Are you? I've been calling to you for a very long time. Please. Where are you, Mal? Where the fuck are you?

THE ONE WHO WAITS

When it comes to the subject of belief, Sad has plenty to say. So, when Mira proposes the topic for her weekly radio program, he is surprised that she does not ask what he thinks. It is the failure of belief that she is concerned about, belief upended. She has a slightly different take than him, as usual— Mira is always one bleak step ahead.

On nights before her broadcast, Mira seems to almost erupt with energy. This, Sad notes distinctly, as she moves slowly through all her other days. Sad has always admired this pacing, feeling himself always playing catch-up to her moods. In the early days of her program, she would talk in love letters, and in every address she would softly call out, "Dear Listeners," to her sparse audience. As the weeks went on, her tone changed. The audience is no longer "Dear Listeners" but possible sparring partners, always charged with the spirit of debate. She eggs people on. She is full of questions that she pelts, one after the other.

Once, during a call about the longevity of romantic relationships between humans and ghosts, Mira got into a heated argument with a caller who insisted that it could never work out due to the different ways in which the two measured time. The conversation became combative, and Mira ultimately declared the caller "dead inside." Sad, who had been listening, cringed as he listened from his apartment. He stopped by her room in the middle of the program to say, *Mira, come on, now.*

She touched him and said, "Let me do this."

Mira spends the night before her live recordings chatting away without pause, and Sad has long stopped touching her arm to slow her down. "Can you believe them?" he catches. "Nobody gets it." When she finally exhausts herself with her rant, he feels her drift off into a heavy sleep. In bed beside her, his thoughts are lost in the whirl of Mira's notions of belief and failure. From what he can gather, Mira has a definitive sense that all belief persists until it meets its end. An idea, once formed, must be perpetually proven until the evidence runs out, eventually encountering the terrible fact of its reality. It makes Sad so uncomfortably crestfallen to hear her, even as some of her words slide by him, that he thinks to ask her, *What do you believe of us, then?* He hates endings and is afraid to know her answer.

Without a head, he does not sleep much anymore, let alone eat. It is a blessing in some ways, with the food shortage, but it also means he stands out even further from the rest of the people in the building. Sure, the elderly Levan grew a boil the size of a second head on his neck from trying to fish in the con-taminated East River, but Sad's particular condition made him a bystander to the building's comings and goings. He touches her face, the curvature of every fine detail of her that he has memorized many times on nights like these, lying next to her. He is a witness to Mira's life, but not his own. It seems point-less to lie in bed when one no longer sleeps, but he knows the routine is important to her, and admittedly part of him appre-ciates the ritual too.

Before Mira, there was Corina, and with Corina his nights had a cadence that he grew accustomed to. Corina moisturiz-ing at 9 p.m., and by 9:15 the two of them taking turns brush-ing their teeth at the sink, always Sad first so that she could remind him to floss in the very back. Then reading in bed until 9:45, followed by a brief discussion of their selected book's highlights, and if the mood permits after, sex with Corina on top. She would ride him and make herself come by 9:55, with just enough time to rinse off quickly and head to bed by 10. Before her, he spent his nights falling asleep in front of the TV, and though this timed regiment was far different from any-thing he had ever known before her, when the night ended with Corina in his arms, he felt it was worth everything.

The topic of Corina never came up with Mira, because Mira never asked. Sad chalked it up at first to Mira not being the jealous type, but after a while he started to wish that she would ask him something about his former life. Instead, these nights with his body awake in bed, all he could think of was his life before Mira, which included so much of Corina.

In fact, it was the topic of faith that Corina often said drew her to Sad. Three months into dating, and with enough fights between the two of them that they had lost count, Sad fell asleep outside of her door overnight, a wilting bouquet of roses in hand. Taking pity on him, she had let him in and bathed him in a milky white soap that smelled like candied flowers. As she ran the loofah over his body, she confessed, "I'm always running. I know I run from relationships. I can't help it."

Sad nodded at the time, said nothing but listened.

"But you, you're different," she continued. "You have this hope for us. What is that? I don't know what it means. But I think that if you can have it, then I can have it too."

He looked up and saw the softest expression on her face. Placing a hand behind her neck, he pulled her close and held her as she sighed.

"I'm glad you stayed."

These memories have a way of festering during the night. Not wanting to think about Corina, who, as far as he knows, is no longer. But that night he remembers her, the echo of Corina's hope suddenly adorning the room.

Without thinking much of it, he gets up slowly so as not to wake Mira and makes his way to the bathroom. He kneels to open the cabinet under the sink. In the very damp back corner is a plastic bin that he pulls out. Rarely does he check on its contents, knowing that nothing changes with each revisiting. This time he feels pulled to open the lid, revealing years of old cards, letters, photos from his relationship with Corina. Although he can no longer read them, he still fingers their paper, imagining the substance of their words and images bleeding into his hands, becoming part of him once more. When he catches himself reminiscing for too long, he shuts the lid and hides the bin once more, a secret that only he can keep.

When Sad starts to make his way back to bed, he feels it, the brush of something cold passing through him. It is the same sensation he feels when Grandpa Why, in his tumbling ghost way, would rush past him, and his insides would be licked with sudden chill. Yet this drop in temperature is different. It feels heavy coursing through him, almost like a veil cast over the whole room.

He spreads his fingers against the cold air. The feeling speaks to him, and it says through pinpricks of ice against his palm, WHAT ARE YOU DOING?

When Sad does not answer, the ghost asks the question again, this time wetting his hand entirely.

Sad feels the room grow damp. Touching his finger to the mirror, he writes: WHO ARE YOU?

The air is still as Sad waits for the ghost's next move. He stretches his hand out, but what the ghost wants is his torso instead. He feels the cold pressed against his chest. It says to him, YOU WAITED.

And suddenly Sad knows, and the knowing aches within him.

He wants to say so much, but when he reaches for the mirror, his finger barely finishes his message before the temperature of the air returns to what it was before. All that remains in the room is Sad, buckled over, and his message on the mirror: CORINA.

⁂

Sad does not tell Mira about his late-night encounter. There is too much to explain. He would have to write it out, but also, where to begin? He racks his memory for the last mentions of

Corina. Of course, the last time he saw her, it was when . . . He shakes the thought away. *If* Corina had died—and Sad was adamant that what he experienced the night before could be something other—her family would surely call or write him. But then again, the way things ended, it was just as likely that they would not even bother.

The other possibility is that he was losing his mind. *Already lost it, remember?* he jokes. How he misses the ability to chuckle at himself.

Sad does not have to worry about Mira picking up on any of his anxious ruminating. She is fully preoccupied with today's radio broadcast, going head-to-head with a caller who insists that the subject of faith pertains to matters of religion only. "Listen," Mira starts—Sad, with the radio pressed up to his neck where the skin has healed and formed a smooth round, can feel her mouth spitting against the mic—"when I say faith, I mean the assurance of something beyond description. This includes God and everything else we don't know the truth about—the Loch Ness monster, unknown particles of the universe bearing some other brilliant red life, the potential for water to become water again." Sad nods with his torso, and then remembers this is what he and Mira spoke about the other night, rattling off examples of things they believe in, no matter how foolish or lacking in hard proof. Sad had circled the skin above Mira's heart to say, *I believe in you.* Mira had placed her hand over his and said, "I believe that the dead are not really dead."

The other callers have a lot to say on the matter. One caller describes his work with the Erasers. It is a widely known fact that no one is able to keep an Eraser job for more than a month before the work finally gets to them, and always out of exasperation they either quit or exit the work in some other more devastating form. It is understandable, Sad thinks as he listens closely, the ways in which one encounters dead body after dead body, always in some unsuspecting location, the corpses littered with red welts and burns. As if that violence alone is not enough, the caller explains, he has witnessed his fair share of vultures, renegades in stolen government hazmat suits who enter the streets right when the rain starts to ebb and the dead bodies are freshly coated in the oily residue of this wet poison. The vultures rifle through coat pockets, shake backpacks loose from the still bodies, emptying out whatever they can into their rubber bags before fleeing the scene. The caller has shooed away his fair share of vultures, often prying the dead's belongings from their suited hands in a fierce tug-of-war, and then sometimes managing a quick kick to their shins when they finally give up and make a run for it.

Mira wants to know why it matters so much to him to stop the vultures. Keeping vultures away from the bodies is a fairly new addition to the job description, and many members of the cleanup crew are too tired, too overwhelmed by the daily onslaught of such scenes, to intervene. Sad can hear the caller hesitate before answering. "Because once you start, you have to keep going," he says, "and once you realize you can't, that's when you know your sense of what is right and wrong no longer matters anymore. Nothing matters anymore. It's enough to make you feel like nothing is worth believing in. It starts to feel like . . . *What's the point? Why am I here? Why are you here? What the fuck are we doing?*"

Sad listens. He always listens. He can feel the caller sniff his nose, mumble an apology about needing to go do something, and hang up. Mira, undeterred, moves on to the next caller.

"Powerball," the person on the next line says, and already the mood has shifted. "I used to believe in it. Way back when the winnings were in the billions. I had all my numbers except two. Imagine that! Two numbers, and I would have been living in an Italian villa instead of this hellhole. So, I say, *Forget it!* Now I bet on weather."

Sad can sense Mira nodding. Quietly, she says, "There's only so much we can blame on the rain."

With that, the show moves toward its close. Sad can hear Mira in the background, moving the needle of her record player and the familiar clicks of vinyl snapping into place for the final song. She pauses a little bit too long. Then he feels a small whisper creeping through the radio: "Mal." The broadcast turns off suddenly with a loud squeak.

The radio static blares across Sad's room, which now feels inordinately empty. The aquarium humming its blue-green glow paints the room in waves, and it seems to make the feeling in his gut sink heavier. *You love her*, he tells himself. Thinking of Corina again, he declares it again. *You love her.*

Sad may have lost touch with many of his former colleagues at the Brooklyn courthouse where he used to work, but he still has one or two people there that he knows have stayed behind to organize the responsibilities of disaster relief. Although he has put this off for quite a while, he knows that it is time to make the call and hear it for himself. He remembers the courthouse's number by heart, and that the extension to the administrative office's line always came with at least ten minutes of elevator music, so he dials another extension instead.

"Hello, you've reached the former U.S. District Court for

the New York Eastern District, now incorporated Brooklyn Office of Law and Disaster Support. If you're calling regarding a lost or stolen rations card, please dial extension—"

HUGH. Sad's nimble fingers type out his old friend's name on the keyboard, cutting off the extended introduction.

The voice on the other end of the line pauses before finally speaking again. "Hey, if this is a prank, this is a government line, and I can have you—"

IT IS ME, Sad declares, and then quickly punches in his full name. How strange it is to type all its letters once more.

Sad can sense Hugh breathing a sigh of relief on the other line. "Well, holy shit, you son of a bitch. You're alive. You sound a little different, though."

If Sad could sigh too, he would. *LONG STO-RY.*

"Yeah? No kidding. These days, going to the market is a whole saga. Man, it's great to hear from you. What's going on with you, man? We miss you here."

NEED YOUR HELP.

Hugh's voice grows serious. "What you need, man? You in trouble?"

CO-RI-NA. FIND HER.

A heavy sigh on the other line, and then cautiously, "Yo, I'm sorry, man. I thought you and her were still . . . I haven't heard anything about her. You would know better than me."

Sad pauses, contemplating what to add next before finally typing, *DEATH REC-ORD.*

Hugh is silent on the other end.

PLEASE.

Hugh's voice is soft when he finally answers. "Okay, give me one minute."

Sad types out all the details about Corina that he knows—

her full name, Corina Maria Esmeralda Vasquez, and her legal date of birth, not her real one, which is unknown, lost to memory and immigration. If pressed for more, he can share her last three phone numbers—personal, work, and a landline she refused to let go of—her Social Security number that he has memorized in the event of an emergency like this, her driver's license ID, the four-digit code to her building, the expiration date on her passport, her alias when she ordered coffee at Starbucks, and so on and so forth.

Hugh's voice stirs Sad, lost in his memories. "Hey, man," his friend says from the other end of the line. He seems to be swallowing something hard down his throat. "I'm sorry."

Sad's fingers freeze on the keyboard. So it is true. He has many questions, not all of them for Hugh.

Sensing Sad's shock, Hugh breaks the ice. "Listen, uh . . . the date on the record says she passed over a year ago, sometime around the start of the downpours. That was a hard time for everyone, man. I lost a cousin and a grandfather then too. But you know, I did a little bit of internet searching, because we still have some connectivity here on site. I found an obituary for her, published in a local newspaper. Family probably couldn't afford anything more, you know. Times like these . . . Anyway, you want me to read it to you?"

Sad has almost forgotten about his keyboard, but when he recovers, he types an affirmative answer.

Hugh clears his throat. "Corina Maria Esmeralda Vasquez . . . born the second daughter of four to . . . avid Knicks fan . . . loves to cook . . . dreamed of children one day . . . Died during the fifth rainstorm." Sad's body caves into his hands. "Lived a fierce life . . . wanted the best for everyone . . . engaged to"—he is surprised to hear his own name—"who has also unfortunately passed."

Sad is stunned. Gone so long, he has almost forgotten this big detail of his life. How could he have forgotten, even in his memories of her? He sinks deeper into his lap, cradling the keyboard in his hands.

"I didn't know about that last part, man," Hugh says on the other line. "I'm so sorry."

Sad thanks Hugh for his time, each of them hanging up unceremoniously. Left alone with himself, he recalls what it was like to sob, to wail so grievously that the walls could shake. He does not remember ever needing an occasion to do so, but now he misses his head more than ever in a heart full of missing. *Corina*, he thinks. *I'm so sorry.*

After the radio program ends, Mira arrives at Sad's apartment and crawls across his body. When she lays one palm flat across his chest, he knows she is thinking about another body that is not his. This other body she craves is more supple and soft. He can feel it in the way her hands cup for breasts that are not there, caressing hips that are fuller and more rounded than his own. The other body has a jaw, a scowl, laugh lines, and hair to grip onto when . . . *It is fine*, he tells himself. *Some of us are more haunted than others.* He thinks to tell her about Corina but does not know where to begin, paralyzed by the stuckness in his chest. It does not matter, though. Mira has already placed her mouth at the center of his chest and is slowly making her way down.

The other body that is not his vanished in a fire and no one knows if she has turned into a ghost. Sad knows this because, as people often tell him, he has a knack for giving everything his deep attention, so much so that he had been listening to Mira's radio show long before they met. It did not take him long to figure out that the confusing letters she would recite before each program's final song were a message for someone called Mal. There are other signs too—the murmurs in her sleep that have the same hum as Mal's name, Mira's obsession with television reports of the buildings in Jackson Heights that caught fire, the fact that every word that comes out of Mira feels like a wail.

Sad has resigned himself to living in the shadow of Mal. In a game of (Not So) Death, he and Mira would take turns pretending to be dead. It was a morbid game, but the circumstances felt fitting. The winning reaction was the scare—to startle, to spook, to commit to the pretend-death so faithfully that it feels close to real. Once, Sad found Mira slumped over the bathtub, her head underwater. He was not afraid because he could feel her body tense when he touched her. When he pointed out that flaw in her faked death, she threw her hands up in surrender. When it came to his turn, he would make a joke of it, hanging a noose from the ceiling and kicking over a stool when she walked into the room. Though Mira knew the absurdity of it all, it still pained her to no end. Cradling his limp body, she would murmur into his chest, wetting the whole of him with her tears. Sad would raise his arm and stroke her hair, causing her to cry out in forgetful fright. "Don't you dare leave me!" she would sob with shuddering fury, beating his chest with her fists. She would curse him a hundred times, and then ask between the swallowing of tears, "Can we play again?"

As a truce, Sad would suggest that they both play dead, and so they would lie together on the kitchen floor beside a butcher knife and a spill of red dye. She would fall into the crook of his arm, and they would stay as still as possible until sleep found them.

A few days ago, he had shown up at Lucinda's door, wanting to know how it would all end. Mira loved him, that much he knew. But it was Mal whom she dreamed of at night. Mal whom Lucinda saw in a vision of an afterlife. Mal whose name is broadcast through every show, the currents of which will never make their way to any plane but this one. And yet Mal's persistent presence is relentless, and the longer her whereabouts are unknown, the more Mira seeks her out. Without Sad having to say as much, Lucinda knew, and she could not console him. She had said that she would find a way to retrieve Mal from wherever she was, would bring her back to this plane so that she and Mira could finally have their peace. He begged her not to; she explained that she had a moral obligation to do so. The ghosts, when they come, they come.

Is that what you are, Corina? A ghost? In asking these questions, Sad is stunned by his immediate acceptance after confirming her death just hours before. Perhaps all it means is that he understands Mira's pain, which she has lived with for some time now. Meanwhile, the fact of Corina's death had occurred to him far earlier, and it was his own fault for refusing to know. It is far easier to imagine someone hating you from afar than permanently no longer of this life. Try as he does to talk himself out of his guilt, he becomes further rooted in it.

That night, Sad spreads his hand across Mira's chest, feeling the rise and fall of each breath and the absence of his own.

The muscle inside his chest thunders so loudly, he wonders if Mira can hear it. He is not like the callers to her program whose sense of belief has been shot. He believes, more than anything, that there is virtue in trying. He has known this ever since Mira came to his door, disheveled by the news he would later discover was the death of her Mal. Still, he had longed to feel the wetness of her face, which was somehow exactly as he had imagined as he listened to her disembodied voice on the radio every week. That day, Mira stayed with him for hours that turned into days. They had learned a new language through sex, through a silence that cut through rain and ash. He touched her and she touched him. Even so, he understands, with perfect clarity, that not everything remains the same forever.

When Mira falls asleep that night, he makes his way to the bathroom once more. He can feel the cold rising in the air, the prick of it spelling out letters in his hands: I MISS YOU TOO.

Corina once said that *to try* was a pathetic hero's attempt at winning. "Can you imagine?" she said, aghast. "What if Superman *tried* to save Lois Lane but timed things poorly and she fell down splat from a fifty-story building?"

What Sad had tried to do was build a home for the two of them—a one-bedroom apartment in Fort Greene, Brooklyn, on a court stenographer's salary. This was before the rain, before he was relocated to his current place on the Lower East Side after the Fort Greene apartment complex could no longer withstand the early downpours and fell apart. It is just a pile of rubble now, much to Sad's despair.

Before he lost his head, he and Corina divided their time between their two apartments, though eventually they were confronted with the issue that she never wanted him to go over to her place and she loathed everything he owned. She used to say, "I was raised to take care of myself. Don't need a man to take care of me. So I like my space and my peace." This speech, he knew emphatically well, coupled with his memory of her confession one night after several glasses of wine—a screaming father, his hand on her mother's throat, waiting in the closet for the crying to be over. He understood now; her solitude felt earned. Still, when she slept over for the first time, she surveyed the light brown water stain on the ceiling, the sticky windows that shut heat within the apartment during New York's hottest days, and the solitary mouse that darted from bathroom to kitchen and back all night. She decided that she needed a place that was the opposite of what he had.

So Sad bought his apartment in the hopes of making it everything Corina wanted. He stripped the tiles and put down new ones, painted the walls her favorite shade of gray, and called in several favors with some old friends in pest control to do a clean sweep of the building. He patched over the water stain, wired up a new ceiling fan, and put in new windows that opened and closed.

With hands veiling Corina's eyes, he led her through the threshold of the newly renovated apartment. When he uncovered her eyes, her gaze quietly panned across the living room. She said nothing.

"Move in with me?" Sad said to the back of her head.

"Oh." The utterance escaped her, though her head remained turned away from him. When she seemed to have collected herself, she turned around, beaming so brightly that it was clear—the grimace tucked recklessly beneath. She ran her hand through his hair and brought her palm to rest against his stubble. Through her smile, Sad read an awful pity.

"You worked so hard," she said, placing one foot over the threshold.

Since Shin left, Sad has taken his place as Ma's weekly tea companion. It just happened, and then it kept happening. One day, upon exiting his apartment, he came across Ma sitting alone in the lobby, the mah-jongg table open before her without a single tile on its felt surface. He knew this from touching the table week after week, feeling the surface for any game in progress, only to find it bare. He gestured to the table to ask if she played, and though she did not answer then, only pulling his arm to have him sit down beside her, she would later reveal that Shin once sat at his place, and through him, she learned so much about how to haunt the living.

As always, Ma pours Sad a cup, forgetting or perhaps not caring that he cannot drink. Often they sit together in silence. To hold a conversation, Sad takes his time with the Fisher-Price keyboard in his hand, an old toy he found while diving through the pile of discards in the back of the building. He imagines it to be ridiculously colored, bright orange alphabet letters arranged for a young typist back when they cared about such things. When he hits enter, a voice calls out the sentence he has typed with a stilted start and stop. It has become so much a part of him that people have started to talk to the keyboard instead of him, as if the speaker is a microphone. Thankfully, Ma exhibits none of this tendency. However, hearing her requires something far more intimate. It took three meetings before Ma would allow Sad to rest his hand on the base of her neck, his thumb against her throat, listening for the vibration of her voice. By now it has become second nature, the sitting down and the keyboard and the hand against his girlfriend's mother's throat.

Sad has wanted to talk to Ma about Mira for a while. He has not heard from Lucinda since his last visit. Mal's whereabouts are still unknown. He wonders if Ma knows anything that he does not know.

Sad fingers the Fisher-Price keyboard tentatively, and then types the following: *CAN I ASK YOU SOME-THING?*

He can tell by Ma's pause that she is startled by his question. Her cup lands on the table with a soft tap, which Sad feels against his elbow. She takes his hand and places it on her neck, saying slowly, "Speak."

Sad considers his words carefully before typing. *I HAVE A GHOST.*

"My boy, we all do." She pauses to see his bodily response to her joke but, met with only stillness, she inquires further. "Who is it?"

EX.

Ma's next response stuns him, her quick, "Okay."

OK?

Ma knocks him on the chest firmly. "Like I said, you are not the only one."

MAL?

Sad feels Ma's throat tense. "How do you know?"

LU-CIN-DA.

Sad feels Ma mutter something under her breath, likely

frustrated at her friend for getting involved. When she finally gathers herself, she places her hand over Sad's and talks slowly. "What do you know?"

Sad feels himself shudder against Ma's throat. *I KNOW. LU-CIN-DA IS BRING-ING MAL BACK.*

"No, she isn't."

Sad pauses, waits for Ma to clarify.

"We spoke. She will not."

She says it so matter-of-factly that Sad hesitates once again. He had begged Lucinda not to bring Mal back as a ghost and should be relieved to hear that Ma has put a stop to it. Something does not feel right, though.

He has to ask. *WHY?*

Ma clears her throat before continuing. The story is told in gulps:

Once, when Mira was seven years old, she ran away to find her father. It was only for a night, and she did not go far, ending up in a park in Bushwick, sleeping inside a tunnel slide. Ma had to tell her the truth—Mira's dad passed away a long time ago. For years, the myth of him had buoyed Mira despite Ma's frequent tales of his good-for-nothing nature. In truth, Ma did not know whether he was a good or bad man, as time has a way of eroding the original truth. All she knew was that he was dead, the remainders of his life shipped to her—a watch, some papers, a pack of cigarettes, and a note in which he inscribed his parting words, 我係個冇用嘅人, or *I am no one.*

The circumstances of Mira's dad's death haunted young Mira. Had Ma known the impact it would have on her daughter, she would have kept it a secret. Mira grew up somber, drinking heavily at age eleven, and then by fourteen would disappear for several weeks at a time. Once, Ma found Mira pale and struggling to breathe in the corner of her closet, and had to call 911 to resuscitate her, pump the drugs from her stomach. Another time, she found her daughter sitting in a pool of her own blood, her wrist limply draped over the side of the tub.

She did not know how it would end, only that one day something changed. At first Ma did not know what it was, but it became clear that it was not what but who. Mira brought Mal home one day, and though they sat a foot apart on the couch, Ma knew. She did not know how to react at first, thinking perhaps it was yet another way for Mira to rebel. But the Mira that came to be was soft and light, reminiscent of a younger version of herself who knew nothing of death. Even if Ma did not understand all of it, she could at least recognize that something had reignited inside her daughter, that this love would alter her forever.

When Mal died, it took Mira several days to tell Ma, and only after much prodding. All she knew was that one day, Sad was in the picture and Mal was not. She knew nothing of Mira's ask of Lucinda until her friend relayed the news to her after the building meeting. It startled Ma to know that something she thought had passed still plagued Mira to this day. She thought of the times she found her daughter lifeless in the back of her closet, the placid expression of her face as she sank into the tub. She would not let her go back there.

"Do you see?" Ma finally says. "Do you see why I will not let this happen again?"

Mira has told Sad countless stories about her life, the whimsical tricks of her childhood, the games she would play, but she's left out these more devastating parts. Still, he loves her.

Slowly, on the keyboard, he types, *WHAT DO I DO NOW?*
Ma pats his hand, tells him, "Wait." She returns after a short
while and places a small square box in his hand. She says, "Do
you know what this is?"

Sad opens the box and feels the interior—satin holding a
hard ring. It could not be mistaken for anything else.

"This ring . . . it is very lucky. It belonged to my mother."
Then, with the clearing of her throat, she implores him, "Make
her happy."

Sad has imagined this moment many times before—he has
seen himself proposing to Mira in the fish tank, at the place
where they both first intimately met, body to body, touching
each other inside and out, kissed by the bubbles of the water.
He imagines the ring box opening like an oyster shell. It would
happen in some distant future when the acid rain has stopped,
the crops have regrown, and the sky is no longer a stretch of
impending doom. Mira would open her mouth into the water,
forgetting where she is, and, in her gasp, would choke slightly
before she recovers, laughing at her own surprise before nodding yes, yes, forgetting that Sad cannot see, and then throwing her arms around his waist to make clear that she chooses
him entirely. It had been thrilling to lean into the fantasy, but
now, before him, the ring in his hand and Ma's blessing floating
between them, he doesn't know if it could ever be real.

Sad has many questions for Ma, but only one comes out.
ARE YOU SURE?

Ma swallows something hard before answering gently,
"Try." She seems to be considering what it is that Mira needs
most, and upon further thought revises her statement to only
"Just try."

In truth, Sad hardly ever used his head back when he had one. He did not floss regularly, kept a number two fade growing out for several months until it resembled a patchwork bramble, and his beard could take apart even the strongest comb. He was often mistaken for being deep in thought when really all he wondered about was the length of the city against the length of sky. It was how, he believed, he came to be the first to notice when the weather started to change in New York.

Part of Corina's dissatisfaction with Sad's job as a courtroom stenographer was her somewhat astute analysis that this profession was quickly becoming obsolete thanks to advanced digital voice recording technology that transcribed audio recordings with increasing accuracy. It did not help that in terms of effort, he was lacking. He noticed all the wrong things—the way a widow clutched her collar on the witness stand, the smell of tuna on the judge's breath when he called the court to order, and the over-starched suits of the defense lawyers. In the courtroom, he inevitably found himself looking out the window, learning to detect the subtlest signs of seasonal shifts, from the first new tint of a leaf to the rain stuck on the bottom of a pant-suited woman's shoe as she crossed the street.

One day, a courtroom officer he had seen several times at Kings County approached him during recess. "Look, man, I'll be straight with you," she said. "People's lives are on trial here and you don't seem like you're paying attention half the time. Not telling you how to do your job, but keep your eyes and ears in the courtroom, okay?"

But he was already sensing a shift in the weather that summer, there was something about the way the clouds formed sinister shapes, their opaque heaviness in the sky. The air, electric with something awry, sent static ripples throughout Borough Hall, and he could see it in the raised hairs of every passerby. The week before the rain turned acidic, Sad called off work and sent a mass message to everyone he knew, telling them to do the same. At first his supervisor sent him a formal reprimand about issuing nonprofessional emails regarding yet another exaggerated weather-related warning with a P.S. that said it was "strike seven" for him. The other times that his supervisor was referring to concerned his miscalculation of impending snowstorms and hurricanes, off by several weeks at a time, too long to give his warnings legitimacy. And of course there was a blizzard that he once claimed would bury the city in three stories' worth of snow that ultimately came in at under two feet. He understood his supervisor's hesitancy, knew his track record was abysmal on the weather prediction front. It was not a precise math, and yet he felt it so deeply in his bones that the next rain to come would burn.

As always, Sad cc'd Corina on these emails, because she deserved to know too. She wrote back, *This is crazy. Please stop. I can't do this anymore.* His mother called to ask if his email had been hacked and then asked what it meant to be hacked. His supervisor called twenty minutes after his email to tell him to send an apology and retraction, and when Sad refused the apology, he was told he should not bother coming back to work.

The day the acid rain came, he found himself walking on Broadway after buying a cartful of portable electronics at Best Buy, anticipating that things would get dire soon. The panic was slowly rising. When he felt the air shift with a distinct sharpness, he stood still to feel the first drops pinch his flesh, thinking that whatever danger might follow, he needed to feel it. But the first water was cool. He knew this to be deceptive by the way its viscous texture slowed it down flowing through the sewer grates. No one seemed to notice at first. Before he remembered how to scream, his feet propelled him forward, and he moved more quickly than he thought himself capable.

He realized later, when his apartment building cracked down the middle, no longer able to withstand the burden of the rain and age at the same time, that he was desperate to recover anything from the wreck that would remind him of Corina. Moving through the rubble, he picked up every photograph and card from their relationship that he could find, unearthed his old records, a beaten-up metal tin filled with photographs of his abuelo standing next to various brightly colored cars, a painted tile inherited from his abuela that was still surprisingly intact, and a note from Corina attached to his old refrigerator's broken door, which read: *SURPRISE ME.*

As army men, dressed in padded gear, ushered him into a white van on the way to alternative housing, he thought with renewed confidence, *Sure. I can do that.*

~

After Sad returns to his apartment from his conversation with Ma, he feels even more downtrodden than before. The ring box in his pocket sharp on all corners. It seems to pierce his flesh. This should be a happy occasion, and yet the swirl of what Ma has revealed of Mira's life and Mira's current fixation with bringing Mal back has been disorienting. Then there is the matter of his own ghost haunting him.

The apartment is quiet when he returns, but he can sense a change in the humidity. The walls seem to swell and are slightly damp with condensation. He makes his way to the bathroom, turning on the hot water until the room fills with steam. When the mirror fogs up, he scrawls a message for Corina: *OKAY, LET'S TALK.*

The silence of the room falls gently upon him. *Fine*, he thinks. *I'll wait.*

By the time Sad emerges from the shower, Mira is already inside the apartment, sitting on his bed. Playfully, she grabs at the towel around his waist, which he interrupts by placing a hand over hers. He sits down beside her, and signals to her, *Listen*. He cannot see her face, but he can read her expression from touch alone, the fullness of her lips, the soft angles of her cheeks. She radiates against him, warm and full of life. It is enough to make him cry.

Mira returns to bed with his keyboard, placing it into his hands so he can type to her. Fingering the keys, he writes, *I KNOW.*

Sad's hand against Mira's throat quivers slightly, and she swallows in turn. "What do you know?"

Please don't make me say it, Sad thinks. He hesitates on the keyboard. *YOU*, he begins. He pauses, realizing that he cannot go back from this. *YOU ARE BRING-ING MAL BACK.*

Mira places a hand over his. "It's not going to happen."

For a second Sad experiences a moment of relief. *WHAT DO YOU MEAN?*

"I mean . . . I don't know if Lucinda can do it. She says she'll try, but . . ."

There it is. Sad's heart sinks again. *WHAT WILL HAP-PEN TO US?*

"What do you mean?"

WHEN MAL RE-TURNS.

"You mean *if*?"

Sad squeezes Mira's hand tightly, so she can feel how desperately he is holding on. *Mira, you know what I am trying to say.* Of course Mira knows. The two of them have forged an undeniable bond. He feels her touch his chest, laying one hand over his heart. Tenderly, she responds, "I don't know."

Suddenly a chill descends upon the room, and the hairs on Sad's back rise with the sudden change in temperature. He senses Corina's arrival, wishing she would come back another time, any time but now. A ghost's cold arms drape around his shoulders, hands reaching down his torso. He wonders with great alarm if Mira can see this. However, she seems only to be sitting quietly, waiting for Sad's response, the appearance of Corina unknown to her.

Sad feels the sensation of a wet mouth pressed against him. He tries to bat it away, but the mouth is insistent, moving across his body. Just as he is about to get up and shake her off, a cold finger draws a message across his back: *I KNOW WHERE MAL IS.*

The message stops Sad in his tracks. At this point, Mira is concerned and tapping against his chest, wondering where he has gone. His body grows cold, and he shudders in his seat.

Slowly, taking its time, the finger pens another message: *I CAN FIND HER IF YOU LIKE.*

At this, Sad gets up suddenly from the bed, startling Mira. He marches back and forth across the room, shaking the cold off him. To Mira, he must seem like he is losing it. He wants to assure her that he is not, but if she cannot see what he feels, then he must be imagining it.

Mira's hands, a warmer set, wrap tight around his waist.

What's going on? he senses her body saying. *Are you okay? Tell me you're okay.*

Sad cannot tell if it is Corina he needs to protect Mira from or himself. Either way, he pushes Mira toward the door. In his haste, he accidentally pushes her too hard, causing her to stumble. Although he catches her, he can tell that she is stunned by the force of his hands and backs away from him. The wind from the door hits his face before he can reach it, and that is when he knows that Mira is gone.

Sad falls to the floor. All around him, the air grows thicker and colder than before. Every part of him wants to cry out, but the cold wraps so tightly around him, holding him in place. *Why are you doing this, Corina?* He is flooded with disbelief. This cannot be her. Something else must have taken her place.

He feels the ghost's hands tickle his spine again. When he backs against the wall, the ghost places her hands on his chest, which he attempts to cover with his arms. *No more messages. I'm done.* But she is not. Her fingers find his torso, tickling him for a bit, taunting him. Finally, she writes her message out with excruciating slowness: *I TOLD YOU I'D BE BACK.*

After moving into the Lower East Side housing projects, Sad was at least in the same borough as Corina, meaning they were only a few checkpoints apart. He wanted to try to make the relationship work again. When he showed up at her door on the Upper East Side, passing the people in hazmat suits handing out flyers for proper safety procedures concerning the acidic rainfall, she seemed frazzled.

"Can you believe it?" she said, aghast, and then, "I can't believe you were right about the weather this time."

Sad wanted to reach out, to touch her face. It had felt like forever since he had seen her, but she was looking elsewhere to make sure that the people in hazmat suits were not damaging the hallway walls with the equipment they were carrying.

Corina's eyes slowly settled back on Sad, though she seemed dizzy with the whirl of events before her. His words spilled out before he could properly catch himself: "I miss you, Corina."

"What?"

Sad clutched at the gift he had for her in his hands. She asked what he was holding. He happily handed her a wrapped copy of Roland Barthes's *A Lover's Discourse*, which he knew was a mistake from the moment her eyes landed on the size of the package. She tentatively peeled the wrapping paper open, careful not to rip the clear tape, as if she were prolonging a root canal.

"What is this?" she asked, holding the book by the corner as if she had plucked it from the floor. "We break up, and this is what you give me?"

Sad turned to the middle of the book and pathetically pointed to an excerpt, brushing aside the dried rose petals caught on the page. "Don't be mad," he said. "I was reading this excerpt and thought of you."

Corina grabbed the book from him and read the passage aloud:

Am I in love?—yes, since I am waiting. The other one never waits. Sometimes I want to play the part of the one who doesn't wait; I try to busy myself elsewhere, to arrive late; but I always lose at this game. Whatever I do, I find myself there, with nothing to do, punctual, even ahead of time. The lover's fatal identity is precisely this: I am the one who waits.

She paused and seemed to consider the passage for a moment. Then her eyes filled with water, and she threw the book back into his arms. She cried, "Do you even know how insensitive you can be sometimes?"

Sad stared back at her, dumbfounded. "What do you mean?"

"You idiot," she said, shaking the tears from her eyes. "You can't give a book like that to a girl, dog-ear that excerpt, and not have her think you're trying to lord something over her."

"I swear! I wasn't!"

"So what are you saying, then?" She waved the open book, her finger prodding at the passage. "Poor you, always waiting for your girl, always the victim."

"Please, Corina—"

"You are always doing too much. Is this even what you want?"

"I'm trying to tell you in a thousand and one ways how much I love you—"

"You don't listen, you don't listen, you don't listen," Corina repeated, listing that same offense on her fingers as if each repetition were different. "You. Don't. Listen."

Sad reached out to her, and she slapped his hand away. She turned her back to him, and he slid his arms around her, letting her flail for a moment before her body quieted to a more contained rage. He said softly, "I want to be the man you want me to be."

She muttered beneath her breath, "Show me."

Once, several years ago, Corina and Sad took two buses and a train to Queens Farm, where they rode along on a haystack in a truck full of schoolchildren. It was a third date gone awry, despite being meticulously planned. The excursion was supposed to be an inside joke about country life (something they had seen on TV, undoubtedly, and lost all context for over the years), but the promise was far from delivered—the day was rainy, the children were loud, and having not been told the details of the date (the intended surprise), Corina wore her suede boots, which were ruined by the day's end.

In considering Corina's challenge, Sad thought back to that day. It was one that she frequently referred to as a close deal-breaker for her. The one saving move apparently was the latter part of the date, unplanned, when they ended up at a tiny pizza shop in Kew Gardens. Sad had dived back into the rain to buy Corina a pair of sunflower flip-flops from the dollar store while her ruined boots sat somewhere by a bus pole. Corina said that it was the flip-flops that won her over—those large gaudy plastic flowers bursting from her toes. They made her laugh every day that she slipped them on, and it was that memory that he clung to in his last-ditch effort to win her back.

It took several days, but eventually Sad was able to rent a patch of land at Queens Farm, which had traded ownership to several local government officials who had yet to decide what to do with the space, considering none of the soil was usable anymore, not after the acid rain. This was in the early days of the rainstorms, when the city had not yet decided when and for how long people were permitted to be outside. He led Corina to the farm and handed her a shovel.

"What are you trying to do?" Corina said suspiciously.

He told her to dig and began digging with his own shovel. They dug until the sun went down and the hole in the ground was the width of a body.

"I love you, Corina," he said, and slid his body into the hole. "Can you please help me fill this up?"

"You're insane!" Corina cried out. She wrinkled her brow and reached for the shovel at the same time. "All the way?"

"Just up to the neck."

Corina eyed him suspiciously. "Why are you doing this?"

Sad looked up at her, her eyes dry and steely. He felt like his heart could pour out of his chest and she wouldn't even know. He said, "I want to show you that I'm willing to do whatever it takes."

She shook her head. "This is crazy."

"Yeah." He laughed, and then his gaze settled on her intently. "Marry me, Corina. I'm on my knees in this dirt, I swear."

She paused her shoveling to look at him quizzically. "Listen, I don't know what you're trying to do here—"

"I've never been so sure of anything in my life."

She groaned, but he could detect that underneath it, there was a hint of a smile. "God, you're such a bleeding-heart romantic."

That little bit of affirmation emboldened him. "Yeah, you love it, though."

"So, what's this all about, then? You want me to live with you as a pumpkin in the ground? Have little gourd babies?"

He shook his head, his voice serious. "No, real babies. A real home. I'm here to prove it to you. I'm not your dad. I'm not leaving you, okay?"

The mention of her father seemed to soften her gaze, and she finally whispered, "Okay."

"You don't need to give me an answer now. If it's a yes, come back for me."

She narrowed her eyes at him. "And if it's a no?"

"Then I'll turn into a pumpkin."

To her surprise, she laughed and agreed. "Fine." Lowering her whole body to the ground, she kissed him on his mouth. "I'll be back. Promise."

Sad waited past the next rainfall, feeling the sting of the droplets pierce his skin. He felt their scalding heat and the steam rising from the top of his head with each wet impact. Every day, he dreamed of Corina, which began with the more carnal parts of his imagination, and then, the objects he started to desire most became much simpler and more distinct. For an entire day, he drifted in and out of sleep, dreaming the same dream of Corina peeling an apple, her knife bent at a careful angle, the single long peel unbroken and seeming to extend for miles. By week's end, he dreamed Corina stuffed one end of the peel into his mouth while she bit the other, and together they bit the peel all the way to the center.

When the first week passed and Corina didn't come for him, Sad felt a dull alarm and heaved into the dirt before him. She could not—no, *would* not come. And why? What good was a promise if it was something you could rescind? Then he thought, *You chose this.* He wiggled his hand beneath the ground, feeling it packed so tight that not even a daily effort could loosen him. He chewed on the dead vines around him when hungry, though he could feel himself slowly wasting away. The rain fell again on the Tuesday of the second week, and it tore his skin apart more severely than the last. He called out for help, but he was miles away from anyone who could hear him. The rainfall

burned so harshly that he blacked out. While he was uncon-
scious, he dreamed that he was in a pumpkin patch surrounded
by overly ripe pumpkins. He was visited by three farmhands,
who tried to pull him up from the ground, but it was no use.
The tangle of vines below threaded through him. They decided
the best thing to do would be to cut off his head.

When Sad woke up, he found the ground around him loosened, and he crawled his way out through the dark. Stumbling
across several thick and dried vines, he tried to pry his eyes
open, and thought with sudden alarm that he had gone blind.
He raised his hands to his face, but they plunged through the
space where his head should have been. Hands gripped his at
that moment and, not being able to make out what was being
said, he flailed and fell to the ground, where he slammed the
trunk of his neck over and over, feeling nothing, not even the
phantom pain of a dizzying head knocking against a hard surface. Every limb of him shook, though there were no places
for the tears to go. When the many hands found him again,
they lifted him from the ground, some clutching his arms, and
others firmly gripping his shoulders. He threw himself back as
if to scream and nothing came out, just the pelt of his body
against the un-seeable others. When the people around him
slowly departed, there was only a single figure left, and this
one slighter in frame, carefully and surely taking him into
their arms. Sad wished the body was Corina's, though he knew
through touch that she was already far away. Though Sad could
no longer cry, he knew this other body was crying for him, and,
feeling their body shudder, he let his arms fall to his side. In
this way, the first feeling he learned to describe in shape and
color as a newly born headless man was condolence. Condo-

lence was blue and patchwork. It had no sound. He squeezed his sympathizer's shoulders. *Don't worry about me*, he tried to say. *I'll be fine.*

⁂

Since Mira left his apartment, Sad has not ventured far from the floor. Occasionally he drags himself to the bathroom to relieve himself, but the ghost of Corina follows with icicles darting across his back. Sometimes he thinks he is hallucinating her, but then the carpet feels moist to the touch, the blankets soaked through. Everywhere he goes in his apartment, Corina is at his heels. Her messages always remain the same: *I KNOW WHERE MAL IS* and *I CAN FIND HER.* He wonders if she is mad at him for moving on, if her taunts are meaningless at the end of the day. Still, he cannot shake the feeling of something gone terribly wrong.

When he is able to finally get up from the floor, he decides to seek Lucinda's help. The walk to the stairwell is painful, so much so that at some point he drops on his hands and knees, crawling his way up the stairs. As he moves farther away from his apartment, the air grows noticeably warmer, and by the time he arrives at Lucinda's floor, he feels his body coming alive again.

When Lucinda answers the door, Sad does not have to read her face to know that she is shocked by his appearance. In his haste, he had left his apartment shirtless with only a pair of long pajama pants barely hanging on to his thinning hips. She rubs her hands against his arms as if to draw heat back into him. He can sense her saying, "My god! What happened to you?"

Sad makes a motion for pen and paper, and Lucinda ushers

him in. He is shaking when she places a blanket over his shoulders, quivering still when she puts a pad and pen in his hands.

I HAVE A GHOST, he scribbles fast.

Lucinda holds his hand to her throat, so he can sense what she has to say. "Is it Mal?"

NO. MY EX, CORINA. I THINK.

"You are scared."

YES.

"Is she dangerous?"

Sad thinks for a moment. *I DON'T KNOW.*

Lucinda holds Sad's hand against her throat and speaks carefully. "Listen. I will gather some things. Find me something of Corina's, anything—a hairbrush, a note she wrote. I will meet you at your place."

WHAT ARE YOU GOING TO DO?

"It's called an exorcism, my dear."

When Lucinda arrives at Sad's apartment, he is not sure what to expect. When she hands him the items in her arms, he feels what appears to be a metal bowl, a saltshaker, and a bag of candles. He senses her body tense as she steps inside.

"My dear," she says, when he sets the items down, "you were not kidding. She is everywhere."

Sad had kept very few of Corina's things, as she made sure to take all her possessions with her when they broke up, even the gifts she had given him. One thing he did keep was a Post-it note she had written him, with the message *CALL ME BACK.* He tries not to think of the irony of it all when he hands the note to Lucinda.

Lucinda blesses the space, blesses their bodies with Florida

Water. Sad feels the curtains drawn shut, the apartment grow-ing colder. He senses the clatter of various objects surround-ing him, and then the soft scrapes of matchsticks against their boxes before they are lit. He feels he should be doing some-thing to help, but she forces him to sit still.

"I'm sorry, my dear," she tells him sheepishly. "There is a chance this might be my doing. All that conjuring and reaching into the spirit world, all this time thinking nothing was hap-pening. Perhaps I conjured your ghost by mistake."

Sad barely senses her as the cold descends upon him again, the air a stricture around him. By now he can sense Corina's arrival, slow and slinking. His heart plummets to his stomach, and he wishes it would all end.

"Stay strong," Lucinda urges, giving Sad a nudge.

He gives her a somber thumbs-up.

Lucinda takes Sad's hands at last, sitting knee to knee in front of him, their feet grazing each other's. He can feel the rough soles of her feet, the soft leather of her hands. Under her breath, she murmurs a prayer, something that he can sense by the vibration alone. She repeats the incantation again and again, more forcefully each time. He does not know what she is saying, only that the walls seem to be expanding and contract-ing, groaning as Lucinda speaks.

Icy hands slither up Sad's back once again. Sad's instinct is to shrug it away, but Lucinda's hands hold firm on to his own. Her grip tells him to hang on, and he does, even as Cori-na's fingers dig deeper into him. She has discovered that her hands can pass through his insides, touch the taut muscles and bones of him, eliciting a chill that rattles him from the inside out.

Finally, he senses Lucinda's voice ringing out clearly. "Be gone! Be gone!"

Corina chuckles against him and then the room is silent.

What happens next, he can only describe as the feeling of falling through a trapdoor. When he hits the floor, the room surrounding him is pitch-black. He is surprised to find that he can see, hear, and even taste the air around him. He moves through the room slowly, searching for walls, but finding none. He turns around and sees that every side is exactly the same. Then he hears the sound of someone whimpering, a smudged edge of the room, as if static runs through the space. He approaches the sound, and moving closer sees the hunched body of a woman with long black hair draped over her arms. He reaches out to touch her, and the body looks up. It is Corina, except not entirely. Her eyes are sunken, and her cheeks puckered as if she'd been starved for months. The grease hangs in her hair, something he knows she never would have allowed when she was alive.

Corina reaches up to grab Sad by the arms. He lets her. She gasps, "Let me go, please."

Sad is taken aback by her plea. "What do you mean?"

She balls her hands into fists and pushes them against her head. "You! Keep! Sticking! Me! In! Places! I! Don't! Belong!" Each word accompanied by the slamming of fists against her head.

He takes her hands gently, trying to stop her. "How am I doing that? Tell me and I'll stop."

She gets up suddenly and starts walking around in the dark, her hands tracing the air. She is searching for something. He follows her as she darts forward, racing until it seems she has found a wall. There she stops. She grabs Sad's hands and guides them until they take hold of something that feels like a knob. Together, they turn it, and before them a door opens onto a gray field, the light from the outside spilling into the dark. Sad squints, not having witnessed something so bright in years, and sees that in the field people are walking aimlessly.

Corina points. "I know where Mal is."

Sad follows her finger, which directs him to a woman wearing all white, her hair in a low ponytail, lost in thought. He feels suddenly flooded with fear. "How do you know for sure it is her?"

At that question, Corina laughs and does not stop. "Been here . . . long time . . . learned many things."

He holds her up by the shoulders and looks her in the eyes. "Corina, if this has been here all along, why can't you go?"

Corina's eyes soften as if she is about to cry. "I'm trying, I'm trying, I'm trying." Her hands ball into fists again. She tries to hit herself again, but Sad stops her. "You won't let me!"

Sad lets his arms fall to his sides. He does not know what to say except, "I'm so sorry. I don't know how I . . . I'm so sorry."

"Make it right." Corina's voice is no longer harsh. "Let me go. Let me tell her. It is time for her to go back."

"Corina, what are you saying?"

Corina points again to the field where Mal is standing, looking up at the sky. "We have to tell her. Mira is waiting."

Sad grows quiet, saying nothing at first. He looks out into the field, where Mal is standing still. She does not see him, and he feels a strange power in his anonymity. Finally, he tells his ghost, "Corina, you can't say anything to Mal."

Corina seems stunned by this pronouncement. "I . . . have to."

"Please, Corina. I'm telling you not to get involved."

Sad's words tip Corina over the edge. She stalks back and forth, shouting, "Don't get involved? Don't get involved! Where is my peace? I am already involved. You put me here! I want my peace. Let me go." She turns to Sad and says the last words softly. "Let me go."

"Promise me. You won't tell her."

Corina shakes her head, holding back tears. "I have to."

It happens so quickly that Sad does not have time to consider the ramifications. He grabs the handle to the door and closes it shut. When the last light disappears, he can no longer see Corina's face, but he can tell she is crying.

Suddenly the room is no longer dark. He feels the heaviness of Lucinda's hands holding his. The apartment is dripping with cold sweat. He wonders if he dreamed it all—Corina, the door, the sight of Mal in the field. Then it occurs to him that what transpired was more real than he will ever know. What did he just do? His heart thumps heavily in his chest.

He feels Lucinda reaching to hold his hand to her throat. She asks him, "Did you do it? Did you let her pass?"

Sad recalls the shock of Corina's face when he closed the door on her, encasing her in the shadows of the room once again. He raises his hand to form a thumbs-up, and he can feel Lucinda's relief.

"Good! Maybe we let our ghosts rest for a while, huh? Let us all have some peace."

Sad's apartment is still and empty except for the sounds his own body makes. He checks the walls, which ripple with the aftermath of moisture. The air is musty, as if rain-soaked, but the temperature does not change. He thinks about sending a message to Corina again, perhaps to apologize, but he knows that it would not be enough. What he has done, he has to live with.

At some point in the night, he feels the sensation of a warm body fold into him. He is alarmed at first, but then feels the familiar softness of Mira's small frame. He caresses her arms, and she lets him, placing her head across his chest. Her hands wander to his back, and she writes a message to him: *I AM SORRY.*

No, I am, Sad thinks. He takes her hands into his, holds them to his chest.

They fall asleep soundly, their bodies nestled against each other. It is the best sleep Sad has ever had.

The next day, Mira tells him what she knows. She had a dream. There was a dark room with a door leading to a bright field. The grass, the sky, and everything beyond it were gray. She knew that whatever she was searching for was there. When she approached it, though, the door shut in front of her. When she woke up, she felt as if a cord had been cut between her and Mal. She placed her hand over her heart, felt something hollow within her.

"Every time I think I am finished grieving, it comes again," she says so softly.

Sad holds her close, willing the grief out of her. This will take time, but he will be there. He will always be there.

It does not happen the way he had imagined it, but the romantic in him has always believed that the gesture matters more than the act. He waits for Tuesday to come, the rain pelting the sides of the building. It seems that every Tuesday the rain falls heavier than the week before. Mira stands by the window, a cup of coffee in her hand. In his pocket is the ring box Ma gave him. In his hand, it feels as heavy as a large rock. He comes up behind Mira, wrapping his arms around her. There is so much he wants to say, how this love can be a revision of the past, can correct everything that has fallen out of place. He lost his head once, and he will lose it again for her. Loss, he will face it time and time again. He sinks to his knees, his arms extending up to her, the ring box opening like an oyster shell. Suddenly the air grows heavy once more, and he thinks, *Not again. No.* He feels Mira's body turn, just as the humidity thickens in the room. Corina, everywhere and nowhere at once, there to remind him of his failures. He will not relent this time. No. He remains on his knees. The floor beneath greets him with a thud, and he realizes it is the weight of Mira's coffee mug dropping. The ceramic shatters, and hot liquid pools across the floor, soaking his knee. He can feel Corina laughing from a distance, but he is undeterred. For Mira, he will wait forever if he has to.

HOW TO SAY YES

Dear Listeners,

So, it has happened to me. On a Tuesday, Sad gets down on one knee and proposes. I love him, so I say yes. Or I say nothing in the moment, hot coffee spilling on the floor, splattering on Sad's pants. I may have said yes after that; it's hard to remember what it felt like in the moment.

Several aunties from the second floor approached me the other day, having heard the rumor. Guess news spreads fast in quarantine. Their advice: You do not have to sleep with him just because he is your husband. In fact, it is better not to sleep with him at all. Have some cake instead. I laugh, but they say, "Listen to us. We are serious." So I will approach the matter of marriage most seriously. Which is to say, this episode is dedicated to the letter *D*, as in "dead serious."

I have only talked about marriage once with a partner. Back then, we were surrounded by anti-marriage queers who wanted nothing to do with the institution. She and I felt differently, though we were too afraid to say it aloud.

"What does it mean to you?" she asked me once. "To get married."

Because I was too scared to begin, I urged her, "You first."

She grinned, and we decided we would speak it together, and what we came up was this: On a day in which the sky is not leaking with acid rain, we would make our way to a rooftop with all our friends. We would haul the ELVIS 3000 karaoke machine up the stairs, where, once it was set up, friends would join in a choral rendition of Mariah Carey's "Always Be My Baby." She and I would eat cake and smash our slices into each other's faces. Ma would be there, fighting her urge to dance and sing along. Her parents too would come back, as ghosts, and they would watch us quietly from the corner, holding each other. Of course, travel restrictions from borough to borough would be lifted by then. Of course, everyone we knew would agree that this was the most obvious thing to happen, and why didn't it happen sooner? The holes in our studio apartment would be miraculously patched. The rain would eventually stop searing our skin, and we would be able to open our windows, let our plants suck in the good air. We would combine our last names into one prettier-sounding last name, one that would go on our mailbox or intercom. We would live thoroughly uninteresting lives of cutting fruit, packing lunches, rushing to the subway to catch the train before work, and coming home to one of us playing disco in the kitchen. We would wiggle our butts at each other until bedtime. Then, one day, after we died, both preferably at the same time, hopefully from fucking, we would be buried next to each other.

But that was then.

After the proposal, Sad and I talk about what it means to be married, and I look at the ring in my hand like it holds a heavy secret. On a piece of paper, he writes to me: *I KNOW IT WILL NOT FIX ANYTHING. NOT EVEN THE RAIN. BUT LET ME TRY.*

With no face to touch, I place my hands at the stump of his neck. I may not always be the best at seeing him, but I do believe he sees me perfectly.

How to say yes: Dear Listeners, having little recollection of joy before this, think about what it means to let go of something, what it means to begin again. I wish there was a proper template for joy. I can love the person who is here, loving me the best way he can. These days, all we have is the rain and each other. Say yes before it is too late.

BELLS, BELLS, BELLS

You can make a myth out of nothing. That was Grandpa Why's special talent—to spin a tale so winding and elaborate, flushed with wild descriptions of talons and scales, of land that split apart from gunfire and soldiers torching the fields, of brutal men and even more terrifying women who wielded weapons like third and fourth limbs. The towering smoke and flesh of his stories could sear a near-frightening smell into the present air.

A younger Ma let her jaw hang down in awe while he regaled her about the time when his mother fought off a gang of men who accosted the two of them when they were walking home from the market one day. One man had a machete, and the others a makeshift club with nails, a broken piece of pipe, a cleaver. His mother had him close his eyes and promise not to peek. He heard the great shuffle of feet, the smashing of limb against limb, the loud grunts of men throttling muscle. He feared for the worst. But when he opened his eyes, there the men were, lying all in a pile, their weapons discarded several feet away. His mother, after wiping the dirt from her face, took Grandpa Why's hand and went home.

"But what *really* happened?" Ma asked. She had not touched her bowl of rice since Grandpa Why began his story. She might have been enraptured, but she had always been a skeptic too.

"What do you mean, what really happened?" Grandpa Why said, aghast.

Ma stammered, poking at the soy sauce that had pooled at the bottom of her bowl. They had slathered the rice with soy sauce then, in the absence of meat, trying to imagine a life of fat and sumptuous things. "I don't know," she muttered cautiously. "I mean, you didn't see anything, you said."

Grandpa Why held up three fingers in the air, slowly pushing each one down as he counted off the reasons. "Your grandmother was so strong, I watched her kill a chicken just by holding it by the throat and giving her wrist one quick flick"; and, "She once pinned a debt collector's head to the wall and made him piss his pants"; and, "Once, she struck me so badly, I was hospitalized for a week."

Ma tapped the chopsticks to her mouth, pondering her father's hand closing into a fist. She narrowed her eyes. "Okay, I believe you."

Grandpa Why ruffled Ma's hair, the way he would a boy-child's. "Like I said," he declared most proudly, "my mother taught them all a lesson."

Years later, as a ghost, his storytelling takes on an even more unbelievable form. The fact of his ghosthood, for instance, is no accidental matter. He chose it. That was the first myth. It does not negate the tragedy of his death, he makes clear ("But, oh boy, is that a story for the century!" he proclaims), but from what he could recall with greater clarity than any of the ghosts in Apartment 9A—the whole building, in fact—was the moment he was plucked out from the underworld through which he wandered for an uncertain amount of time, and then was brought back as a spectral body.

Before Shin disappeared, he had questions for Grandpa Why, like "What was that underworld like?" and "How did we spend our days?" Grandpa Why would feign stroking the little ghost roach's back as he pondered his answer. "Well, little guy, it was a strange and unfamiliar place far beyond anything you could ever imagine," he would say, and leave it at that. Shin, who could not remember anything before the day he arrived in the apartment, would begin to ask for more, but Grandpa Why would always glare, insistent that the drama of his statement's end remain ever so pregnant with silence. Shin vanished before he found out anything about the last place he came from.

Grandpa Why told his stories the way one laid mousetraps, slowly across the span of a home, watching the busy rodents of the apartment scatter, descending from their rooms during those Tuesdays when the darkening storms would cast light-and-shadow patterns on every surface, and those furtive animals, so lost and aimless, would hide and go into their little holes, just watching. He would wait for the inhabitants of the apartment to emerge, and caught in step with them, launch into a narrative as if it had already begun, telling the tales in pieces.

"There was a field."

"The ghosts all gathered there."

"We lived in apartments much like these. They rose up into a sky that was permanently gray."

"I was told to forget, and when I would not, they sent me here."

Ma and Mira listened sometimes. They would nod as they went about their days. "That's great, Ah Ba," Ma would say, and Mira would echo, "Very interesting, Gong Gong." But Grandpa Why would not be patronized this way. He kept weaving his tales.

Meanwhile, the world he stumbled back into continues to churn toward a more awful path. The storms have not subsided since he arrived, and in fact seem to be worsening. The weather bears no consequence for him anymore, but he sees the growing fear in his family's eyes, the skittishness of building residents who have taken to boarding up their windows with more inventive pieces of debris every time—splintering plywood, discarded cardboard, chopped-up pieces of old shelves, a disaster collage plastered over the windows.

Ma and Mira sit near the radio to listen to the daily updates. Each month, the task force for their zone issues a new system of disaster assessment, the latest being a color code—gray is ideal, and on the other end of the spectrum red indicates imminent danger. Most days the color hovers around orange, which means that people are to keep three feet between themselves and their windows, and anybody seen outside during quarantine faces both felony charges and a hefty fine. Even Grandpa Why finds this system hard to keep track of, the conditions shifting so often that the assessments can barely keep up. He watches as Ma and Mira take matters into their own hands, sometimes so careful that they stay huddled in the middle of the room during the storms; other times, throwing caution to the wind after enduring so much preparedness, they plan a big party.

Such is the case with Mira's wedding—which comes as a surprise to everyone, especially Grandpa Why, whose sense of his granddaughter is that of a sullen girl, not suitable for adult matters like marriage. Wedding planning preoccupies much of Ma's time, which she seems secretly glad for.

Ma says that Mira's wedding is to be on a Tuesday, because everyone will be indoors due to the storm anyway, and what else will anyone be doing? When word of Sad's proposal comes out, the building is abuzz with questions: "Where will the wedding be?" and "Seems inappropriate to celebrate during a time like this, doesn't it?" and "How many people can I bring?" Before Mira can protest, Ma has already given verbal invitations to everyone she has passed by in the building. As to how to accommodate everyone, the plan is to hold the main ceremony in the apartment, while each floor throws its own party afterward. The seed of the idea planted, the party planning spreads from floor to floor, and soon every apartment is prepared to offer something by way of food or music for the occasion, however little they have.

Grandpa Why witnesses Ma and Mira arguing often about the wedding.

"I told you, I didn't want to make a big deal about this!" Mira complains.

Ma lets whatever pan she is holding fall to the stove with a loud clang and retorts, "You need to think about other people, not yourself!"

Mira lets out a groan. "What does *my* wedding have anything to do with anybody else but Sad and me?"

It is the same dull argument each time, and it never holds Grandpa Why's attention for long. He thinks of his own wedding, which was spectacular. Sui, Ma's mother, a woman with full cheeks like white peaches with a permanent blush. At a time when extravagant weddings were frowned upon, at the emergence of Communist reign, he planned everything in secret. The invitations to the people in his little pocket of Guangzhou he whispered in passing. The location, an alleyway that could barely contain a full man's body with arms outstretched. There, lights were strewn, and folding chairs held up stacks of little cakes. For his bride, who loved steamed buns filled with lotus paste, he created a mountain of them at the end of the alleyway, so that when she moved toward him, she would beam at both his proud face and the warm sweetness that awaited her.

He did not love her at first, as he barely knew her when the marriage was arranged, but he felt he could, and that was what mattered. All his life, he watched his father and mother at a standstill—his hand on her throat, her fist digging into his torso. If his mother could take on a handful of thieves, his father could lay siege to an entire town. It was not so much a contest of brute strength as how much pain each was willing to endure on any given day. He once watched his father wrest a knife from his mother's hand and beat her to the floor. In protest, his mother forced everyone to watch while she sliced open her arm from wrist to elbow. Had it not been for the women next door barging in with cotton rags to stop the bleeding, her knife would have hit a crucial vein.

Once, Grandpa Why asked her, "When did you know that you loved Baba?"

If his mother gave an answer, he could never remember what she said.

Love felt like a grand delusion, but Sui was full of potential. During the wedding, she stood next to him and could not stop laughing. Was it the image of Confucius, a peeling, half-hearted painting of the man, looming over them in the alleyway? Grandpa Why did not know what to think at first. At one point, she doubled over and nearly tripped over her tears. The spectacle of it all, really, was too much. She could hear the water bucket from a squatting toilet being splashed about, a sound even the mandolin could not drown out. She tried to signal to Grandpa Why the absurdity of it all, but the more she widened her eyes to send this message, the harder it was for her to compose the rest of her face, and so all of her dissolved into body-shaking chortling. Grandpa Why could not help it; he laughed too. And then the whole assembly of people, even the ones blockading the alleyway, trying to obscure the business of celebration behind them, were beside themselves as well.

Sometimes when Ma and Mira shout at each other about the wedding, Grandpa Why tells them about this very event, feeling the laughter stir up inside him again. Being a ghost is such a hollow thing, so emptied of sensation, but memory is a root; it anchors. It is the closest thing to being flesh again.

Ma and Mira rarely hear him.

At the mirror, Mira looks at her pale reflection, the cheongsam hanging off her, lifeless as a dress on a hanger. In her moments of grief during those early days of the acid rainstorms, she starved herself on purpose, but as time went on and the rations grew smaller, her hunger came gnawing back. This time, she feels the lack.

"That's fine, I can take it in a little at the waist," Ma says, pinching the loose fabric at Mira's torso.

Mira, who has been quiet all this time, offers, "What if I don't wear a dress at all?"

Ma frowns. "Only lesbians wear pants to their own wedding."

Mira pauses and then speaks slowly. "I mean . . . what if we just go down to the courthouse and get a certificate? Isn't that all there is to it?"

Ma's face disappears from the mirror. Behind Mira's back, her frown deepens, sinks to the floor. Mira has suggested this before, and each time, Ma has said nothing.

"What does Sad think about that?" Ma finally counters.

Grandpa Why's eyes fly open at the mention. Sad, the headless and hapless lover, Mira's radio darling. Many times, he has floated through the floors of the building to Sad's apartment to see him with Mira, their bodies intertwined. Mira whispers into his torso, so softly that only Sad can sense her words. When she is not there, he mostly sits by the window, at a cautious distance from the rain, flinching at times when the storm outside wails too loudly. Sometimes Grandpa Why joins him, not quite sure if Sad knows he is there or simply does not care.

Grandpa Why has noted, however, that this routine has recently changed for Sad. Now, whenever he visits Sad's apartment, he senses that the air has been gravely altered, has become colder, as if visited by something heavy. He watches Sad pace around his bathroom, drag his nails across his chest until he is raw and pink. He has begun writing messages on the glass. From what Grandpa Why can tell in the smudged mirror, he has written the words *LEAVE ME.* Each time Sad writes on the glass, he bangs his fists against the bathroom sink with such force that Grandpa Why braces himself for the mirror to shatter. And while he cannot confirm it, he has a growing suspicion that some other ghost resides in that apartment.

Mira surely knows it too. Although her visits to Sad's apartment have been less frequent since the proposal, she has started to feel the dropping temperatures of the space and has taken to bringing sweaters and extra blankets with her. She tells Sad that being in the apartment is like "being held by a body of ice." At first she thinks it is an issue with the insulation, checking the apartment for cracks and holes that can be patched. Then, when all logical reasons for the sudden cold are disproved, she begins to wonder otherwise. When Sad and Mira move to hold each other, she suddenly feels the iciness pressed upon her chest and has to pull herself away. They sleep separately now, with Mira bundled in blankets, and Sad bare-chested beside her, sleepless.

This Grandpa Why watches while hovering at the ceiling corner, wanting to know what haunts the space aside from him. He has taken a mental inventory of every ghost that has appeared and disappeared in the building. If Sad is, in fact, haunted, he would know.

Unfortunately, Sad's troubles do not seem to end there. At some point, a distressed Yee is banging on Sad's door. Sad opens it, and there before him is Yee, a man half his size. Yee looks up at the flat surface of skin that tops Sad's neck, a little ashamed at first for coming to Sad in such a wild state. He has not bathed for days, the odor of many dumpster-diving trips still sour and foul on his body. Grandpa Why can smell the ripeness of him, suddenly envious that Sad has none of his senses but touch, or else he would find himself similarly offended.

Yee recovers quickly, though, and puffs up his chest. "You can't have her," he protests. "She doesn't want you."

From the ceiling, Grandpa Why rolls his eyes. He has seen his fair share of cowboy westerns to know what comes next. But Sad's lack of response is a surprise to everyone.

Sad stands still. His arms remain at his side.

Yee shifts from foot to foot. He has anticipated a short fight in which he would be the obvious loser, his track record foreshadowing such a fate. He is under no illusions about how this would go except that he has something to declare about Mira that this headless man can never understand. He loves her more and he loves her better—that is fact. He has come there to prove it, though that seems momentarily stalled.

"Hey!" Yee eventually shouts. "You in there?" He raises his fist and begins to knock against the stump of Sad's neck.

This is a mistake. Sad's hand flies to Yee's wrist, and with a quick thrust he shoves the offending man against the wall.

"Geez, ouch! Okay, sorry." Yee rubs his wrist when Sad eventually lets go.

Grandpa Why, who has been watching quietly until then, cannot help but let out, "Boring! Bored! You two are bores!"

Neither Sad nor Yee seem to notice, the two still facing each other, their bodies in a lingering scowl. Yee looks up, still rubbing his arm, Sad towering over him. He expects Sad to shove his head into the wall, but the bigger man continues to stand there.

Yee gives Sad a quick shove before ducking out of his way, racing toward the stairs. When he thinks he has reached a safe distance, he shouts behind him, "You don't even know her! She doesn't love you! You'll see!"

Sad does not go after him or show any signs that he recognizes the patterns of Yee's voice, what he has said, or how petulantly he means it. Grandpa Why notes that when he does eventually turn back to his own apartment, he clutches the frame of his door, squeezing it tightly. He looks slightly hunched over, as if Yee has dealt him a blow to the gut. It is only for a second, and then he straightens up, retreating behind the closed door.

What does Sad think? Mira unbuttons her cheongsam, letting it fall to the floor, much to Ma's annoyance as she rushes to pick it up. Mira considers Ma's question for a while before whispering, "What does Sad think? I don't think he'd care."

Mira shares little about Sad's proposal. She had come back to the apartment one early morning from Sad's place and crawled into bed with Ma. When Ma turned over to complain about being woken up, she saw the bright green jade ring on Mira's finger and smiled so wide that her teeth flashed against the dark.

"Is it . . . ?" Ma asked with cautious excitement. She held Mira's wrist so that she could see the ring more clearly.

Mira nodded and fell asleep.

Since then, others have asked about the proposal, tugging at Mira's arm when she passes by to see the ring up close. It was a disappointment for many, especially those who expected a diamond, which would have been a rarity during a time like this, with every jewelry shop on Bowery and Canal boarded up indefinitely. Jade they did not anticipate, and though it is the quality of stone that has possessed the other building residents, Grandpa Why begins to suspect something else.

The ring is vibrant, and it beams under a fluorescent light. There is not a single scratch on its surface, from what Grandpa Why can tell. He has no way of knowing its heft, but he can see that it is no imitation jade. The stone, circular and flat against a gold band, is a perfect patch of dark green except for a pale line that runs down the center, not a crack, but a deliberate line in the pattern, as if painted on to remake the stone as something less perfect.

The ring feels eerily familiar to him.

He remembers that Sui loved the color green. She wore a deep green scarf during the winter seasons, the cloud of it cupping her round and ecstatic face. He loved to gather the scarf around her, so that her head swam in the ocean of green, and there her laughter would explode again.

Together, they chased each other through the sugarcane stalks, which hovered over them, row after row of emerald. During their working hours, they took turns slicing the stalks at the bottom with machetes and peeling their leaves. On one particularly cloudy day, they shed their straw hats and chased each other through the field. Sui was short but quick on her feet, and Grandpa Why, being lanky and long-limbed, found himself crashing too often into the sugarcane with too-rapid turns. When he finally caught up to Sui, scooping her in his arms and tossing her into a pile of dirt, he dug his face into her breasts, sticky with sweat. Playfully, he rubbed his damp forehead against her chest. When she recovered her breath and realized what he was up to, she bumped his forehead with her palm, threw her head back, and let out a laugh so loud that it shook the field.

Grandpa Why gazed at the folds of flesh around her chin and neck when she laughed, convinced she was the happiest person he had ever met. "You are so beautiful," he caught himself saying aloud, but Sui, lost in a joke that had taken on new life by then, never heard him.

That was two years into their marriage, and what shocked him most was how quickly time had passed. They argued mainly about Sui's carelessness, how she hacked through the field of sugarcane with such speed that she often nicked herself. Once, she nearly sliced Grandpa Why's neck, and then made a joke of it. He was furious for days until she came to him one evening with two fistfuls of grass and dumped them onto his head. "Time for you to stop being mad," she said, and before he could protest, she revealed a string of dried mackerel tied around her waist. Had it not been for Grandpa Why's love of salt, he would have remained angry several days longer.

When Sui died, there was no green. He and several men from the town buried her in a dirt field during the summer when the ground was mostly sandy debris. The cost of a granite tombstone drained nearly all the money he had, but he thought she deserved at least that. As for how many people came to mourn her, Grandpa Why could barely recall. He could only remember the sky at the time, clear blue and cloudless. As the day was unbearably hot, the men departed as soon as the last three bows were completed and the paper offerings burned to ash.

Grandpa Why remained at Sui's burial plot, just a few feet

from the sugarcane field where they had worked, day after day. He stayed there until the joss sticks burned to their red stubs and the air became charged with the nighttime breeze. There was little solace but that patch of dirt where he lay, devoid of any laughter.

That night, he dreamed a thousand dreams, each one beginning at a different corner of the sugarcane field. Each time a dream began, Sui's back was to him, lost in the sea of green stalks. When he reached out to her, she raced forward and stopped, only to rush ahead again when he approached. Sometimes he would dash toward her unrelentingly, quickening his pace as she ran faster. Just when he thought he was close enough to catch her, she would increase her speed, and he would be left behind once again.

In the final dream, he fell to his knees while Sui stood just a few paces before him. "Please," he begged, though he did not know what he pleaded for. When Sui shifted, as if to turn around, her hair covered her face, so that all he could see was a black curtain. He tried to call out to her once more, but she ran ahead until she vanished into the thick mass of the field.

On the ground, he saw that she had left behind something small. When he neared it, he saw wedged in the dirt a bright green ring.

When Grandpa Why woke up, the ground was damp beneath him. It was still night when he opened his eyes and saw row after row of green and brown stalks surrounding him, their long and drooping leaves sweeping against his bare feet and face. He assumed he had walked into the nearby sugarcane field in his sleep, but when he turned around, he saw Sui's tombstone planted in the ground.

His first thought was to cry out, but the wind crashing against the sugarcane sounded out a series of *whomps* that drowned out everything else. Suddenly it was as if the green of the sugarcane sung to him too, softly at first and then growing in volume—it surrounded him. He had felt so alone, but he could now tell he no longer was.

Then he noticed the smallest object sitting atop Sui's tombstone. It was the ring from his dream, a gold band with a round jade stone, so perfect in its shape and color that it permitted a single white line down its center, as if to denote where they both would live, apart but side by side.

When Grandpa Why finally recognizes what he has seen on Mira's finger, he feels the song of the sugarcane field besiege him again. The memory is heavy this time, so heavy that he feels something dense course through his spectral body, as if his blood and bones have returned to his form. It takes him a minute before he realizes that what fills him is a slow-building fury.

He finds Ma in her bedroom, the television playing *Kindred Spirit*, a Hong Kong soap opera that has long stopped running. It is a VHS tape, one of many that Ma keeps stored in the back closet, and which is always so disorderly that each recorded episode is a surprise when pulled out.

Grandpa Why holds his finger to Ma's face. "It is not yours to give."

Ma's eyes never leave the television. The actress Nancy Sit appears on-screen, offering some comedic relief from the high drama of the previous episode. Grandpa Why's finger near her is only slightly damp and cold, but not easy to ignore.

She relents, "Ah Ba, what are you talking about now?"

He steps in front of the television, though the transparency of his body only partially obscures what plays on-screen. "The ring, you ungrateful child. Your mother's ring!"

Ma blinks, her mouth opening and closing. It seems to take her a minute to recognize his complaint. Grandpa Why had kept the ring in a box in the back of his closet. Beside it were several watches, a tiny anklet that was gifted to Ma when she was a baby, and the jade ring, all of which he considered to be the most precious remainders of his now-departed life.

Ma seems to think otherwise. "Well, yes, I gave it to Sad to propose to Mira."

Astounded, Grandpa Why sinks to the floor. "You gave it to Sad?"

Ma, who has rarely seen Grandpa Why in a solemn moment since he has come back as a ghost, takes a moment to pause the television. "Yes. What's the problem, Ah Ba? It's only natural. What we inherit, we pass on. You left me this ring when you died. I gave it to Sad so he and Mira could be married."

Grandpa Why shakes his finger in her face. "No, no. This is no good. They are not right." He looks around the room, locating a framed picture of Mira on the wall. He points. "She is not right."

Ma's mouth turns into one tight line. "Ah Ba, you don't know what you are saying."

It takes all the energy he has to anchor himself to the floor. He feels his head float up, his body trying to leap toward the ceiling fan. He has long forgotten the sensation of pain, but perhaps the pinpricks that run through him are close enough. He shakes his head at her once more. "You disgrace your mother's memory."

Ma rises from the bed, her gut roiling. She is so hungry these days that she has only enough energy to lie in bed. Getting up, she feels her legs tremble, struggling to hold her weight. "Listen, Ah Ba," she states sternly. "When you died, everything you owned stayed with me. I kept this ring because I recognized it as something my mother would have owned. I don't know how I knew—I just did. I think it is lucky, that ring. I gave it to someone who could give Mira a good life. Do you not want that too for your granddaughter? After all the terrible luck she has had?"

Grandpa Why continues to shake his head, then hitting himself with his fists. "No. No. It is not right."

"Ah Ba, it is a very hard time for her. She needs this. We need this."

"Selfish!"

"Ah Ba, come on, now."

It grows instantly quiet in the room—Grandpa Why glaring at Ma; Ma looking back at her father, expressionless.

Ma finally speaks. "What can I do now?"

With his hands outstretched, Grandpa Why's voice almost comes out a whimper. "Give it back. It does not belong to you."

"It's too late, Baba."

Grandpa Why resumes hitting himself. It is no use. His own blows course through him, and he remains untouched.

This he does for several days whenever anybody walks by. Mira asks after him, and each time he thinks to tell her about her mother's double-crossing. When that complaint comes out, it sounds like "Selfish!" and "Ungrateful daughter!" And upon hearing those accusations, Mira assumes they are about her. Wounded by his words, she avoids her grandfather whenever she can.

Ma continues to say nothing of her tense exchange with her father, even as the wedding nears. Meanwhile, the task force has indicated that the threat level has been elevated to red. Every morning volunteer workers post notices on every apartment door, detailing in tiny print what precautions each resident should be taking as the next Tuesday storm nears. Ma and Mira have been following the news on television too, endless montages of different parts of the city in ruin—the smashed-up concrete block that was once Delancey, the nearby HSBC Bank ransacked and left with a floor of shattered glass, the BQE officially too eroded for any car to pass through, now blocked off by military and metal fences.

By the way the building residents move through each floor, it appears that nothing of what transpired outside has any bearing inside. The remnants of everybody's dollar store party decorations have taken over the hallways of each floor—tattered tissue paper streamers, deflated balloons in black and gold, glow-in-the-dark stars, lanterns, dirty confetti, and whatever else was found buried in the backs of closets have come back to haunt the walls and floors of the building.

Grandpa Why drifts through each floor, overseeing the party planning as it becomes more involved as the day goes on. While he is usually zipping through the hallways, amused by the racket the living put themselves through, he cannot forget that the only thing he has left of Sui is no longer his. As a ghost, he has delighted in the delicious freedom of it all—the absence of worry, no more obligation to work until his body gives out. For the first time, he feels himself bound again to the living, to feel something so unbearably human as regret. Why can he not forget that, at the very least?

Sui, on the last day she was alive, gripped Grandpa Why's hand as the contractions moved through her. The baby inside her refusing to come out, though her body willed it. She told Grandpa Why that the pain was unlike anything she had experienced before, and while she had anticipated the terrible aches of labor, she was not prepared for what eventually arrived.

"What can I do?" Grandpa Why asked helplessly. He had defied tradition and remained by Sui's side during childbirth, bracing for the tumult ahead.

Sui's forehead was slick with sweat. She had only strength enough to move her head slightly back and forth to say, *Nothing*. Then, wordlessly, she collapsed into the sheets.

The midwife swiped a cold towel over Sui's forehead while Grandpa Why looked on. In the months leading up to labor, he and Sui would lie beneath the stars and talk about their soon-to-be child. The child was to be strong, full of milk and meat. She was to run through the grass, barefooted and unafraid of the critters that lived there. Fat, happy, and fortuitous—the three, one and the same. To resemble the god of peaches, the god of coins. Sui had leaned over one night and whispered the name of the baby to him. He held that name inside him until the day of the baby's birth.

Before him then, Sui, with her hair soaked wet, looked so far beyond those dreams. He felt flooded with fear.

As the hours passed into the dark and early morning, Sui's eyes fluttered open, and she gasped. It startled Grandpa Why, who had just begun nodding off during a rare moment of quiet. Sui held his hand tight and let out a wail. The baby was coming.

The midwife squatted in position, lifting the baby up from between Sui's legs as if it had come from a seed in the ground. Red, gelatinous, and small. Grandpa Why could see the thin veins behind the baby's pale skin.

Sui too was pale, and dehydrated. She was given water, the sweat wiped off her again. Still, she never stopped shedding water, and the blood between her legs kept spilling out.

The midwife cut the baby's cord and held the child before the parents. Grandpa Why glanced only briefly, regarding the alien body of the child in front of him, before switching his gaze over to Sui, whose lips parted once, twice, as if to speak, and then she was motionless again.

The next day, the bleeding still did not stop for Sui. The child, too weak to cry out, could only let out tiny whimpers for milk. While the midwife tended to the baby, Grandpa Why remained by Sui.

When Sui could finally speak, her voice only came out a whisper. "Don't forget me, okay?"

Grandpa Why shook his head, refusing the future Sui foretold. *There is nothing to forget*, he thought. She would outlive him.

Sui passed quietly the next night, so stealthily in fact that Grandpa Why did not notice at first. He touched her cheek, and when she did not react, he knew. The shock of it was almost too much.

When the midwife came to ask him if he had a name for the baby, he could not hold back his cries. He wailed as if it were his own passage into life. He placed his arm around Sui's torso, which would no longer move, and the only reply he could offer was the nodding of his head.

On the day before the wedding, Grandpa Why finds himself at Sad's apartment once more, the quietest place in the building despite the festivities in the floors above, where Sad and Mira can often be found, not talking, just speaking through touch. This time, the two of them are lying inside an emptied aquarium tank. Once filled with brightly colored fish, pieces of luminescent coral, the tank only holds two living bodies now—Mira and Sad, the transceiver from a ham radio resting on Mira's bare stomach. She holds the mic above her as if she is about to bite into it like an apple.

"Dear Listeners," Mira speaks into the mic, and she appears to pause before opening her mouth to continue, "it is with deep regret that I share that this will be my last show."

Grandpa Why rolls his eyes. For him, this news is nothing worth remarking on, as he is sure the audience for Mira's pathetic excuse for a radio show does not extend beyond four or five people, all of whom likely reside in the floors above and below them.

Mira goes on. "I began this show in search of a reason for everything happening around us, to find the words to describe a time of disaster. I wanted most of all to talk about loss."

Sad lies quietly beside her, one hand gently holding her elbow as she talks. As Grandpa Why looks on, he recalls that he too once held Sui's arms the moments before falling asleep.

Suddenly Mira begins to cry. "I wanted to do so many things with this show. I wanted . . . to make so much happen. I don't know what I was thinking."

Grandpa Why moves closer, sees Mira covering her face with one hand, seemingly surprised by her own tears.

"I think it is time to say goodbye, Mal. Wherever you are. Goodbye."

Mira hits a button to turn the radio off and sighs as if her whole heart has fallen out of her chest. Sad holds her, though she has stopped crying after her last "goodbye." It is a curious scene for Grandpa Why, to see the sadness in the bodies before him, the day the wedding is to take place. If this is not further proof that they are too young, too mismatched for marriage, then he does not know what else could convince them. He spies the ring on Mira's finger and grows resentful once more.

Sad places his hand on Mira's throat gently, signals to her a question: *Why?*

She places her hand on top of his, and responds, "We are getting married tomorrow. I think it may be time for a new start."

Mira continues to speak in murmurs even as the room grows cold. Grandpa Why would not have noticed at first if not for the thickening fog on the glass of the tank, the hair standing up on Mira and Sad's arms. He has seen these signs before, of some other presence in the room, but has never known where to place them. Everywhere he turns, he sees only Mira and Sad with him in the apartment.

"Do you really want to do this?" Mira asks Sad.

Sad tightens his grip on Mira's body. *Yes.*

"Do you promise we can start over?"

Yes.

"I don't want to be haunted anymore."

Sad holds her so close that they appear to merge. Against his chest, she has started crying again, her sobs muffled by the tightness of his embrace. Surely he can sense the loudness of her cries, feel the reverberations against his skin.

All around them, the room seems to groan. The walls too become dewy with cold sweat. Grandpa Why can see drops form on the surfaces. He looks to where Sad and Mira are lying close to each other, the water accumulating on the sides of the glass surrounding them. They do not seem to notice what is happening, though they start to shiver from the sudden cold.

Grandpa Why also feels a light static run through him, as if light were flashing inside his ghostly frame. Nothing has been able to touch him since he has come back as a ghost, but now he feels the presence of something other passing back and forth through him.

"Hey, you two!" Grandpa Why shouts. He hovers above the two bodies in the tank sinking deeper into the pebble base. "Get out of here!"

Neither Mira nor Sad notice Grandpa Why. The water rises from the tank, but they do not notice that either—it is unclear where the water comes from, only that it has filled the tank again, the two of them like fish in a tight caress. The water lightly rolls against the pebble bottom, grazing the base of their elbows. Mira cries, and Sad holds her, the two lost in the moment of their perpetual grief.

When the water touches Mira's chin, Grandpa Why calls out once again. "Up! Get up! You're going to be drowned ducks!"

Not long after Grandpa Why's cry, Mira's whole head is submerged, and she seems happily adrift—her face an empty and floating gourd.

It is that moment that Grandpa Why recognizes Sui's face in Mira's own, the fullness of both their cheeks, hooded eyes that fall at the corners like a pinched teardrop. He sinks to his knees, seeing not her, but her countenance, behind the many layers of Mira's flesh. The vast history that lives within this young girl, his beloved being only a small part of it.

After Sui's death, the baby's life felt almost as inconsequential as Grandpa Why's own. The infant, to his surprise, never cried out beyond her first day of life. He would recount this to Ma later, remarking that she had an incredible stillness to her, that even the loud smack of a hand against a fly would barely cause any reaction.

When Grandpa Why's parents declared that there was no way their son could raise a baby on his own, they welcomed him back home, still so heavy in his grief that he could not protest. For a while the presence of a baby in the household brought Grandpa Why's mother and father a measure of peace, so focused on spoiling the tiny child that they seemed to have forgotten how to fight. While Grandpa Why moved through the house without any affection for life, his mother and father doted on the baby, so that she eventually grew to be of healthy weight and size.

The harmonious era was short-lived, however. One day, Grandpa Why's mother dropped a bowl of food she had been spooning into the baby's mouth, and, irate about the waste, his father backhanded his wife for her clumsiness. Then the fights began again, enough to wake Grandpa Why from his mourning stupor. The baby watched as Grandpa Why's parents took turns swatting at each other's heads with their fists and open palms, her eyes wide and watchful.

Grandpa Why prayed that in her adulthood she would not be able to recall such memories from this age. He decided that she should never have to.

The plan was to acquire papers that would bring him to Hong Kong and then to the U.S. Someone in town took pity on his misfortune, told him about a cousin in Hong Kong who had access to forged documents—a family in the U.S. who could claim him as a son rejoining them with a child in the new country. It cost him nearly everything he owned, but he could not risk staying even in Hong Kong for fear that his parents would find him one day and return him and the baby to the violence of their home.

Grandpa Why had never told Ma about those early years of her infancy, how she was bundled so tight for the journey by boat at first and then by plane, she could only stare blankly at her father. Her face at birth resembled a prune more than anything else. But after her first year of life, she began to look more like Sui, and it occurred to him that everything that came after Ma would carry some part of the woman he loved, and so she would live on in this way.

At the sight of Mira floating in the tank, this realization overwhelms him again. Still, Mira has not woken up from the water. Her body and Sad's have become untangled, neither of them alert to the water that is now overflowing and spilling beyond the tank.

Grandpa Why marches up to the tank just as the groans in the apartment grow louder. The picture frames on the walls have started to tremble, close to falling off their hooks. Once more, he cries out, "Wake up!"

Nothing. Mira's body still lies flaccid in the water.

Grandpa Why has had enough. To experience a death, and now this? He throws his head toward the ceiling and howls. "Awoo! That's right! Come out, wherever you are, ghostie! Let's see your face!"

There is a heavy thump against the wall of the tank. A second one follows.

"Oh, so you like to play hide-and-go-boo, huh? Well, watch this." Grandpa Why belts forward, running along the walls of the apartment. As a ghost, his speed is three times what it was when he was alive, and he makes several circles before he starts to shout again. "Come out now! Show yourself!"

The glass tank rattles, seeming to tilt left and then right. Grandpa Why lets out a long scream, and several seconds in, the glass begins to crack. He does not stop screaming, and the crack widens until a large split in the middle yields to the weight of the water. The glass shatters, gushing forward water and the two lovers, shaken from their almost-drowning. They land on the floor, coughing and sputtering.

Mira sits up and gasps, water spilling from her mouth. She looks at Grandpa Why with terror, and says between gulps of breath, "I saw it."

Startled, Grandpa Why says nothing, only watching Sad slowly prop himself up beside Mira. He reaches over to brush the hair from Mira's face, but she flinches and shudders away from him. In the water, they each must have encountered something different, their bodies turned away from each other. The room is quiet now, the walls dry, with no trace of water. Grandpa Why listens but cannot sense anything beyond Mira and Sad's harsh breaths on the ground. Without saying anything more, he backs out of the room and leaves.

Grandpa Why returns to Ma's home, where she sleeps, the television a low hum in the background. He waits for her to wake up enough to tell her—about what, he is not so sure, but he knows he wants to express something to her about where they all come from. Perhaps she will understand something of him then.

Mira does not return to Ma's apartment that night, nor can

she be found the morning after. Her disappearance is first noted by Lucinda, who arrives at Ma's apartment before dawn with a tin of thread and bobbins for some last-minute alterations to Mira's dress. Sleepily, Ma lets Lucinda in, and her friend darts through the apartment, scouring for Mira.

"Where is the bride, anyway?" Lucinda asks aloud after ducking her head into every room. "I was just at Sad's apartment, thinking she was there. I wanted to give her a good-luck charm for her big day, but Sad said she left a while ago. I assumed she'd be home."

Ma swats her hand in the air. "Oh, you know her. She's always everywhere at all times of day and night."

Lucinda frowns.

Outside, the clouds have started to amass into thick and load-bearing shapes. On Channel 7, the meteorologist warns that the day's storm will be arriving earlier than expected, that sheltering procedures should proceed on a level red for all zones an hour ahead of the usual time. In the hallway, two task force members in hazmat suits have been going door to door, making sure that everybody is accounted for and indoors. They are less than happy about the parties set to begin on each floor, kicking aside the fallen streamers as they pass.

Ma remains unconcerned until the hazmat suits come to her door. Grandpa Why watches as she says yes to the question "Is everyone in your household accounted for?" And then yes again to "Do you understand that missing persons will result in a fine and felony charges applied to each member of the household, the amount and severity of which will be determined at the discretion of the courts?" Without any more follow-up, the suits click their handheld tally counters before moving on to next door.

An hour passes, and Mira still does not come through the door. Ma leaves at some point to find Lucinda, and the two split up to look for Mira on every floor. Ma ducks her head into every open apartment door, calling out to her. The neighbors, thinking it is a joke, say, "Uh-oh! Runaway bride!" But Ma is not amused. No one seems to have seen Mira.

When Lucinda finally returns, shaking her head, Ma's alarm grows. Turning to Grandpa Why, she asks, "Ah Ba, you've seen her, haven't you?"

Grandpa Why nods but looks away.

"Where is she?"

From the corner of his eye, he sees Ma swallow the words to her question. He turns his body her way to speak. "Something happened at Sad's apartment. I do not think she will be returning there."

"Ah Ba, if you know something, tell me. Did she say anything to Sad? Anything about where she might want to go?"

Grandpa Why thinks about the look on Mira's face when she poured out of the aquarium. How familiar her fear had felt. He shakes his head.

Ma purses her lips and glances nervously out the window, where the sky is starting to grumble. "She couldn't have run away. Not during a time like this." Ma paces the living room, muttering to herself. "Just stay put, I try to tell her! But no, she keeps leaving. She leaves me again."

Lucinda places an arm around Ma's shoulder, giving her body a tight squeeze. Grandpa Why watches Ma fold into herself, her back sloped and heavy with worry. "She won't leave you," Lucinda consoles.

Ma does not hear her. Pushing Lucinda's arm aside, she rummages through her closet, pulling out a pale green hazmat suit from its far reaches. She shakes it out, still creased and unused. She starts to put it on.

Grandpa Why asks, "What are you doing, silly woman?"

"I'm going out there to find her."

"Don't be crazy."

While the hazards of this world are no longer a concern for Grandpa Why, he has seen his fair share of death at the hand of the acid rain on the endless parade of televised images of the city. It does not surprise him that Ma would keep a hazmat suit for emergencies, but by the looks of its shoddy make, it is guaranteed to have little effect once the storm begins. Just as he is about to protest once more, Lucinda chimes in, "Give me the other suit. I'm coming with you."

Grandpa Why throws his hands into the air. These ridiculous women marching to their deaths. "Fine! Let's all go find that stupid girl, then."

In truth, Grandpa Why has not stepped outside since he became a ghost, feeling confined to the building he once lived in as a human. He has never tested the bounds of where he can go, the thought never occurring to him until now. It surprises him, suddenly aware of how dulled his desire has become, and how eager he is now to find out what lies beyond the building.

Grandpa Why looks at Ma and sees her face surrounded by the green of the suit's hood.

Ma catches her father staring. "What is it, Ah Ba? Are you still mad at me about the ring? Listen—"

"You look just like her."

Ma pauses. "Ah Ba . . ."

Grandpa Why feels a shudder run through him, a sensation

that he only remembers as sadness. He reaches out as if to touch Ma's face before taking back his hand. It will do no good; the hand will only pass through.

With some softness in his face, Grandpa Why says at last, "I have so much to tell you when we come back."

It occurs to Grandpa Why that there are places he rarely frequents in the building—the basement and the rooftop being two of them. In the basement, he rummages through the piles of old blankets and broken appliances, discards from building residents that they cannot bear to permanently throw away. He looks under the piles, peeks in the corners, and still, Mira is not there.

Outside, the sky darkens, the way it always does right before the storm begins. In just a short while, the heavy tarp will fall over the facade, shuttering everyone in complete darkness. The wedding festivities will kick up then, music blasting from stereos on every floor, and the bodies packed tight in the hallways will be anticipating the fanfare of Sad and Mira shimmying up and down each level.

Grandpa Why makes his way from the basement to the roof. He has seen the locked door to the rooftop, covered in caution tape, many times. He has heard the rumors of kids who know how to pick locks, leaving the door sometimes propped open with a rock, so that they can gather there from time to time to chain-smoke or feign a taste for cheap vodka. This time the door is closed, but he passes through it easily to find himself standing on the gravel surface of the rooftop.

In the decades that he had lived in the building, he had only been on the roof twice—once when he first moved in to look for Ma, thinking she had wandered there for some trouble, only to find her huddled under her bed, drawing in a little notebook; another time, he had gone up there to cry, wondering how he could raise a child all by himself. How strange it is to return to the roof as someone who has let many years go by, seeing how little it has changed.

On the far edge of the roof sits a small figure that Grandpa Why can barely recognize as Mira or a crow. When he moves closer, he sees the shadowy remnant of his granddaughter, her legs dangling over the building. At first he thinks she has become a ghost too, but as he finally stands beside her, he can see her corporeal realness, how burdensome it seems to weigh on her. She looks like she has been crying for a very long time.

"They're looking for you," Grandpa Why says slowly.

Mira nods to show that she understands. "I know this. I'm not going back, though."

Grandpa Why looks out toward the city skyline, where he can just barely make out the tops of the buildings down-town, seemingly shaved off on all sides. The rain erodes what time has only just begun, the buildings' foundations bearing the marks of accelerating age. He can see tiny flickers of light inside these buildings, not as bright as they once were, but bright enough to offer evidence that people are making their way slowly inside. As the storm's roar grows louder overhead, the buildings respond with their own quiet aliveness, as if to say, *I am still here.*

Grandpa Why looks down at Mira, who stubbornly will not budge. He says to her, "Dying is no fun, silly girl. You need to go back inside."

"I'm. Not. Going. Back."

Just then, Ma and Lucinda come rushing through the door to the rooftop, Grandpa Why forgetting in that moment that humans move slower than he does. The two women, upon seeing Mira, breathe a sigh of relief. As they make their way to the edge, he insists again, "Do you want to end up like the bodies you see on television? Their flesh burning up like barbecue? They'll be scraping you off the rooftop. What are you thinking, girl?"

Mira shakes her head and digs her face into her knees. "I saw it, Ah Gong. What you were telling all of us about *that* place."

That place was an underworld Grandpa Why barely remembers, having only visited for a moment before he was returned to this world. In truth, he has embellished his stories about that place. It makes no sense that a living girl would see any of it.

Lucinda interrupts. "My dear, what did you see?"

Mira narrows her eyes at Lucinda. "I saw *her*. Very briefly." She shows everyone her wrist, which bears the light touch of finger bruises. "Someone found me, took my arm, like they were saying, *Here, come with me*. And then I was dragged into a strange field, where I saw her. It was so quick and there were so many people. But I spotted her there, and I called out, but it was like no one could hear me, like I wasn't really there. It was like I was just . . . visiting."

Ma makes her way forward to say, "Mira, it's time to come home."

At the sight of Ma inching toward her, Mira hangs over the edge as if ready to leap. "No! You're not listening."

Grandpa Why glares. "Who is *her*?"

Ma backs away slowly, and, watching her still, Mira avoids Grandpa Why's gaze. "Someone I still love very much."

They are quiet together for a moment—Mira suddenly self-conscious about her admission, and Grandpa Why, letting the thoughts roll over in his head. Ma and Lucinda are silent too. Finally, he says, "So you see someone you love very much, and she is dead. And now you think that if you stay here a while longer, you can die and join her too?"

Mira says nothing.

"It is a very stupid plan."

Mira's scoff comes out a laugh and then a cry. She places her forehead against her knees. Grandpa Why has rarely felt the impulse to embrace her, touch being something he had once reserved for Sui and Ma alone. But now, seeing his granddaughter so close to death, helplessly coveting it even, he wants to offer her something, anything.

He says to her, "Can I tell you about the ring on your finger?"

Mira looks down at the jade ring on her hand as if suddenly remembering that she had it all this time. "What do you know about this ring, Ah Gong?"

"That's your grandmother there."

"You mean, it belonged to my grandmother?"

Grandpa Why swipes his hand in the air. "No, I mean it is your grandmother. All that remains of her lives within that ring."

Mira looks at Grandpa Why skeptically, trying to puzzle out his pronouncement in her head. She argues, "But Sad gave it to me. Are you saying that he took it from you?"

"No, no. That was your mother's doing, but that's beside the point now. You must know that when your grandmother died, the force of her life grew an entire field around me and forged this ring from the ground. Some people do not die very easily, you know. And when they do, they still find a way to live on somehow."

"But you loved her."

"Yes. Very much."

"So, when you died, did you find her?"

Grandpa Why opens his mouth to answer, closes it. After thinking about it for a while, he responds, "It doesn't work like that, silly girl."

"Why wouldn't you try to find her? If you knew you could?"

"I made your grandmother a promise a very long time ago. And I kept that promise all throughout my life and even after I died. I will never forget her, that was the promise I made. And all the years in between, I raised Ma as best I could, and then Ma raised you. All this time, your grandmother was with us." He pointed to his chest. "All blood and meat and sticky bones. That goes for you and your mother too. You have her face, just as Ma carries your grandmother with her in everything she does. It does not matter if you don't see it. I do. You think we die, and then that's that? Oh, then you do not understand death or dying at all."

Mira is quiet, her lips pursed in reflection.

Grandpa Why continues. "Do you understand now? Your grandmother. My life's big, big love. She persists."

Mira turns her face up to the sky and sighs. As she takes in a new breath, a siren begins to blare loud and clear, the sound surrounding them. She winces at the volume, more pronounced now that she is hearing it from outside rather than indoors.

Lucinda finally speaks. "I'm so sorry, my dear. I should have never intervened. I—"

Ma places her hand on her friend's shoulder, turning to Mira, her heart heavy. "我個心," she says. "My whole heart."

Mira looks down at the ground many stories below. "I know that."

Turning to Lucinda and then again to Mira, Ma offers her next admission. "All I ever want is for you to live a good life."

"I know."

Ma's eyes never leave Mira. "It is still possible."

Mira shakes her head. "I'm not going to marry Sad. I do love him. It's just . . . it isn't right."

It is Ma's turn to shake her head now as she says quickly, "That's not what I mean."

Mira turns to look at Ma expectantly. "What do you mean, then?"

All eyes turn to Ma now; the older woman sighs and looks out toward the cityscape. The pointy needle top of the Empire State Building pierces the sky. She gestures at it. "Look. I forget what a view we have here sometimes." She points behind her to where the East River roars, the all-too-common accompaniment to the impending rain. "I am always looking behind me."

Mira looks at the cityscape, the river, and then back at the skyscrapers again. Finally, she whispers, almost to herself, "I forget sometimes to look around me at all."

Ma's face turns into a soft plea. "My daughter, I look only at you."

Grandpa Why watches the scene unfold—a mother, a daughter, each exposed to the crackling of the sky and the rain to come. Lucinda, hiding under the awning over the roof door, yanking at Ma's sleeve to come back inside.

Suddenly Mira turns her attention to Grandpa Why, which

startles him. "Ah Gong, do you believe that there is more out there? Will you tell me what you've seen?"

Grandpa Why nods so hard, if he were not dead his head would roll off his neck. He looks at his own daughter, whose eyes are beckoning him for help. So he offers it. "Come back inside and I will tell you."

Mira tentatively accepts, getting up and walking toward the rooftop door. Everyone lets out a collective sigh, carefully observing the coming storm. The siren continues to blare, louder than before.

"I'm going elsewhere after today," Mira adds while rising up. "I don't know where yet. But I can't stay here."

Grandpa Why watches Ma fight her every urge to protest. Lucinda holds her hand. Finally, Ma relents. "Okay."

Mira looks back at her mother, tenderly this time. "Are you going to be okay without me?"

Ma nods, though her arms are wrapped around her own waist, already mourning what is to come. "Ma will be okay," she assures her. "I don't always understand, but I am okay."

Mira turns to Grandpa Why now. "What are you going to do?"

Grandpa Why is confused by her question. "What do you mean?"

Mira gestures to the whole city before her, the clouds blanketing each building in a thick gray swarm. "I mean, what happens next for you? Are you going to poof like Shin and pass on?"

Grandpa Why grins. "Ah, like I said. It doesn't work like that." He pounds his chest and howls.

"Huh?"

"Silly girl, there's no rules to this. I will be fine, though." He turns to his own daughter, who seems surprised by his answer. With a wink, he adds, "Like your mother."

Mira looks at Grandpa Why for a while with a raised brow before finally giving him a nod. Lifting herself off the edge, she joins hands with Ma and Lucinda as they make their way back into the building just as a crackle of lightning flashes from the sky, the thunder following not too long after. Suddenly a roar emerges from the East River, and they all look back, expecting to see a row of ghost girls climbing their way to shore. Nothing. Just the vast rolling back of waves, crashing into each other, eagerly waiting to catch the water from the sky. There is no fear, every woman and ghost taking their time to return inside.

GHOST TRANSMISSIONS

"This is so silly. Why are we doing this again?"

"It's just a little experiment. Try it."

"I don't even know what to say!"

"Just say hello."

" . . . Hello."

"Okay, maybe something more, Lionel Richie."

"Mal! Geez." [laughter]

[singing] *"Hello . . . Is it me you're looking for?* That's what you sound like."

"Stop! People are staring, and I'm trying to cross the street."

"Yeah, where are we anyway?"

"Not sure. I wrote the directions down and it said turn right on Forty-Sixth Street a while back. So I did . . . Might have gotten distracted by someone's recording antics, you know?"

"Just trying to have some fun here! You do say I should lighten up every once in a while."

"I did say that. Yes. Having a sense of humor looks good on you."

"Thank you, thank you. So, remind me again, what are we doing here?"

"Getting supplies. The notice says we are scheduled for pickup somewhere around here . . . Do you think it's that red building over . . . Wow, look at that line."

"Yeah, geez. It's looking real bad over there."

"I think that's us, Mal."

"No way."

"How long do you think it'll take?"

"No idea. Glad I peed beforehand, though."

"Glad we're recording this for posterity."

"Oh shit, I forgot. [laughs] Should we close it out, then?"

"With song and dance?"

"Maybe just a dedication."

"Let me think."

"Don't think too long. It's getting noisy over here."

"Fine, fine. Okay, this is dedicated to the letter U. Happy?"

"Oh, very. Love that you'll still flirt with me even when the world is about the end."

"Oh shut up. We'll be fine."

WELCOME TO THE
UNCOMMONS

Many ghosts like myself come to the Uncommons by accident. Yanked from the earth and hurled onto a patch of gray grass, I look up at a sign that says: WELCOME TO THE UNCOMMONS. WHEN YOU'RE HERE, YOU'RE HERE. The sign lights up for me like a tarmac path for planes. Above, the sky is pallid, full of milky debris. The gulls fly overhead, not in V-formation, but in a tight oblong; they seem to know the parameters of the place and stay within it, looping themselves inward once they fly too far off. It seems that everything but the newly arrived ghosts of the Uncommons know the order of this city.

It is unclear why we are here and not elsewhere, circling in the field as if making a shape with our bodies will give us some answers. Others appear beside me as if they had been neighbors in the field all along, just waiting. They hold their glassy hands up to their faces in close examination. Watching them, I come to understand that something must have changed in me too. I hold my hands up, make them pass through each other and pull apart in sticky transparency. I touch a blade of grass. I hold it in my hand for just a few seconds before my fingers pinch through it. We all make the same curious motions almost synchronously. It feels like we are part of one great outdoor calisthenics routine. Occasionally someone exclaims, "Where are we?" A futile question answered only by unhelpful gesticulations to the sign. Had we forgotten? We are dead. This is a dead land.

There in the field, I remember little of my life. When the shuttle comes to pick us up, I can barely iron out my own name for the driver: *Mal*, as in the perpetually awful, short for something I can no longer remember. I say my name aloud and the ensuing joke, hoping to get a laugh, but to no avail. The driver points to the seat beside him, and there I sit quietly for the entirety of that short journey to the Uncommons' main headquarters. There, the driver explains via the loudspeaker that we are to register ourselves, get our affairs sorted, hold our questions for the end. I wonder what affairs I have, if I can barely remember who I am. My insides are hot and burning, a tightness of breath like a spectral feeling in my unbodied body. It comes and goes, not quite a panic attack, but somehow similar. I must look frightened, because the driver turns to me and whispers conspiratorially, "Don't worry, you'll forget that too."

Forgetting has an unforgiving pallor. In the Uncommons, the pewter brick buildings seem to pile one on top of the other.

Within each of these buildings scaling over a thousand stories are units, each one occupied by a single ghost. Wherever you live, there is the same washed-out view of sky cutting between you and a neighbor's living room, where they are likely just sitting, not doing anything but pursuing their stillness. I once thought it strange, how in the boundlessness of empty time in the Uncommons no one thought to set off fireworks in their apartments, throw themselves out the windows, or even host a party. I thought this until I experienced the gradual lull too, how I eventually exhausted myself with all the doing, chasing activity after activity—developed an elaborate dance routine, baked a five-layered cake, held a solo drinking contest where liquor of every pungent form slid and trickled out my ghost body—and found myself on the same recliner that came with every unit.

At the corner of each block is the same identical lamppost, its light always shining. The sky's permanent dimness means that every walk through the Uncommons is cast in shade. So many passing ghosts on their way to nowhere. Occasionally I catch someone's eyes. They begin, "Going for a walk?" and I return, "Yep! Just like I always—" but stop there, unsure if walks are something I enjoyed once upon a time. During that pause, we both quietly acknowledge the hole inside each of us, and with a nod, part ways. Never does it occur to us to ask the other why we ended up here.

I count the trees along my walk, their sparse branches with only speckles of pale leaves, one on each block, two hundred from one end of the Uncommons to the other. There are plaques on every building declaring this fact, but I count them anyway, waiting for some idiosyncrasy to happen, some answer from the gods to smack down onto the land about the circumstances of my dying. Whether this is punishment or limbo, it is unclear. I walk and hear the sky rumble without storm. Inevitably, when all things are counted, at the absence of anything more I return to my unit, where I sit again.

Sometimes, during these elongated periods of sitting, there is an attack of memory. It happened to me once at a building meeting where we gathered in the basement to listen to the Uncommons representative give an overview of the different services offered at the Uncommons Registry, a talk accompanied by pamphlets and a bullet-point presentation. In this meeting, the Uncommons representative stood on a makeshift stage, expounding upon the merits of "community," how he himself had risen in position at the Registry to advocate on behalf of those like ourselves, his fellow ghosts.

"I have always believed in the virtues of giving back," he said, brandishing a laser pointer against the presentation projected on the wall, "which is why I'm here today, asking you all to trust in this system, to let us help you, our community."

As he started to list the reasons why, I felt heat in roaming patches across my body. When it made its slow crawl into a loud fire, I burst into the middle of the aisle, swatting at myself and crying for help. It seemed that no one knew what to do until the Uncommons representative at the meeting cut through the crowd, his hand in the air summoning everyone to gather around. He crouched slightly, though I was still upright and spinning, and with a firm voice he repeated, "Stop, drop, and roll!" He turned around to the crowd of ghosts behind him, gesturing with both hands to repeat after him, and so everyone started to chant it too: "Stop, drop, and roll! Stop, drop, and roll!" Occasionally someone would chime in with, "You got this, mama!" It was all so discombobulating, the voices blending together and some ricocheting off the rest. Eventually the heat subsided, and I found myself standing still, no longer bellowing. The Uncommons representative must have sensed my embarrassment, because he shot me a crooked smile and immediately turned around to continue his presentation.

Later, I approached him to thank him and asked tentatively, "What does it mean? Why is this happening? Am I sick?"

He blinked hard, and his careful grin wavered when he said, "We welcome all questions here at the Uncommons, but we try to dissuade equating your afterlife state with sickness."

"Okay . . ." I saw that he was gesturing for me to leave. "But am I, though?"

His smile was so taut, it seemed close to snapping. "I'm afraid that's not my department." Sensing that the answer would not suffice, he added, "Listen, just go to the Uncommons Registry. They'll tell you where to go to address . . ." He looked at me from the sides of his eyes before walking away. "Your situation."

At the Uncommons Registry, the queue spans around the block. The line moves quickly, but each time someone enters the building, a new ghost steps up to the queue. I stand for some undeterminable time, the sky pooling white and gray and always dim. I think of how many years might have passed since my first day at the Uncommons, how without the fatigue in my body I may never know the true length of this waiting.

By the time I arrive inside the building and at the counter where a single receptionist waits behind a desk, I have forgotten what I am there for and why. The receptionist sticks her hand out, palm up, and it takes me a while to register that she is asking for my ID. I fumble for it while her fingers wiggle impatiently, and when she finishes considering its contents, frowning every step of the way, she finally says, "Okay, what do you need?"

I look around. "Um, am I supposed to talk to you, or . . . ?" I feel her frown deepen with each pause. "Something really strange happens to me where . . ." I begin, and then look around, suddenly growing anxious at the sight of the ghosts lined up behind me. "I'm sorry, but can you point me to a clinic in this building or something?"

She wags her fingers. "No, dear. Not how this works." She reaches into her desk and pulls out a numbered pad. Tearing the first page off, she splits the tiny ticket in two, handing me one of the halves. "Hold on to this, now. We've got a whole cadre of ghosts seeking treatment. That there is your number in line. Once we get to your number, we'll take a look at your case file, see if you're a viable candidate, and then we'll give you a call."

I look down at my number: 100672. "Wait, candidate for what?"

But she is already on to the next ghost in line.

⁂

Of waiting, I know it so well by now that it has become a sort of non-skill. I meditate on the recliner, pushing myself to sleep and dream, but sleep is not something a ghost body does in the Uncommons. I will my body to think of something, anything, but I always return to the same place—the gray field, its lit-up welcome sign, the blurred faces of each ghost turning around and around. The burning does not happen again, but I feel it in there, like the sole living organ in me, rushing with blood.

One day the phone rings. It comes with the unit, an ornament until that moment, lacking the ability to make outgoing calls. Its noise is jolting, unfamiliarly sharp and urgent. I pick it up and place it against my ear, and an automated voice says, "Congratulations! Your number, 100672, was selected as the next guest for our services. Please head to the Uncommons Registry as soon as possible to claim this opportunity."

I place the phone back carefully, its dial tone stopped short with a click. I pause, thinking someone is going to come out of the corner with further explanation, but the room greets me with its usual silence. I pick up the phone again, more dial tone, and place it back, thinking perhaps I had imagined the call.

At the Uncommons Registry, though, the torn ticket has a certain currency, such that when I get back in the queue, an official cuts through the crowd to find me, the other half of the ticket in hand, and beckons me to follow. We skip the line at great speed, the faces of each ghost amassing into one disaffected blur, and before I know it I am in front of an elevator tucked somewhere in a far corner of the building. We do not say a word to each other the whole way, but he does reach over at one point to press a button in the elevator for the 444th floor before stepping out and waving goodbye.

The hallway on the 444th floor is drenched in some awful yellow paint with equally sallow-looking lamps punctuating the hall every three feet, and it stretches for what seems like miles. I walk along it, looking left and right, each glass door fogged and absent any lettering to distinguish one from the other.

When I finally reach the end of the hallway, a woman in tweed opens the door.

"ABNA," she says, sticking her hand out. I look her up and down, startled because it is the first time since I have arrived here that anyone has introduced themselves to me by first name.

"Ab-na?" I repeat dumbly.

She sits down, indicating that I should do the same. "Well, actually, it's A-B-N-A," she clarifies. "I'm a ghost just like you, but instead of numbers, officials of some ranking have letter-generated names. But you don't need to say every letter out loud for me." She smiles, her mouth taut like a wire. "You can call me ABNA."

I nod, looking around her office, which is filled with small framed paintings of horses standing still in a field or in a barn or some other idyllic setting. It is the first art I have seen in the Uncommons. I think to ask ABNA about the rest of the Uncommons, whether any of us can ever walk past the 200th tree to the 201st, and what lingers there in the beyond.

ABNA begins her line of questioning. "So, you signed yourself up because you want to talk to someone about the discomfort you're experiencing, is that right?"

Did I sign myself up for anything? I am not sure. "Yes. I'm usually fine, but sometimes, out of nowhere, I'd feel like my whole body is on—"

"Fire, yes," she interrupts. She writes something down on a pad of paper, repeatedly circling a word that I cannot not make out until the pen almost drills a hole through it.

"I'm just curious," I interject before the pen breaks through paper. "How does this whole thing work?"

ABNA's lips curl in such a way as to suggest that she grants a smile only once every couple of years or so. "We're not at liberty to say, at this stage. We'll address that if we decide to move you forward."

For the rest of the session, ABNA takes copious notes as I talk. I mention the building meeting, how my body felt like it was scorched from the inside out, a sensation that felt impossible in the Uncommons, where I had learned that sensations happen on a more subdued scale. She asks questions about my time in the Uncommons, how I go about my afterlife, and the hobbies I have taken on. ("Do you enjoy your chair? How do you enjoy your chair?") After a while, she puts her pen down on the pad and places her two hands over it, announcing, "That'll be all for today. We'll let you know what we decide."

Back in my unit, I wait beside the phone, which does not ring. I think of my meeting with ABNA, how I left with more questions than I had going into it. Whether she is a caseworker or a doctor, I have no clue, only that she studies me in such a way that every motion seems to conjure some significance for her. I worry I might never see her again.

When the phone rings at last, the voice on the other end is the same one from the first automated recording, except this time it declares, "Congratulations, 100672, you have been selected to move on to the next stage. Please head to the Uncommons Registry as soon as possible."

The same official waits for me outside the Uncommons Registry, but he wears his smile brighter that day, and chirps, quite sincerely, "Congratulations!" He brings me back to the elevator in much the same way, only on this occasion he offers, "You can press the button this time." He winks before waving goodbye.

At the office, ABNA greets me with a clipboard tacked with several forms, which, upon skimming, seem only to note vaguely all the ways in which the Uncommons is not liable for what happens when one decides to move forward with these sessions.

"How many more sessions are there?"

ABNA does not answer, crossing out my signature on the form and gesturing to the page with her pen to sign it again with my number. When she determines that the signature is sufficient, she gestures for me to follow her to another room, the size of a closet. In her hand is a VHS tape with my number and my date of death labeled on it. She does not say a word as she pushes the tape into a tiny TV in the room, and nothing still as she closes the door behind her.

On the screen, my name appears in funny font along a scrolling marquee. And then it is my life. Someone has picked out all the critical moments, which seems at first like a highly presumptuous gesture, but then, thinking about it, I find it a gracious move, how the many years of my life can be condensed into a two-hour action-packed video. Like, who knew pissing my pants in first grade in the middle of playing "Hot Cross Buns" on the recorder would become such a momentous event?

I see myself. I see that my first life inside my mother was a bright pink nightmare, and I came out wet, sopping, and with hair like an angry, slow creature rising from the sea. I see that I missed the word "apocalyptic" at a school spelling bee, and the next day the lump on my father's throat blossomed into cancer. I see the stench, the brutality of a hospital room, its blue corners singing of death until the rasp of my father's breathing was no more, and when they covered his body, the stench disappeared with him.

I see that I made some girls cry, most of whom I loved maybe too haphazardly in bathrooms of basement dance parties or with our hands frantically searching for each other in the shadowy sidelines of the pier. I see how being loved back in that same way made me girl, made me estranged from myself, and goddamn did it feel that way with Mira. Sure enough, there was Mira, scene after scene. Mira kissing the length of my back from nape to the base of my spine. Mira fanning her fingers over the softest parts of my thighs, tossing me onto my back, her face descending between me, licking all of me clean. Mira, bringing my hand to her breast, and the rough squeeze that elicited a yelp, followed by a sheepish "Not too hard." After these occasions in which our bodies are lit up on-screen, I see another scene in which Mira asked me if I was afraid of death, and when I said, "Hell, yeah," she looked at me all serious and said, "Well, don't be." She had that way of knowing things before they happened. She said it was because she died twice, and it was dull both times. I grabbed her close, told her, "I don't want you to die," and she chuckled: "Okay."

I see that we fought often. A forgotten call, some confusion with an ex that didn't even matter anymore, a heated text exchange detailing all the petty wrongs we had committed throughout the course of our relationship—all of that insignificant now. I see us reading together, her wet fingers on a copy of *Giovanni's Room*, sitting on the side of the bathtub, the water running and running. Then Mira's boots crashing onto the floor, the door slamming. ("If you want to fuck her so badly, then go do it!") Her face in her hands, full of wet. Mira and I, practicing our duet for the next karaoke get-together, one

K-Ci & JoJo song away from our voices cracking. "Leave!" I said. "Get out of here, then, if you want to go so badly." Mira dancing on the subway platform, her lucky dance, she said, to conjure the train's arrival, which never worked. Forgotten birthday, forgotten anniversary. We did not yell, but we cried loudly at each other. Mira with her head pressed against my chest, whispering, "Let me," and I held her as close as possible to my heart's drumming.

Then one day, my mother died, and the world kept turning. I looked in the mirror and whispered the word "orphan" until the glass fogged and became clear again. I see the other queers who said, *Dude, that sucks*, and kept right on dancing, their tank tops soaked in sweat and disco light. When Mira and I broke up for the fifth and last time, they said the same thing, except I stopped dancing altogether and no one called.

I am sobbing by the end of my video, which is strange, because I cannot for the life of me remember the last time that I cried for myself, or for anyone else, for that matter.

The door opens and ABNA stands in the light, her pad in hand and the same rigid smile. "You did very good in there, 100672," she praises. "Very, very good."

At ABNA's recommendation, I spend some time after my life review sifting through the memories on my own. Although the video showed only a handful of them, other memories would popcorn throughout my time in the unit. I turn on the sink and can see my younger self sitting there while my father thaws my winter feet with warm water, his hands rubbing the cold out of my flesh. I can recall that stinging sensation of a body coming back to life.

With some flexing, the memories become a patchwork, as if threaded together to make a certain type of sense. I remember, for instance, there was a time when both my parents held on to their lottery number for a studio apartment in Fortuitous Plaza, an old historic building in Lower Manhattan that was then recently renovated and opened for new vacancies. As with all openings in low-income government housing, the chances of getting an apartment were slim. One day my mother got the call that the apartment was hers. She was busy cleaning the floor of their basement apartment with bleach and lemon when they called. Overjoyed, she must have gotten up too fast, the smell of the cleaner and the thought of living in a place that was at least central to the city dizzying her, making her stumble, and she collapsed on, thankfully, a spotless area of the floor. Later, at the doctor's, she found out she was pregnant, a fact that destroyed the Fortuitous Plaza dream altogether. For what kind of life could she and her husband have with a child who would only grow and grow until they reached a monstrous size, taking over the whole damn place? I remember this, not because I saw it, but because it was told to me by someone, and though I have sifted through my memories over and over, I cannot not see the mouth that spoke it.

I told ABNA about these memories that web together, how they fit beside one another, often with holes. When seen from another angle, the narrative looks entirely different, yet there is no way to tell which memory is right and which has been mistaken.

"What does it feel like to possibly be mistaken?" ABNA asks in our third session.

I think of my mother, and the pungent smell of lemon and

bleach pierces the air. The thought of her floods me and leaves just as quickly. Perhaps she is the mouth and the telling. It occurs to me that perhaps she too could have been mistaken, and to that I confess, "It feels like devastation."

When spoken, the word "devastation" has a suddenness to it, the way the video of my life had me enthralled for its duration and only after it ended did my body give way to tears. I hold devastation in my ghost body, and when it comes out it feels as if I myself am spilling. ABNA presses for more, but somehow I think it wise to keep certain things to myself. She takes notes furiously, and often without skipping a beat, dodging those questions about my place in the Uncommons, where this treatment is going, and whether we are going to address what I came here to remedy. To be honest, I am not sure about why I am there.

"It's okay to cry," ABNA emphasizes, giving a name to what is happening in my body. "That's a residual response from your human life. If you give it time, that will dissipate."

I touch my face, its lack of hardness, and my fingers go through me. If my face is wet, I will never know that feeling again. "You know, they keep telling me that."

"I am very happy about your progress, 100672," ABNA declares happily. "Your honesty, your openness, your everything. Let's keep this going, shall we?"

I nod, because it seems the thing to do and because there seems no other recourse.

Sometime before my fourth session, I see my mother. There, in the corner of my unit, she sleeps on a hospital bed. The image of her bone-thin body is impressed upon the room like a stenciled scene beside the window and plastic plant. When I move close to her, her image crackles like static and only becomes clearer when I watch from afar. I think perhaps I am imagining it, but then I hear her breathing husky with tubes running in and out of her body. I wonder if it is possible for memory to haunt a ghost the way a ghost haunts the living. I wonder this while standing on the opposite end of the room, watching her open mouth heave out a bit of stale air with each breath.

After a while, the smell of her breath fills the unit such that even cracking open a window does little to dispel the odor. I stand on the coffee table and hold several issues of the Uncommons magazines, fanning the air around her to no avail. My mother just lies there with her eyes closed. "Umma! Wake up!" I yell, but her breathing is even and slow, and she seems permanently sedated.

At one point, I leave the unit and returned to find that in her place, my father is sleeping. His lips, chapped and purple, look to me like a bruise. "Appa?" I whisper. He does not respond. The air grows thick with the smell of cancer.

I spend less and less time in the unit, taking long walks around the city, watching its murky sky unfold in fits of gray and white. I rent a bike from the public lot and ride it down one street after another. I ride it all the way to the city's edge, the welcome sign exactly as I remember it. In the field, a fresh batch of ghosts. I walk among them, searching their faces for someone familiar, someone I might know. It occurs to me that I am as lost as they are.

At one point, an older woman approaches, and she calls out something that I cannot hear. Her face has a soft transparency to it, as if she is more ghost than I am. She speaks again, trying to grab hold of my hand and failing. Suddenly there is the twinge of something familiar about her, and I tell her so.

"I remember you," I whisper. The words feel powdery as they escape my mouth. I can trace her face but not her name. I search my memory feverishly for it.

She mouths something once again, but I cannot hear her.

I repeat myself. "I remember you."

The woman's eyes flicker with recognition, and I will the volume of her voice louder so I can hear. Finally, her words pronounce, "I have a message for you from Mira."

"Mira?" The name falls out of my mouth so easily. I must have said it countless times before. The memories from the video jolt me back. Mira. Of course, Mira. My mind races. Where is she?

The woman's voice grows urgent, but it fades again, and this time I can no longer make out what she is saying. From the distance, I hear the familiar rumble of the white vans, coming to retrieve the newly arrived ghosts. I turn to the woman and say once more, "Mira?" The vans blast their loud horns, and instinctively I put my hands to my ears. When I open my eyes, the woman is gone.

I turn quickly, surveying the field, trying to see where she might have gone. The faces of each ghost now train themselves on the arriving white vans. I hop back onto my bike before they mistake me for one of them, and ride as far as I can toward the thick line of trees on the field's edge.

As I pedal forward, the image of Mira appears before me, and I see her sitting on the handlebars of the bike I am riding, her long hair grazing my face as the wind blows. I close my eyes and can smell apples, the sweetness of her neck. With my eyes still closed, the front wheel hits a rock, and Mira falls forward on her hands and knees, her hair a cascading mess on the ground. I stop and rush to her, pulling her body from the grass. Her face is scraped, and her nose is bloody.

"Mira!" I shout.

Mira blinks once, twice. She raises her arm over her eyes to block the sun. Slowly, she groans, "Ow."

I do not know whether to laugh or cry, only that in the Uncommons, it feels one and the same. Overhead, the gulls circle the sky, and I watch their loops bounce against one edge of the city and retreat to the center. I look before me and see that I have pedaled to the farthest edge of the Uncommons, the thick line of trees like an impenetrable wall before me. I walk toward it, and suddenly all of me stops. The air is draped with a heavy curtain, though I can see the field stretch out for miles, dipping into a horizon of speckled ash.

This is it, I realize. I fall to my knees, the fire inside me spinning and whirling, threatening to recall something my body cannot stop. My parents and Mira, all three of them gathering around me in the field with a birthday cake in hand, too many lit candles to count. They are singing "Happy Birthday" in unison, Mira in the middle, holding the cake steady so that I can see. But this is not right. This is not the right memory. The timeline is off. I hear myself yelling, "This is not real!" No one seems to hear me. They keep singing. Suddenly Mira's nose starts to bleed, and she raises one arm to wipe it, surprised at the sight of her own blood. My mother and father too take turns coughing and sputtering. The scene fills with smoke, and Mira calls out, "What's that smell? It smells like burning."

I tear at my body, where the fire seems to be catching on

everything. I roll and roll on the grass, shouting at the sky, rattling the birds from the branches. The heat presses against me, and then it stops so suddenly I almost do not notice it. Mira and my parents are no longer singing the birthday song, and are in fact no longer there. It is just me alone, no fire, just the field unspooling behind me.

I heave myself onto the grass once more, this time feeling the anguish in my heart come out in waves of tears. What I am crying for, I do not know anymore. Once the tears subside, I pick myself up, more tired than I can ever remember being. With all the remaining energy I can muster, I pedal my bike back to the city center.

Back at the unit, the phone is ringing. I pick it up to listen to its latest message: "Congratulations, 100672, you have been selected to move on to the next stage—" I do not have to wait to finish the message to know what it will say, and so I let the phone fall back into its place.

At the Uncommons Registry, the same official who greets me at the queue every time pulls me forward in line. "Something very strange is happening," I whisper to him. "Please help me." He looks at me with a smile that wavers only a crack. The elevator button is pressed but he does not say, *Congratulations!* He does not even wave this time.

ABNA welcomes me to her office, a fresh pad in hand, and I think to say something about what is happening. "I think I'm being haunted," I say to her, and wait for her response.

She is unwrapping the plastic cover on a new pack of legal pads with much difficulty, using a fingernail to puncture a hole.

With the other hand, she holds up one finger to indicate, *One moment*, still fighting with the plastic.

"What's happening?" I whisper.

ABNA finally breaks through the plastic and relishes the tear, both hands stretching it apart. "Oh, goody!" she squeals, and holds the freed set of pads up in the air like a trophy.

I feel a low boil move between the inside and outside of my ghost body. Every cell feels pinpricked—singed. I look down to see my arm charred to the bone, exposed in patches beneath flesh. At some point I must have fallen to the ground, because when I look up, ABNA is standing over me, her pads tucked under her armpit.

"Oh dear," ABNA exclaims. "This is all happening way ahead of schedule."

"Help me," I say, reaching my arm up from the ground and toward her.

She crouches down beside me. "What did you see?"

"This." I gesture to the arm in the air, which is no longer charred. "It was all burnt."

ABNA stands up, and I can hear her pacing back and forth on the carpet. Eventually my body loosens its hold, and I get up to catch the tail end of her muttering, " . . . too soon for the next phase."

"Why is this happening?" I cry.

ABNA holds her brand-new set of pads in front of her and sighs mournfully. "Won't need these today, I suppose."

"What's going on with me?"

"Follow me."

ABNA exits her office and makes a right down the corridor. I push myself up and quickly follow. At the elevator, she brandishes a long key, which she uses to unlock a compartment beneath the trail of buttons, sliding open its tiny door to reveal a hidden set of unmarked buttons. She pushes one of them and we sink together far down into the bowels of the Registry.

"Forgive me if I'm a bit nervous," ABNA tells me as the elevator plummets. She seems jittery, excited even, as she speaks. "I've never taken a client to the basement levels before. Mind the clearance process. It can be quite tedious."

Tedious is what I have come to know in the Uncommons. What's another session? Another infinity? I think of my mother, father, Mira, their stony faces locked in a forever pattern of death or its approximate. My arms tingle again, and I will the sensation away.

I look at ABNA, her stern face giving way to worry, and offer her something. "I'm sorry you never got to use your new pads."

At an unnamed basement level, the elevator stops and opens its doors. Before us is a warehouse of neatly arranged shelves that stretch farther than I can see and contain, in staggering height, black boxes of identical size, each one with one white label affixed to the front. Too small to be coffins, I think. But then, what use do they have for our human bodies?

"Here we are!" ABNA announces, her arms held above her in a V. She points to an official in a jumpsuit standing next to her. "This is the Uncommons Collections foreman. He'll walk you through the clearance process."

The foreman looks at ABNA and then at me. "Your number?" he asks.

"100672."

"Are you dead?"

I pause and answer tentatively, "Yes . . ."

His shoulders shake with gentle laughter. "I'm just messing with you. We don't get a lot of visitors here, but it still gets me every time. All right, let's see, here . . ."

The foreman takes an instrument from his belt and scans me head to toe. Its bright red light beeps once upon completion, and with little ceremony the foreman shrugs and nonchalantly declares, "100672 checks out. Congratulations." He seems not to know what to do, and he does a quick bow before turning to ABNA. "Head to Row 724, Column D. Her box should be labeled there."

ABNA seems surprised by the ease of the clearance process. I gather that perhaps she had only read of the regulations and had never been to this level herself. ABNA gestures for me to follow her to an unattended forklift, and she drives me past aisle after aisle of black boxes. I imagine ABNA and me on a cross-country trip, something that has never come up for me thus far in my memories, so I gather that perhaps it is something I never did. Still, for a moment I feel ABNA and I are journeying somewhere the sky cracks open, pouring its gray silk and clouds onto the road, and its contents cover us such that we wonder if we can survive it.

"This is a unique opportunity," ABNA shares emphatically. "I advocated for you in front of the board. We don't get a lot of cases like yours, but even with the few we do get, the board often turns people down after one or two sessions. Says residents always end up forgetting over time, that we have fine-tuned our treatment to the point where we can address someone's concerns in an instant."

I say nothing, but stare at the aisles rushing past me, wondering what it would be like to witness it all in Earth time. At that moment, I recall riding in a car with my parents as my mother held a lottery ticket in her hands. It was a sticky, hot summer, and the car's air conditioner was permanently broken. With the windows rolled all the way down and the radio turned all the way up, my father, who was behind the wheel, shushed everyone in the car as the announcer read the winning numbers. I could see the ticket in my mother's hands, gripped as tight as her attention. When the announcer finished giving the final number and thanked everyone for participating, my mother burst into laughter. "What's so funny?" my father asked, his eyes still on the road. My mother swiped the air with her hands, still recovering from laughter. "Huh! We might have gotten the jackpot had we not used Mal's birth date for the last two numbers." In the backseat, I sat in shock while my parents teased me about the millions that I owed them. How would I ever pay them back?

Back at the Collections floor, ABNA continues talking. "We never used to be so thorough about documentation until we started testing out recollection therapy and realized that reviewing the past could be good for working out the trauma. We keep records of everyone here. Isn't it marvelous?" She gestures to the aisles that sail by us. "I don't even get the privilege to see mine, since it would interfere with the integrity of my job. Still, I'm glad they implemented the lottery system for this, made room for some checks and balances. This was partially my idea, you know? The board just took it and ran with it."

"Why are you telling me this now?" I whine, suddenly agitated by the monotony of the black boxes. "I've asked you so many questions before about the what and the why."

She takes her eyes off the wheel and stares at me for a long moment before turning her gaze back to driving. Firmly, as if talking to the path before her, she states, "You have to have faith."

I give up on conversation with ABNA, and it is just as well, since we are arriving at our aisle. Operating the forklift with surprising ease, ABNA lowers a box from Column D from its place on the shelf and places it on the floor.

"Well, this is you," she chirps gleefully. "Congratulations!"

"What is it?"

ABNA leaned in to whisper. "It's your death."

Lifting the cover from the box, I see only one thing—a tiny cassette tape inside a small tape player.

"I don't remember this." I fidget with the buttons, switching the tape player on until the following recording sounds out:

Happy birthday to you! Happy birthday to you! Happy birthday, dear Mal! Happy birthday to you! Haha! It's silly, I know, but wherever you are, listening to this, I bet some birthdays have passed, so I'm just making up for lost time. I know you hate this day, but let me make it special for you, okay? Anything you want! The beach? A box of cannolis from Ferrara's? Sex on the rooftop? Unfortunately, these things are a little bit inaccessible right now, what with the rain and all, so I'm going to have to get back to you on all of this . . . Anyway, you're going to wake up soon, and I'm going to make pancakes and you're going to love it. Don't worry so much. I love you, after all. Forever and always. Love, Mira.

Just like that, I remember the time of my death, the way the fire spread and ate up the walls around me. At the time, I understood I should be trying to escape, as I heard my neighbors next door doing their best to break through the metal bars. Instead, I sank to my knees, whether in panic or submission, I am not sure. As the memory grows in form, I see myself still, praying.

I forget for a moment that ABNA is standing behind me, until she speaks. She mutters with unusual softness, "Well, that was disappointing."

Although I am not allowed to take the tape player back with me to the unit, I have permission from the foreman to check it out anytime while it is on the Collections premises. It will not go anywhere, he explains, as all objects are trapped in the time of death.

I turn to ABNA. "What happens now?"

"How do you feel?"

Unknowingly, I make a gesture to cradle myself. "Calm. Empty."

"Well, congratulations!"

"For what?"

She raises one eyebrow. "For a successful treatment."

"That's it, then?" I look at her, bewildered. "What happens next?"

She kisses her fingers and lets them unfurl in the air. "Poof! It all goes away. All the obstacles to forgetting."

"Do you mean—"

"Rest in peace, dear," ABNA says assuredly, her smile returning to its taut position. Now that the matter has been taken care of, she is resetting. "For now, you should go home."

Back at my unit, no one waits for me. The corner, once populated by my family and Mira, is vacant, save for the houseplant that shines in all its plastic brightness. The odor has gone as well, returning the unit to its original smell, which is to say that it smells like an empty room that knows no life or speck of dust.

I stand in the lonely corner and let its emptiness touch me. Is this vacancy a type of resolve? I am not sure.

Some time later, I receive a call from the automated messaging system. "Thank you for your participation," the message says. "Please stay on the line to take a brief survey of your experiences with the Uncommons Registry services. If for some reason you are dissatisfied with the services you've received, you are welcome to apply again. Please keep in mind you'll have to visit the Registry to collect a new number and complete the evaluation process once more."

After a while, the memories appear less and less clear, as if peering through the scenes of my life through a thick gauze lens. I catch a memory once, before it slips away, of asking my parents why they never applied for the housing lottery again, settling instead for a place in the outskirts of East New York. We were broken into so often that we stopped replacing the television and kept our electronics hidden in the far corners of closets, though they were stolen too eventually. My father said, "It's important to know when to let things go. That's how you learn the difference between tragedy and disappointment." They seemed like separate lessons then. Perhaps I understand it better now.

The last thing I remember of my life: On the first day of the acid rainstorms, Mira and I rushed home at the same time, our umbrellas and clothes soaked through and burning. We washed ourselves with soap and water, shuddering from the cold. We held each other as we cried, knowing somehow that our lives had forever changed.

"Remember what I said?" Mira's words shivered between her teeth.

I shook my head.

She took my face in her hands, kissing me deeply. When she pulled away, she rested her forehead against mine, and said, "Don't be afraid of dying."

"How? It's everywhere. It's . . ." I gestured to my apartment, its piles of boxes full of my parents' things, everything I could not part with. I could not finish my sentence.

She said it again. "Don't be afraid."

"Mira, how—"

"Don't be afraid."

I nodded, pressing my forehead harder against hers.

She pulled me close and whispered into my ear. "Wherever you are, I'll find you."

Between gulps of tears, I nodded again. "Okay."

There was something else. Did I promise her something too? There was that look in her eyes, and I knew she meant what she said.

"Don't be afraid."

She said it so simply the final time that it was hard not to accept it as fact, so easy that I felt my insides weep for something I did not know I could lose. How can anyone ever bear it?

ACKNOWLEDGMENTS

This book was more than ten years in the making. It would not have been possible without my teachers, including Dana Johnson and Aimee Bender, who read the earliest iterations of these stories and helped me breathe life into these pages. Thank you to Keija Parssinen for leading the first fiction class I have ever taken and from which the first story in this collection was born.

My gratitude to my agent, Hafizah Geter, for your belief in this project and the future of my work to come. To Mo Crist, as well, for your diligent read and editorial eye, for warming my heart with your deep comprehension of my New York City–specific references.

I am indebted to the literary journals that believed in this project enough to publish the stories within it: *Fairy Tale Review* (particularly Benjamin Schaefer), which published the earliest version of the titular story, "How to Fall in Love in a Time of Unnameable Disaster," *Joyland* magazine, which published "To Molt, to Love You," *Indiana Review*, which published "Welcome to the Uncommons," and *Paper Darts*, which published excerpts from "The *Ma (妈) Like Mā, Not Like Horse (马)* Radio Show."

To my sister, Jean Chen Ho, thank you for leading the way with *Fiona and Jane*, a story about the family we choose, and for loving me so fiercely.

My deepest gratitude to my VONA Speculative Fiction Rocket Ship crewmates, especially to T. K. Lê, whose careful insight has been instrumental to the heart of this work. My fellow crewmates, thank you for the work you do to change the landscape of speculative literature: Jacqueline Barnes, Nia Hampton, Ariel Eure, R. Cielo Cruz, Joseph Earl Thomas, Maya Beck, Stefani Cox, Junauda Petrus, Aaron Talley, and LaTanya Lane.

And, of course, where would we be without our captain, Tananarive Due? Thank you for teaching us.

To Patricia Tolete and Abigail Devora, whose friendship over the past fifteen-plus years has inspired the funny connections and unpredictable hijinks within this book. I guess I like you both okay.

Thank you to the staff of Blue Mountain Center, Sundress Academy for the Arts, Kimmel Harding Nelson Center for the Arts, and the Community of Writers who have worked so hard to provide the kind of writer haven where these pages can be written. I have been so nourished.

To my beloved *Apogee Journal* family, especially to long-time friends and comrades Joey De Jesus, Zef Lisowski, and

Alexandra Watson, thank you for the example you continue to set when it comes to living a politically ethical life in the arts.

My best friend and platonic life partner, Dan Lau, with whom I have been co-dreaming a future in which we may live off the grid—I cannot imagine this world-building without you.

So much love to my friends who have fed me, watched me cry at the dinner table, given me advice, and roasted my bad decision making: Tiana Nobile, Kati and Gustavo Barahona-Lopez, Veronica Garcia, Vanessa Angelica Villarreal, Kyle Casey Chu, Claudia Leung, Truong Tran, Angie Sijun Lou, Mihee Kim, Neha Deshmukh, Kino Hsu, Michelle Lin, Kazumi Chin, Kim Acebo Arteche, MT Vallarta, Vickie Vertiz, Kenji Liu, Michelle Penaloza, Alex Cummings, Jane Wong, Sally Wen Mao, Billy Gong, Debbie Gong, Saretta Morgan, Monica Sok, Luke Rampersad, Sam Cohen, Neela Banerjee, SA Smythe, Margaret Rhee, Viola Lasmana, Ruben Miranda, Alexandra Chew, Kay Ulanday Barrett, Addie Tsai, and Matthew Siegel.

To my family on both sides, those who have suffered the pains and joys of coming to the U.S. with the hope of a life with more possibilities. However imperfect this journey was, I would not be here without the soft embers of your hope.

From the immigrant working-class bustle of Queens, to Lower East Side housing projects, to all the Chinatowns that have raised me—however far I am, my dreams always take me home to you.

AJ Kim, there is not a world (acid rain or otherwise) in which I would not want to meet you. Let us walk bravely into the future together. I love you.